Rocky Point Road

Joe Allen

Published by Rogue Phoenix Press
Copyright © 2015

ISBN: 978-1-62420-120-2

Credits
Cover Artist: Amanda Kelsey
Editor: Kitty Carlis

Chapter One

The apartment was cluttered with art.

Denis Rosa's unfocussed appreciation of different styles ended up in a kind of warehouse approach to everything. There was a rubbing he'd bought in Cambodia, and a pair of late Ching dynasty vases, probably not worth a lot. An early Chinese brazier or incense burner, coppery green on a Noguchi glass-top coffee table with his grandfather's crystal pipe ashtray that took two hands to pick up. Then an old Syrian inlaid wooden chair with bits of shiny mother-of-pearl diamond shapes here and there, a ragtag assortment of flat-weave kilim rugs, a Barcelona chair, a walnut harpsichord. His grandmother's heavy sterling candlesticks with Christmas red candles, an African table carved from a single ebony tree trunk, and a mismatched assortment of African sculptures bought here and there, one a red-faced West African piece with monkey fur for hair. A dark, moody painting of Chief Joseph in television pixel patterns, a ghostly painting of shadowy figures on a bridge, an abstract oil of student riots in 1968 at the Gare du Nord, a couple of big academic nudes, a late impressionist picture of two people on the Staten Island ferry with the Brooklyn Bridge, a gaggle of Victorian tourist watercolors of Italian stereotypes (a cleric, a street musician, a woman with a big hat), two Persian miniatures of animals, a pair of impressive storytelling copperplate etchings from the 1960s, and five non-objective mystery pieces in bright colors by a well-known Irish artist. That was plus two dozen or so family photos scattered around the room and seven or eight pieces of high-fired ceramic bas relief.

What a fucking mess. Why did I accumulate all this stuff?

His wife had died and he was walking in circles with his back to the walls, looking from the walls toward the rooms, trying to make sense of something that didn't make sense no matter how you looked at it. *I could just start hitting things, pick up that African ebony head shaped like a scythe and just hit the canvasses until they are all ripped and shredded.* But like the temptation to throw her wedding ring in the river, the impulse subsided. Till death us do part. Death was here, and they were parted.

Why do you make a home after all? So it will be a place where you are comfortable, where you feel safe, where you can store all your pieces of string into a huge ball if you want. Then you pull away one of the foundation stones and what happens? Ashes, ashes, we all fall down.

He walked out the front door of the building. *It's odd how lucid I feel while I am nearly unhinged in the way I am thinking. Almost like I had taken some kind of designer drug that would make me high, but let me drive a car.*

It was chilly outside and the sidewalks were wet. He scuffed through the puddles in the pedestrian mall that used to be Broadway, stopping to watch the lights dance across the buildings. A man on stilts with a tall red hat was handing out flyers for a comedy club, or maybe a nude club, and that man with white underwear and a cowboy hat was strumming a guitar for a group of people who were busily snapping smartphone pictures of him and probably giving him money. How does he stay warm enough to play the guitar? How does his guitar stay in tune when it is so damp?

He turned onto 46th Street and headed for St. Mary the Virgin, hoping the door would not be locked. It was Sunday afternoon, so there was an even chance he could get in and smell the ghost of stale incense that constantly floated in the air. The door was, in fact, open when he pulled on it. There was to be evensong. Could he wait for that? He looked at his watch, which he had buckled on upside down, so he had to twist his wrist around and cock his head to read the clockface: four thirty. He scooted into a pew on the side. There was a scattering of people: a couple of ladies, a man who seemed to be dressed as a Gray Friar with a rope around his waist, and a man with a young child walking the Stations of the Cross.

He stared at the beam that crossed above the old communion rail that formed a rood screen about thirty feet off the floor. It had a life-size crucifix, and six pendant, red glass altar lights in gold or brass fixtures at regular intervals across the span, swaying slightly from the motion of the earth, or the vibrations of the subways. The church couldn't get a permit for a crypt even though it was well over 150 years old because, basically, the idea of burying dead bodies under the theater district was too gross for the city to consider. And you can't dig very far in midtown without hitting something that makes the city run anyway.

Someone started to play the organ, stopped, and started over. *If you play the organ you have to practice on an organ. Makes sense. Hard to have a full organ in your apartment, so you have to practice in a church. Well, evensong, after all, is only an hour or so away. Maybe that's it.* The organist stopped again, and there was silence for half a minute. Then he started to play Bach's Toccata and Fugue in F Major.

Tony Perkins was speeding along a cliff edge in his little sports car yelling goodbye, John Sebastian, and singing along with the organ music on his radio. *Odd the things that music makes you remember.* "It's raining," Melina Mercouri had said shakily, staring out the window with half a pound of mascara on her magnificent burning eyes. Her husband would kill her, of course; that was the fate of Phaedra. But Tony Perkins had to drive his car off a cliff into the water with a randomly chosen Bach organ piece playing as he flew through the air toward the rocks.

His eyes filled with tears, remembering that time long ago when he could take Phaedra seriously. Hell, his wife had died out in California and he had so far felt no discernible emotion other than anger and a certain level of disorientation, even though he'd been alone when he got the call and could have cried. *But crying is a communal thing.* He'd cried fountains in the past; it wasn't that he was so macho that he couldn't cry.

"Yeah," he said, "I'm OK, I'll be OK. I'll get a flight right away, I'll, um, I'll call you later."

Sitting in the church listening to the organist practice made the knot in his stomach loosen up a bit, although he still felt on the edge of nausea. The slightly bitter sweetness in the air was restorative. In most churches you smelled candle wax, but in this church you smelled frankincense. They call it Smoky Mary's because they use so much incense it makes your eyes water if you sit in the front of the church. He knew to sit in the back on the side, and even so his throat sometimes coated with phlegm when the deacon came down the center aisle to read the gospel, and flung the censor back and forth, creating a cloud of gray-blue vaporized resin for the congregation to suck into their lungs.

He couldn't just sit there and wait.

He took out his smartphone and looked up an airline flight service, walked out the front of the church and booked a flight to LA Monday morning, getting in about noon. "Yes, first class, upgrade with my miles. I'm not made out of money."

Bond 45 was dismantling the afternoon brunch. He waved at the maître d', walked over to the long bar, and ordered a vodka straight up, a little dirty, with olives. A drink would help. He asked the bartender for some roasted vegetables, too, cauliflower, string beans, and eggplant.

You'd think something would be different when someone dies. Something would happen, people would not watch ballgames or something. But I'm looking around and Times Square is normal, even though Elissa drowned in the back yard hot tub on a sunny late afternoon at the south end of Santa Monica Bay.

The vodka had little bits of ice floating in it from having been shaken vigorously in a theatrical, over-the-head show that the bartender did. *Show-off. Well, it's Times Square.* It was deliciously cold and there were three big olives. The salty olive juice took the edge off the alcohol and he took a big loud slurp from the martini glass while it was sitting on the bar. He put his phone down on the bar and waved at the bartender, pointed at the restrooms, and mouthed *Be right back.*

Well, something was different. He had never felt like masturbating in a public restroom before. Just as he didn't destroy the paintings, though, he just peed, rinsed his hands, and went back to the bar.

The apartment was chilly because he had left the windows open. The vodka had cleared his head, and that businesslike avatar of his took over when something dislocating happened. He packed a few things, but didn't need to take much other than a suit because he had plenty of clothes in the house in Palos Verdes Estates (PVE).

4

He had to inject himself with a blood-thinner after a deep vein thrombosis years before, and if he waited until after he got on the plane because he did not have a membership in the right airline club, he did it in the head after he got seated in 4D on the aisle. He had never learned, after all those years, to just jab himself with the needle, had to push it into the fleshy part of his thigh and then push the plunger down. It seldom hurt, and frequently was almost sensationless, but there was a sense of dread when he pulled out an orange-wrapped syringe and wiped his thigh with an alcohol swab with his jeans around his calves. He threw the used syringe back in his cosmetics bag after the protective plastic sheath snapped up to protect anyone from getting stuck with the needle. And for some reason after he finished the shot, he felt more relaxed, as though he could fall asleep before the plane took off. There was still the minute coal-like bit of blood clot in a vein just below his left knee, and he had to be careful. He pulled on the doctor-prescribed, tight rubberized support stockings before he put on his jeans. *They're so tight I can't wear them.* But he always managed to forget about them and today was no different. He only had to wear them in the air, and it seemed like a penance.

The flight attendant gave him a screwdriver with an extra little bottle of vodka that he dumped into the drink. He reclined his chair a bit and stared out the window at the sky that was blue and glaring at the same time, left his eyes unable to focus momentarily when he looked back into the cabin. How could she drown? She was afraid of water because she was a bad swimmer, but you don't need to swim in a hot tub. Did she fall? Did she have a heart attack?

Theirs was not a standard-issue marriage, although they'd had children who had dutifully reproduced and given them grandchildren, so on Christmas Day they seemed Norman Rockwell-ish. They'd both been unhappily married before, but the scars from the previous experiences were deeper than they had thought, and they were not able to achieve that easy trust and companionship that some enviable couples had. They didn't distrust each other, and they usually got along well. They shared some interests, notably baseball and classical music.

Things danced around in his head. A strong practical streak in him thought about what to do with the house, a house that meant even more clutter to deal with over and above the apartment that had driven him to the brink of despair the day before. He wanted "Simple Gifts" to be played. He would have her cremated as they had talked about, and he would scatter her ashes at sea. He saw himself dropping a lei of plumeria flowers onto the blackish-blue choppy water of the Catalina Sound.

They loved each other, but they found after the children were grown that they couldn't get along without bickering, and he had moved to New York and opened a new office of the consulting business he had founded. He learned to cook because he did not want to eat at restaurants all the time, and she had taken up with a string of short-term boyfriends, some of whom tried to take up residence in the house with her, but she apparently drew the line at that. Backwards, right? He was supposed to be tomcatting and she was supposed to be cooking, but it didn't work out that way.

He wondered if one of the guys had been with her when she died. His business partner had not said anything other than that Elissa had been found by the gardener in the hot tub with the Jacuzzi function still running. She had apparently been there for a day or so. Ignoble to be all wrinkled and partially parboiled. The coroner had taken her, of course. He had not talked to the rest of the family; not a word. *In centuries past the women in the family would have cleaned her up and packed herbs around her in a plank-made coffin, strong-smelling herbs--basil and verbena and rosemary and mint.*

Chapter Two

He had to identify her. She was in a drawer on ball bearing-type rollers and she wasn't red and parboiled, but gray-blue and cold looking. Yes, it was her. They rolled her back into the wall of refrigerated bins and took him back to an office, him clearing his throat to get the smell of that room out of his body.

He'd worn a tie for whatever reason, because he was used to wearing a tie. He still did not feel like crying, although seeing her like that was a shock.

That was the woman who had given him three children, or he had given her three children.

He didn't think much about the sex anymore; that had become a non-issue for him, though clearly not for her. She had played around a good bit in her youth, before he knew her; they were both clear with each other that they were sexually experienced. He had always felt that sex was a bit overrated. It was fun, and his cock responded quickly to visual or physical stimulus, but the act itself never took him to the heights he had read about in novels, or the ecstasy his gym buddies talked about. He seldom felt like cuddling or talking afterward, just wanted to roll over and close his eyes. He knew that was not what she wanted, but sometimes he did it anyway. *Sex is a bother.*

"Don't clam up on me!" she shouted. It was the same argument they had indulged in over and over. How they didn't communicate anymore. He was replaying it as he told the people at the hospital-like counter that he would have her picked up by the Neptune Society whenever the coroner was finished with her. They had to do an autopsy to find out why she died. He signed some releases and left. He would have to see the children, and they would have to see each other; as adults they were sometimes not close with each other.

He went home to PVE, to the lovely house on the cliff with waves crashing onto goldish-yellow rocks a couple of hundred feet down, and brown kelp trees growing downward from the surface of the water to the bottom--like ropes hanging down from heaven. Maggie was there already, waiting in the living room with a pair of big, dark glasses on to signal that she had been crying. She had poured herself a glass of red wine. They hugged wordlessly and he went to the kitchen and poured a glass from the bottle of pinot noir that she had opened. He was not a pinot noir fan usually, but Elissa had stocked the house with it.

"So," he said.

A key turned in the front door and they both looked up. It was Paul, the first-born. Denis stood up. They were the same height and clearly related: the same blue eyes, the same straight, lank brown hair, the same scarecrow-like, squared-off shoulders on a skinny frame.

"When did you get here?" Paul asked.

"Went from the airport to the coroner. The Neptune Society will be picking her up when they release her--the body, that is."

Maggie made a strangulated sound and both the men looked at her.

"You insist on cremating her," Maggie said.

"That's what she wanted, kiddo," Denis said. "We talked about it and agreed years ago. That's what I want when the time comes, too. But the coroner hasn't finished examining her yet. I mean, apparently it is obvious that she drowned, but not why she drowned. Maybe she passed out from sitting in the hot water drinking wine. I don't know."

"Don't you even care?" Maggie said with little inflection, and with her eyes still hidden beneath the glasses.

"Yes, I care," Denis said. "We all do. I also care enough to want to know what happened, and to do what she wanted with the Neptune Society. There is no point buying a cemetery plot that's going to be resold in ninety-nine years anyway. If we had a family plot it might be different, but our relatives are buried all over the place. If you want, we can put a

8

memorial slab someplace so that you can put flowers on it with the kids, but Mom and I agreed years back that we will both be cremated and scattered at sea. You know that, it's not news." He put his hand lightly on her shoulder and she shook it off, but did not respond.

The back door opened and shut and footsteps came down the hall. Richard, the middle child and, thus far, the champion procreator with four boys of his own.

"Dad," he said, and did a bro-hug with pats on the back.

"Rich," he said. "Glass of wine?"

"Dad," Paul said, "what are we going to do about a funeral?"

"Well, I guess it will have to be at St. Francis over by Hollywood Riviera. We were not regulars there, especially since I have been in New York, but we sent them a check a couple of times a year. Father Yamaguchi will be well-disposed towards us. But unfortunately, we don't know when we can have the body because they're still doing, um, tests of some kind. Maybe I will call St. Francis and see what they suggest," Denis said. "I want them to play 'Simple Gifts.'"

They gradually loosened up, and the boys sat down instead of standing with their arms crossed, but it was the way it always was, with tempers ready to flare and old grudges not far from the surface.

"Look," Denis said, "it would be very helpful if you boys went over to St. Francis and talked to someone there. Tell them what we know, that the coroner is doing an autopsy since Mom drowned and they want to know why she didn't just get up and walk away from the water instead of inhaling it and, well, drowning. I suppose there is the possibility of foul play, although the police report apparently did not say anything was out of the ordinary."

The phone rang. It was Melanie, Richard's wife.

"Well, we're trying to figure out what to do since the coroner hasn't released Mom's body yet. I don't know. Paul and I are going over to St. Francis to talk to them about that. I don't know, a couple of days I guess. Worst case, they cremate her and it is a memorial service instead of a normal funeral, I guess."

Maggie sucked in a deep breath.

"Look, everyone, I just got off a plane and came from the

coroner's office here. I need to take a shower and have something to eat. Maggie, you're welcome to stay while the boys go over to Malaga Cove. I have no idea whether there is any food in the kitchen." He walked into the kitchen while he was talking and opened the fridge. Eggs, milk, plastic containers of stuff he couldn't see, margarine, some soft drinks, a couple of beers. A couple of different kinds of cheese.

"Maggie, see if there is any basil outside," he said, staring into the pantry. Garlic, onions, potatoes, cans of tuna, plenty to make dinner with. The freezer was chock-full of things from Trader Joe's that could be nuked in the microwave. *What the heck is this?* He picked up a thumb-sized, dark brown bottle stuck next to the icemaker. No label. He shook it; it made a clicking sound, like there was something in it. It was cold, frozen. He twisted the lid and it came off easily. He sniffed it and the smell ran up through his head like a knife. Smelling salts? Why would they be in the fridge? He felt a little weak in the knees and plopped down in one of the kitchen chairs. He handed the little bottle to Maggie.

"What do you make of that?" he said. "Don't open it. I think it is smelling salts. "She opened it anyway and took a small whiff, and then he smelled something like old gym socks.

"It's amyl nitrate," she said. "The stuff that we used in college to make us laugh."

"Why is it in the freezer?" he asked, not expecting an answer. "Hmm."

He put the little bottle on the counter and poked around in the freezer. There was a plastic container with something green in it. He pried the top off and looked at it. Rosemary? No, it was marijuana, that's what it was. He took some of it out and held it up. Maggie looked at it, reached out and took it. "What the fuck?" she said, "Mom was using pot? Fresh leaves?"

They went up three stairs and into the master bathroom and opened the medicine cabinets. There was a bunch of prescription bottles.

"I didn't know Mom was taking meds for anything," he said. "Not that she would necessarily have told me, I guess. I think we need to call the police and have them look at this. It may have something to do with what happened."

The police arrived in minutes, and he showed them to the bathroom, where the medicine chest was still open. They were all over it, and they interviewed Denis and Maggie separately, asking what they knew about Elissa's medications.

"I thought she was drinking," Denis told the cop who was questioning him. "You should know that we have not lived together for more than ten years, although we've always been on friendly terms. We were never divorced. I haven't seen her for about six months, but the last time I was out here, she was not taking these drugs, or at least if she was, they were not sitting in the medicine chest, because I would have seen them." The cops were wearing white stretchy gloves and put each of the prescription bottles into a separate plastic bag. Denis showed them the bottle and the plastic box with the marijuana leaves he'd found in the freezer, too.

"Why were you looking in the freezer?"

"I was hungry. I just got in from New York and was trying to find something to eat. Maggie was here, she can tell you."

"So before today you were--?"

"In New York."

"Including the last week?"

"Including about the last six months."

The men were polite and sympathetic, and apologized before they searched the rest of the bedroom. They took some bags of stuff out, and gave Denis a receipt for the items they had taken, including several bottles of vitamins, some aspirin and Aleve, and some allergy capsules.

"Was there anyone living here with her?"

"I honestly don't know," Denis said. "She hadn't mentioned anyone, but she had boyfriends or lovers, I know that. It was one of the reasons we started living apart. That was back in the 90s."

After they left, he said to Maggie, "You go through Mom's jewelry and tell me what you want and we can try to give the rest of it to Melanie or Christie. I have no use for it. Her engagement and wedding rings should be yours and maybe one day one of your kids can wear them." The engagement ring was an emerald surrounded by small diamonds, not a big ring, but all he could afford when he bought it for her.

Maggie started dumping things on the bed and sorting through them. He stared at the boxes as she dumped them out." She had a lot of earrings," he said. "I always gave her earrings." And watching Maggie, he knew he was going to cry, finally. And he did, not wracking, sobbing tears, but real tears, big tears, silent tears that ran down his shirt. He had loved her those years before. He walked out the back door and stared at the swimming pool and the hot tub. He stripped off his shirt and pants and dived into the pool in his briefs. The water was cool, almost cold, and he swam several lengths of the pool before he was accustomed to the temperature. Maggie came outside with a towel and he climbed out of the pool and wrapped the towel around his hips.

"I don't want to do that today," she said. "I put it all back." They ambled back to the bedroom.

"Well," he said, "we're going to have to do something soon, because I need to put the house on the market. She borrowed some money on a mortgage a few years back and I need to stop paying it, it costs an arm and a leg." He pulled a plastic baggie with a wedding ring in it out of the pocket of the pants he had been wearing and handed it to Maggie.

"She was wearing this, but not the engagement ring, so that must be here."

"Don't you want to bury her with her ring on?"

"No. We haven't been close for a long time, and marriage vows end with death anyway," he said. "She and I are not married anymore, but there's no reason to toss the ring into the ocean. It has an inscription inside it, did you know that? Just the date we were married and our initials."

He went into the kitchen, found a bowl and cracked three eggs into it, whisked in some water and some dried herbs, some pepper and a couple of drops of vinegar, threw them in a frying pan with some butter and lifted the sides so the egg could run under. A minute later he flipped it and found some of the yellow cheese, grated a bit on the top, folded it over, and the smell of a calming omelette filled the kitchen.

"Want some?" he asked Maggie. She shook her head and poured another glass of wine. He found some orange juice in the fridge and poured a large tumbler for himself, thought a minute, and then grabbed some vodka and spiked it. He sat down at the kitchen table and started to eat the omelette, realizing how hungry he was as he ate. He took a big gulp of the orange juice to wash it down. He stared out the window at the eucalyptus trees and the camellia bushes in the back yard and made a mental note to speak with the gardener, because the shrubs in the front yard were looking a little too bushy and he was going to have to put the house on the market.

As he stared, the trees developed halos and the room started to expand. He wasn't hungry anymore and he felt like he would throw up, cold sweat on his forehead. It was the drink. "Something wrong with the vodka," he said as he collapsed into a heap by the side of the chair and hit his head on the tile floor. As Maggie looked on, a small pool of blood began to spread from under his face. She screamed and ran to him, shook his shoulder and got no reaction, then realized that if he were hurt she should not be shaking him. She grabbed the telephone from the wall and called 9-1-1.

"My father, he just fainted, or maybe he had a stroke. He was mumbling something when it happened, but he was slurring the words and I couldn't understand what he was saying. Please hurry!" She knelt by her father and noticed that his eyelids were fluttering as though he were trying to wake up. It was really too much to think that her father might die just a couple of days after her mother drowned in the goddamn hot tub. The doorbell rang and she ran to the front door. Paramedics.

"In the kitchen!" she shouted, and pointed across the entrance hall. They ran with their oxygen tanks and medical kit, talking into Bluetooth-like microphones that stuck down in front of their faces from a headset. She pulled out her smartphone and dialed Paul.

"What is it, Mags?" he said. "We're talking to Father Yamaguchi."

"It's Dad. He collapsed or fainted or had a heart attack or something. The paramedics are here. You need to get back over here."

He said something reassuring and hung up. She ran into the kitchen and the paramedics were working on Denis. His nose was streaming blood. "Did he have a heart attack?"

"We don't know, ma'am, but we're going to have to get him to Harbor General so they can get him stabilized." They strapped him to a board and lifted him onto a gurney. He was breathing, she could see his chest moving, and his face was twitching. *Oh, God, he's had a stroke.*

Paul and Rich ran in the front door a few minutes after the paramedic truck pulled away with the siren wailing. She told them what she knew, and they headed to Harbor General, fortunately not far from Rocky Point, where the house was.

They were not allowed into the area where their father was taken, and all the staff would tell them was that he was in guarded condition, but they did not believe his life was in danger. An hour and a half later, a resident in green scrubs came out to talk to them.

"We believe your father had taken a drug, but he told us he had not. Do you know if he had taken anything that might lead to his passing out?" he said. "I'm not the police, I am a doctor, and I just want to do what is best for your dad."

The three of them looked at each other and no one had any idea what was going on.

"He was eating an omelette and drinking a screwdriver. He just arrived from New York today because our mom died two days ago and he had to identify her, so he's probably under a lot of stress," Maggie offered. "I wasn't making it any easier for him, giving him a hard time because she wanted to be cremated."

Paul offered, "Dad is kind of a health nut. As far as I know, he's never taken anything stronger than a stiff drink since he was in college a long while back."

"A screwdriver? Orange juice and vodka?"

"Yes."

"In a bar?"

"No, at home. Why?"

"Where did the vodka come from?"

"The cabinet."

"We think he may have had some GHB, which is a drug that can be used for narcolepsy, but is often abused at clubs. It's inclined to make people pass out and stay unconscious in certain quantities, and it appears your dad had a good hit of it."

"GHB? Is that the date rape drug?"

"Yes."

"Can we see Dad?"

"He is very groggy and we are trying to keep him awake until the effect of the drug wears off. We think he is going to be OK, but maybe it would be best if you let us work with him for another hour or so. If you think the vodka might have been where he ingested the drug, I'd suggest you talk to the police right away and have that bottle tested."

Maggie looked at her brothers. "Mom probably drank that same vodka."

Chapter Three

The two policemen had asked him a lot of questions, but basically, he was no help to them. He did not take any "fun" drugs. He had injected himself with a blood-thinner before he got on the plane to LA at JFK, but he had not taken anything else, other than a screwdriver on the plane and a screwdriver after he went for a swim at the house. He thought he remembered thinking there was something in the vodka, but then the next thing he remembered, he was throwing up in the cubicle at the hospital. He had no specific memories. It was the omelette on a plate, and then the omelette splashing into a bedpan.

They'd told him that they believed, based on lab results, that he had most likely ingested some GHB, which occurs naturally in the human body, but in small amounts. It could make you pass out and stay passed out, which is why its reputation was established as a "date rape" drug.

The kids had taken the policemen to the house and given them the bottle of vodka, which was still sitting on the kitchen table. Russian Standard, good vodka.

He was feeling groggy and his stomach hurt from throwing up. Someone had slipped him a mickey. *What an odd phrase, must look it up. A mickey.*

Now he was at the house, and Maggie had made the bed with fresh sheets so he wouldn't feel like he was sleeping on Elissa's sheets, although there were no sheets on the bed because the police had taken them. The huge expanse of plate glass at the foot of the bed looked out at a waterscape with Catalina Island painted on a scrim in the distance, and vivid hot-pink ice plant in a carpet extending from the house to the edge of the cliff. The window was ajar and he could hear the surf hitting the rocks down below. He had climbed those cliffs as a boy when his parents had owned this house. There was a time when he knew every foot of these cliffs and could scamper up and down them like a lizard. Time, however, had made him less agile, and had worn away the paths and sturdy footholds he had known, and he was certain that if he tried to scale down the cliff now, he'd be impaled on a pointed rock.

He held his head and got up, wandered out toward the living room. Rich was sitting there, apparently taking whatever watch it was.

"What time is it?"

"Hi, Dad. It's about eleven." He didn't wear a wristwatch, but like his grandfather, he always seemed to know what time it was. An internal clock, his father used to say. His father always woke up when he needed to, as well. He said it was the "Holy Souls" who woke him up: the people in purgatory whom he was praying for. He doubted it was the Holy Souls who were telling Rich the time.

"I guess I slept through."

"Well, we kept checking on you, but you seemed to be OK, so we didn't see any reason to get you up. I bet you're hungry. Want a screwdriver?" Big grin. "Probably not, huh?"

"Very funny. Anyone ever try to poison you? The thought of humor doesn't come up in the same breath."

Rich looked down at his hands.

"But you're right. I am hungry. Do you suppose there's any cereal?"

He poured a stream of Grape Nuts into a bowl and found some raisins, scattered them on top with a spoonful of sugar, shook the milk carton, opened it and smelled it. OK.

He poured it all over the cereal and started to eat.

"Hey, Rich, did the police say anything about what happened?"

"I think they're going to come by this afternoon to follow up, but no, I haven't heard squat from them."

He stripped off the T-shirt and boxers he was wearing. "I'm going for a swim," he said, and headed out, buck naked, junk jiggling, and jumped in the pool. He dogpaddled around a bit, enjoying the warmth of the sun in a way that only a New Yorker in November can appreciate. Rich pulled off his shirt and pants and jumped into the pool in his briefs. He made as though to dunk Denis, and they both swam underwater a few strokes.

"You're it," Rich said, and backed away, arms over his head and held back in fake flight. He jumped backward and did an upside-down frog kick, which propelled him into the side of the pool. "Ow," he said, and laughed a goofy laugh that had been his ticket to get away with things since he was a toddler. The middle kid, always had it rough in some ways, but he sure did study his brother and learn from Paul's mistakes.

"What are you doing?" came another voice. This time it was Paul, and distinctly disapproving. "I thought you were in bed."

"Clearly not. And naked as a jaybird, so I hope you haven't brought girls with you, because they'll want me if they see me." He splashed a wave of pool water by pushing his hands forward and up, and soaked the front of Paul's shirt. Paul was not amused. Rich was faking a laugh attack, grabbing his stomach and dancing like a trained bear. Why were they clowning around a couple of days after Elissa was killed?

Killed. He climbed out of the pool and Rich tossed him a towel. While he was drying off, he said it. "So, do we think someone killed Mom with whatever was in the vodka?"

All the fun fell out of the scene.

"Yeah," Denis said. "I thought so."

"And they tried to kill you, too," Paul said.

"No, probably not. No way in the world anyone could have set up to kill me with a bottle of vodka in California when I was in New York. More likely whoever it was had planned to dump the rest of the vodka down the sink and throw the bottle in the recycles. I just got in the way and the truck hit me because I was in the wrong place."

None of them wanted to say it. Mom was always dating younger men, if "dating" was the right word. She was hanging out with younger guys, probably having sex with some of them, and everyone in the family had always looked the other way. Like you ignore when someone has bad skin or a shriveled hand, or if they forget to zip their fly or leave a spot on their jaw unshaved by accident, or don't realize they have snot showing in their nose. Women mentioned those things, but guys didn't.

"Do you suppose Maggie would know who Mom was seeing?" Denis asked.

"I doubt it," Rich said. "They weren't getting along very well."

"Maybe we shouldn't be talking about this until the police get here," Paul said, looking at his shoes.

"Why the fuck not?" Denis was suddenly angry. "Maybe someone killed my wife--OK, my estranged wife--and your mother, and why wouldn't we talk about it? I'm not going to grab a double-barreled shotgun and go looking for the bastard, but I will talk about it all I want!"

"OK, OK, I just meant..."

"I know, I shouldn't cork off like that. I'm sorry. I got knocked on my keester by a drug that wasn't intended for me, Elissa drowned in the hot tub, and I bet there was some of that same drug in her when she passed out in the water. Really, Paul, I'm sorry. I don't have a lock on being angry, I know."

He rested his hand on Paul's shoulder and realized Paul was crying. "You know I loved her for years and I love you guys, too."

He went inside and put on dry clothes, brushed his hair and teeth and came back out. The boys were sitting in the living room; Rich was reading the paper and Paul was looking at his smartphone.

"I can never get my thumbs to hit the right letters," Denis said. "Fat finger problem I guess. I think you have to have been born after 1980 to do it right. "He did his best crooked sorry smile, kind of pushing his lower lip against his upper like he didn't have any teeth. Paul smiled and kept sending whatever email he was sending.

They were bonding the way guys bond, and he wondered how he had let himself be so absent from them for the last ten years. He just couldn't live in the house with Elissa, and neither of them wanted to divorce, or at least he hadn't wanted to, so he ended up saving face by taking over the New York office of the company he started, ostensibly because they couldn't find anyone else to do it. At first he had traveled back and forth every six weeks or so, but as Elissa became more interested in her boy toy of the moment, he found it impossible to stay in the house with her. She would smoke cigarettes and drink vodka and get testy and short-tempered, so his visits became fewer and shorter, and more oriented toward holidays or birthdays. They didn't hate each other; they had a shorthand that allowed them to communicate wordlessly, and they liked many of the same things. As he used to say with a smile, we have no common interests--I like opera and Elissa likes oratorio. He had always intended that to be funny. Well, that was over.

He looked at his sons and wondered what could have happened if he had hung out there instead of going away. Fishing trips to Catalina maybe, stuff like that, tickets to the Rose Bowl, although he was not a football fan, picnics with the grandkids.

The doorbell snapped him out of that. It was two plainclothes police officers, a stocky man of about fifty with salt-and-pepper, short-cropped hair and a well-tailored suit, and a fit-looking woman of about the same age with pants, a white blouse open at the neck, low, stacked-heel pumps and her dark hair up in a bun. No ring. They were Detective Ron Furman and Detective Sue Mason from the LA County Sheriff's Department.

He showed them into the living room and offered to make them some coffee. They declined.

"Mr. Rosa," Furman said, "we got the results of the autopsy, and you were right that there were indications that your wife had ingested GHB, as you apparently did yesterday. The bottle of vodka had GHB crystals dissolved in it. Alcohol is an excellent solvent for GHB."

"So she died of a drug overdose?" Rich asked.

"No. She died from drowning, her lungs were full of chlorinated water from the hot tub, but she was certainly unconscious when she slid under the water, or was pushed under the water. There were no signs of a struggle."

"She was murdered then."

"That is a possibility," Furman said. "We need to investigate more. She could have taken the drug on purpose. It is called Liquid Ecstasy in the clubs and lots of people abuse it recreationally. And you did find marijuana in the freezer, and some poppers, and there were a variety of uppers and downers in the medicine chest."

"But you'd have to be suicidal to take a drug and then sit in a hot tub," Denis said.

"Or just drunk," Detective Mason said, looking directly at Denis without blinking.

"Was she drunk?" Paul asked.

"She had a lot of alcohol in her system, yes."

"Then she was murdered," Denis said, standing up. "I had some of that vodka and it threw me on the floor in a matter of minutes. I could not have drunk enough of it to get even tipsy before I passed out. Someone must have added it to the vodka after she had been drinking."

"That's a possibility," Mason said. "Or she could have added it to the vodka herself."

"And who put it back in the pantry?"

"She could have done that herself, and then taken the drink outside in the hot tub, although according to the report there was no glass found at the hot tub, so maybe she just chugged some vodka and then got in the water."

She's trying to find a logical sequence of events. He looked at her making notes. *She's pretty. But that doesn't change the fact that Elissa was killed by someone else.*

"We want to have a funeral," Denis said. "And she wanted to be cremated."

"The coroner will release her to you for the funeral and there is no reason you cannot carry out her wishes. The coroner has some specimens, x-rays and photos if we need them."

"One other thing," Furman said. "There was sperm in her, so we have DNA from a guy who was with her fairly recently."

"That's not a surprise," said Denis. "She had an eye for guys, I guess you would say."

"Does that bother you?" It was the woman asking.

"It used to. That was mostly why I moved to New York a decade ago. I stopped worrying about her sex life at some point."

"And you were in New York when this happened?"

"Yes."

"Well, we're very sorry for your loss, as I am sure others have said," she offered, looking like she meant it, not a trace of sarcasm or

21

officialdom.

The detectives gave them all business cards and said they should call if they had information or questions. Then they left.

"They don't know whether to call it suicide or homicide," Paul said. "I wonder what the final police report will say. God knows who was fucking her that night."

Denis walked out to the retaining wall that was attempting, unsuccessfully, to keep the clifftop from eroding. The adobe bricks were uneven and water from the spring rains had formed little channels under them. He stared at the beautiful vista that he had known since childhood, the blue hulk of Catalina Island taking up most of the straight-on view, and a clump of pine trees on the point that formed the southern end of Lunada Bay.

"It wasn't suicide," he said. "It just wasn't. We may not have gotten on well enough to live together, but I knew her, knew her bad habits and her good impulses. She would not have killed herself. Someone did this to her, whether it was the guy she was with, or someone else. Someone murdered your mother. Someone murdered my wife, and if I had gone swimming after that drink instead of before, that same person might have murdered me without even being here."

Chapter Four

PVE is a pocket suburb of almost other-worldly beauty just out of the main line of traffic and commerce in the South Bay area of LA County. Much of it was designed in the early part of the twentieth century by the son of Frederick Law Olmstead, who laid out Central Park and Prospect Park in New York City, and who designed most of the city parks in Boston and Montreal, and the campus at Stanford University. The younger Olmstead created a completely manmade environment at the southern end of Santa Monica Bay, but in the nearly one hundred years since it was originally executed, the vegetation had gone wild, with thick eucalyptus forests forming a backbone that enclosed the picture-perfect country club and which ran in controlled strands through the divided highway, around the Italianate adobe brick library, and encircled the picture-postcard shopping area that the locals call The Plaza. This has a huge, ornate white marble fountain surmounted by a trident-brandishing Neptune in the style of Canova, with naked boys riding idealized fish squirting water from their mouths into a basin surrounding the whole. The buildings around The Plaza have a uniform colonnade with Roman curved arches and vaguely Ionic capitals and pedestals. Visitors say it looks like Italy or the French Riviera.

To build a house in the controlled areas of PVE, you had to get permission for everything from a local power broker group called the Art Jury. Your roof was required to be red tile. The color of your house had to be approved. The front yard landscaping had to be approved. Your mailbox had to be approved. You were not allowed to park on the street overnight. If your trees obstructed someone's view, you were required to cut them back or cut them down. If ever there was a town that strived to look perfect, it was PVE.

Needless to say, it took money to live there, but the Rosa home had been in the family for over sixty years and the statewide controls on property taxes kept a lid on the cost of owning the home. The original mortgage had been paid off in the 1970s, and the house had been mortgage free until after Denis moved to New York, when Elissa decided she needed cash to redecorate and to travel and whatnot, and he agreed to take a relatively small mortgage on the house and to hand the proceeds over to her. He had been paying on that fifteen-year mortgage for eight years, and it was a burden because his income was decreasing in an economy with a global downturn squeezing it.

The funeral was set for Friday morning in a small church, St. Francis, near a bluff looking down to the ocean near Malaga Cove. The rector was a woman, though Father Yamaguchi was usually there, too. He had never gotten used to women as priests, although he had no objection. It was like having a woman for a doctor; he'd had women examine him in the hospital, but never got over feeling awkward dropping his pants. Not that he had to drop his pants with the priest, but it still felt odd. He engaged an organist and told him to play some Bach, after which his playlist included "Simple Gifts", "Amazing Grace", and "Long and Winding Road." All three were guaranteed weepers for him, but they were signs of his respect for her that he would expose himself like that.

But in the meantime, he stopped at a real estate office in The Plaza and found an old-timer, someone who had been there since before the newbies started arriving, when most of the hill had been covered with Japanese truck farms and, for whatever reason, miles of garbanzo beans. The white-haired man introduced himself as Jim Kearny, and of course he knew the Rosa house on Rocky Point.

"Perfect location, isn't it?" he said. "Right above where that ship cracked up a while back."

"You *have* been here a while," Denis said. "That was when I was in high school back in about 1961. It was called the *Dominator*. The captain was drunk and hit the rocks out by the end of the point. It was full of grain, and when it fermented the whole neighborhood smelled like beer for a while."

They had a good chuckle about the old times.

"I haven't put a house on the market in my whole life," Denis said. "I have no idea what to do first."

He would need to find a copy of the title, or get one from the county or the city. If the house was community property he would need a death certificate, and Kearny suggested he get twenty or thirty of those, because he would need them for lots of things. Then someone would have to try to figure out the asking price, which would certainly run into seven figures. Denis took his card and said he would get back to him in a few days, then drove home.

Home. It had been home most of his life until the last few years when he was in New York. Then it was her home, not his, and she had changed things around, taken some of his paintings down and bought different furniture. No idea where some of the stuff was, but wherever everything was, he felt it all as a burden. Imagine trying to empty this house so someone could move in. A daunting task. There was virtually no attic and certainly no basement, so if the old things were still somewhere, they had to be in a storage depot someplace. He did not feel like going through Elissa's desk, but he had to, and might as well do it now as later.

He had not expected to find a will, and there was none that he could find. There were a variety of bills to be paid, but nothing apparently overdue, and her checkbook had been balanced through the week before; there was a notation to the effect that she had balanced it with the statement. There was plenty of money in the account to pay her current bills. He looked at the open balances on the credit cards. There was a Visa card with a $20,000 balance, but the others--if that was all of them--were low. If he could sell the house, the proceeds would be enough to pay everything off and still have a lot left over. His father had bought the house in 1956 for under $40,000 and he suspected the asking price now would be over $2 million. Although she had lived in the house, it belonged to him solely, because it was inherited from his mother, along with all the contents, when she died. He was an only child. He had paid some estate taxes at the time, but not much, because the appraisal on the house came in lower than it might have, given the heated-up real estate market. So there would be long-term capital gains tax on the house now, but that was fairly easy to pay if he could sell the house.

It made his heart ache to think about selling it. There were so many memories. And a lot of ghosts, too.

He found the handbag she had been using parked on a side table in the television room, a large multipurpose room with old-fashioned cork flooring that had been there when he was a boy. He opened the navy calf bag and dumped it out on the bed. Other than some wadded-up tissues, there was no junk in the bag, no stray coins or deformed, old sticks of chewing gum or safety pins. He opened the paisley-patterned make-up bag and there were the usual: a compact with skin-colored stuff in it, a couple of lipsticks that had obviously been used, a small container of hand lotion, a small brush that he thought must be for mascara, and a small container of a black inky-looking substance that was probably put on with the brush. There was also a tiny bottle of cologne. He sprayed some of it on his hand and smelled it. Lemon verbena.

There were some receipts in the bag, one long one for groceries dated about a week earlier, and one from a Mexican restaurant in Redondo Beach out on the fisherman's pier at a place called King Harbor. That was for $210.84, a high total for most Mexican places, which tended to be low cost. There was a website address on it, and he turned on the computer in the bedroom, launched a browser and had a look. It was a taco–enchilada type place with a bar, looked like a hundred other places. How would you spend that much money on dinner? He put the receipt aside. There was a piece of paper with a phone number on it, no area code; he put that with the receipt.

He looked through the directory on the computer, found Microsoft Office, and went to Outlook. It wanted a password. He looked all over the desk pad, which had notes all over the calendar pad. In the lower right corner was a printed phrase, "rockypoint3." He put in her name and then typed rockypoint3 into the password. It opened. If she was at all like other people, she would have used that same password for other programs, too. He flipped through the Contacts section of the Outlook file looking for the phone number and found it: someone named Ricardo Espinosa, no address, no email. He dialed the number and it went to voicemail.

"Hi, this is Ricardo. Leave a message and I'll get back to you."

He looked through the bills and found the phone bill. The same phone number was on the bill seven times in two days, but it was two weeks ago. He circled the number each time he found it. Then he looked for other repeating phone numbers, his curiosity getting the best of him. There were many. The kids' home numbers and Rich's office number were there. A number with the same exchange as the one here, probably a neighbor. But after he eliminated the ones he could recognize or sort of recognize, there were still six others. He put asterisks by them and wrote the numbers down on a pad.

Then he went back to the Outlook file and looked up those numbers. Three of them were there. All of them were Hispanic names; none had an email or an address. They all went to voicemail, but it was a time of day when most people would be at work, so that didn't prove anything. They were distinctly different voices, and one was a woman, though the name on the Outlook file was Edgardo. The wife maybe.

He realized he was prying, looking at things he was not intended to see. It didn't make any difference, he wanted to find out what happened, so he kept going. He pulled the center drawer of the desk out and turned it over on the bed, dumping out all the bits and pieces, paperclips, old matchbooks, business cards that were wrinkled and old. He looked at each bit of paper both sides. Nothing of interest.

He went to the closet, pulled out all the other handbags, and looked through them. The occasional bit of paper or receipt for something, but small amounts and no phone numbers.

The Outlook mail file had nothing of any interest in it. As a matter of fact, it had very little of anything in it. He looked at the Discarded Mail file; it was empty.

The phone rang. It was Maggie. Did he want to come over for dinner? Or could she bring him some food?

"Oh, kiddo, thanks. I'm just sorting through some things here and I doubt I'll go out. There are things in the fridge and I'll just make something here."

She said she wanted to come over and she would bring Alix, her daughter, who was in second grade. Maggie was divorced, but on good terms with her ex, who took Alix on the weekends and paid child support.

"OK, if you want," he said. "I haven't seen Alix in a while. I bet she's grown a foot."

He put everything back where it had been and tidied up the bedspread where he had dumped things out on it, brushed his teeth, and then went into the living room and looked through the CDs. He was distracted, but there were some chamber music discs that were probably his originally. He put on a Louis Lortie disc that was all Ravel, starting with "Pavanne pour une infant défunte" (Pavanne for a dead princess); a chestnut, but a pretty one. He went into the kitchen and poured himself a scotch on the rocks with a splash of tap water. He tasted it gingerly and waited. Nothing. He took another swallow. Nothing. Elissa was not a scotch drinker, never had been, so there would have been no point putting drugs in the scotch. He looked in the fridge to see if there were soft drinks. There were a few cans of this and that. He got out some crackers and cheese and put them on the kitchen table. Odd that people seldom used their living rooms anymore.

He opened the sliding glass door out to the pool area and could hear the waves breaking; the late sunlight sparkled glaringly on the water in the pool.

Alix brought her own sunlight into the room with her: a smile that lit up all the dark corners of his mind. He picked her up and swung her around, then set her back down.

"You're getting too big for that, aren't you?" he beamed at her.

"Oh, Grandpa, I love you," she said cooing. He could see Maggie in her, Maggie with blonde braids and little rubber bands in the ends, the kind of rubber bands that you used on braces, the little ones. He glanced at Maggie and she was looking at him looking at Alix and smiling.

"Yes, people say she looks like me more and more."

"People are right."

He took them into the kitchen and offered crackers and cheese and a soft drink. Alix wrinkled up her nose at the cheese, so he asked her if she wanted some peanut butter. Yes.

He and Maggie stood by the counter while Alix merrily made mini sandwiches with Triscuits and peanut butter, and then crunched into them.

"This is kind of an odd thing to ask, so I apologize. But did Mom have a Latino boyfriend that you know of?"

Maggie stared at him for a moment as though he had spoken a foreign language and she couldn't understand him. Then she looked down at the sink and out the window at the ocean.

"I don't know for sure," she said softly but without whispering, "but I think so. As a matter of fact, there were probably several, but I tried to keep my nose out of that. I always felt like it was something that was best left alone. I saw her with a young Chicano one time when I drove by The Plaza and they were obviously not discussing business, if you know what I mean. I almost waved at first, because I was driving around looking for a parking place, but I left and went back later instead."

"Did she use any drugs that you know of? There was a variety of things in the medicine cabinet in the bathroom, and there was some marijuana in the freezer, and that little bottle that smelled like smelling salts, whatever you call it." He tried to put zero inflection on any of the pieces of the question, just as though he were writing it out instead of speaking it.

Alix cuddled up to him, and said, "Grandpa, can I go swimming?"

"Ask your mother. You can't go swimming alone, so she would have to be there with you, at least sitting by the pool watching you," he said, smiling at her.

She beamed back and said, "Mom, can I go swimming in Grandma's pool?"

"Why don't you watch TV instead?" Maggie said. Alix shrugged and walked slowly down the hall toward the television room.

"She was hanging around with younger guys, you know," Maggie said. "I guess it would not surprise me if she was taking something, but I never knew her to be high when I was around, or to act embarrassing other than kissy-face stuff with a hunky Mexican kid."

"Kid?"

"Well, not kid, exactly, except she was beyond cougar age, you know, and she didn't have face-lifts or whatever, so she really looked like, I don't know, out of place kissing him on the mouth."

He didn't mention the sperm in her vagina from the autopsy.

Maggie was already on the verge of crying.

"Don't worry about it, kiddo. Mom was a good person. She always put you and the boys first, you know. And I left, so she was alone a lot of the time."

She said, "I think I should see what Alix is watching," and walked down the hall dabbing at her eyes with a paper towel.

Chapter Five

There was no viewing.

The funeral was simple and the coffin was closed. The three Rosa children--Paul, Richard and Maggie--had a chance to see Elissa before the coffin was closed, and all of them declined. Denis was the only member of the family there when the coffin was closed.

The family were all there, kids and grandkids. Even Alix's father came and sat with them. Rich, Melanie and their four boys sat with Denis, and Aunt Elsa, who was in her mid-90s, flew in from Alabama. Paul and Christie were there with their two girls. Elissa's two cousins from Santa Barbara drove down, and there were thirty or forty longtime friends of the family: two nuns from a hospital where Elissa had volunteered, several local policemen, and an actress Elissa had gone to school with. Elissa had been active with the PTA when the kids were in school and there was a small group of past and present PTA officials. Denis gave the eulogy, which ignored the manner of her death and the peccadilloes of her sixties. Rich stood up and took his boys up to the altar with him, knelt in front of the coffin and cried for his mother, but never said a word.

The organist played the prescribed music and there was widespread sobbing when "Long and Winding Road" started; it continued for four long choruses with some people singing along and holding hands. That brought back to Denis the woman he had married, all giggles and practical jokes, wobbling on her high heels walking down the aisle.

Maggie and Paul formed a reverse receiving line outside the church, thanking people for coming. Only Denis went with her to the crematorium. He waited for a while and then decided to just let the

Neptune Society take care of it. A few days later the ashes were scattered from a small private boat halfway to Avalon from Long Beach harbor. Ashes to ashes like her ancient namesake, Elissa returned to the sea.

Denis took a call from Jim Kearny, who said he had done some computer surveys of comparable sales and was ready to talk about how to go about listing the house.

The good news was that there were no other comparable homes on the market right now. The bad news was that there had been no sales of cliffside homes in the area for more than eighteen months, so Kearny thought they would have to extrapolate from noncomparable sales and mark them up for views, ocean access, etc.

"You mean wet your finger and stick it up in the air to see which way the wind is blowing?" Denis asked.

"More or less. Fortunately, you are the only game in town, so we can see what kinds of offers are made, and raise or lower the price based on interest," Kearny said. "Either way," he advised, "you should clean up the landscaping a bit in the front and paint the interiors. Don't do anything fancy, because whoever buys it is likely to rip it apart and remodel anyway. Given the age of the house, it could even be a tear-down."

Kearny said he had looked at recent sales in Laguna Beach, sixty miles or so to the south, but a similar kind of community, and a similar kind of buyer most likely. One house with about the same square footage, but a larger lot, had recently sold for $6,695,000, so discounting for the smaller lot, that might suggest something in the range of $5–$6 million. It was a ranch-style house, which was a zoning requirement, no multiple storeys allowed, and whoever bought it would have to stay within the same envelope or battle with the Art Jury to get it changed, which was unlikely.

The number itself was shocking to Denis. He had worked hard all his life and had not come close to earning $5 million, even if he had kept it all, which he hadn't. And his father had paid less than $40,000 for the house in 1956 and expected it to depreciate from there, because like anything else, it would be worth less when it was used. At that point, with miles of cliff unbuilt, there was no thought that the waterside unobstructed views, clean air, and the sound of surf would be such a scarce commodity in the twenty-first century. By 2000, most of the available seaside lots in LA County had been built on, and they did not change hands often. In Orange County, for instance, the Irvine Company, no longer in the hands of the Irvine family, had subdivided oceanside land mercilessly, and sold it in tiny lots with huge homes virtually touching each other on the sides, all homage to the ocean views. Those homes were selling for £2 million plus, and there was no safer investment in California, because once they were built out, there was no replacement inventory.

Even so, it was like finding a gusher in your back yard. He had inherited some ranchland halfway between Houston and San Antonio, and he had been through several oil leases and zero drilling, so he knew what it meant to wonder what a gusher would do. This was no gusher; all he had to do was sell the homestead to whoever had enough clams to buy it. Otherwise, he would have to continue paying the mortgage for another seven years, and at the age of sixty-eight, the payment was too much for a house he had no intention of living in.

He went out into the side yard where his father had planted a peach tree, looked at it, twenty feet tall, and knew it had dropped peaches all over the ground every year. Big, juicy yellow cling peaches, nothing wrong with them other than the occasional bird peck. Trouble was they all got ripe in a two week period, so if you didn't want to can them or make a heck of a lot of pies, they rotted on the ground and brought gnats to the pool area. And the cactus garden in the front was his mom's idea, the night-blooming cereus one of the wonders of nature--you just had to see it at 10:00 p.m., and it was gone by morning. He had fallen into the jumping cholla on his bike when he was in seventh grade and it took hours to pull all the barbed thorns out of his leg.

Old Duke, the black lab, was buried behind the garage; he died back in 1965. Best dog ever.

Well, ghosts were everywhere. Friendly ghosts for the most part. Elissa was still there, waiting for closure; he knew that, and he would have to either take her with him to New York, or leave her there with whoever bought the place. On the other hand, he would be able to retire finally, and most likely could leave a real inheritance to his grandkids.

Not a bad trade-off.

He signed Kearny's exclusive and they decided they would list at $6,550,000. They would do a broker preview on Saturday and then it would hit the multiple listing service on Monday.

Rich and Melanie had invited him to dinner. He didn't want to go, but wanted even less to offend them.

"Hi, Mel, it's Denis. Hey, I was thinking, I never get any good Mexican food in New York. What do you say we all go get some Mexican food tonight instead of you having to cook. We could take the boys if you want, or we can leave them with a babysitter if you could use a night off."

Put that way, she agreed, and said she would get a sitter.

"Great," he said. "And tell the boys I want them to come over this weekend and go swimming. I'll make hotdogs on the grill." He could see her smiling on the phone.

"So," he said, "I think there's a Mexican place out on the pier at King Harbor, don't remember the name, Casa Adobado or something like that. Nice to be out on the pier anyway. I can meet you there, or you can come over here and pick me up."

They agreed to meet at the restaurant at six. That would be right at sunset, Melanie said, a pretty time out on the water.

Good. I'll be able to see how much you'd have to eat to spend that much money.

He decided to hike over to the canyon that was formed by a runoff stream and cut through the soft clay and diatomaceous earth to form an easy path down to the rocky beach from the clifftop. It was about a half-mile walk to the top of the pathway, and then another quarter-mile down to the beach, the way smelling of sagebrush and slippery leather plant that could land you on your butt if you stepped on it: more slippery than banana peels in a Three Stooges movie.

No one could describe the smell of a kelp bed at low tide. There were little crabs scuttling around under the wet rocks, and soft anemones waving in the tide that would close on your heel and feel like they were sucking on you if you stepped on them. He was carrying his shoes and stepping gingerly from rock to rock, avoiding the sharp barnacles with his soft feet that were used to sturdy leather shoes instead of rock beaches. *How life changes.*

The smell was fresh, not stale, but salty and wild, not something you would come across away from the beach. There were kelp bass out there, little ones that made a perfect individual serving of flaky white fish. Striped or spotted, and about twelve or fourteen inches long, spiny, and capable of drawing blood if you grabbed them wrong and stuck one of the spinal spikes in your finger or palm. Problem was, of course, your hook would grab the kelp more often than a fish, so it took patience and luck to bring in supper.

There were mussels everywhere, one of his favorite foods. If he lived here, he would gather them and make the best cioppino in the history of the world. All the fresh fennel growing up the sides of the cliff: lacy, fernlike, licorice-smelling foliage. And that wonderful white root that made the cioppino taste Italian. It was like a cioppino Garden of Eden. Wow, and a kelp bass would make it perfect.

He had walked these rocks with Elissa when they were courting. Mom loved her from the get-go. Who could look ahead? Nobody. He was besotted with her. She was a high soprano with an agile voice, but a fainting inability to audition. He took her to auditions and she would hyperventilate and get light-headed. She was fine in the quartet at church, quite OK, and read music no problem at all. Good pitch, even better solfège, reading intervals. He'd never been able to read a vocal score, although he could pick it out on a keyboard, but she could read anything if you gave her a starting note. A pitch pipe would do.

He sang out, rolling the Rs in an exaggerated fashion to make it sound more Scottish, "Out from the sea came a little green crab/taking the sun, the morning being very drab... The tinker and the crab." Couldn't remember the words in between.

The sun was lower in the sky than he realized, and he turned around before he got out to the point and walked purposefully back to the easy path up the cliff. He passed a group of teenagers on the cliffside path along Paseo del Mar, cut between two houses to get to Rocky Point Road, and fast-walked out to his home at the end of the point. It was nearly five and he was to meet Rich and Mel at King Harbor in Redondo Beach, a good twenty-five-minute drive if you didn't want a speeding ticket.

He slipped off his jeans and put on a pair of gray slacks and a plaid shirt, a pair of loafers with silver buckles, and a blue blazer with dark colored buttons. He grabbed his keys and automatically went out into the garage. No. It was her car there, not the rental that he had driven over. He went back through the house and got in the rental car, a white Chevy Malibu, which was sitting in the driveway.

The drive from Rocky Point through PVE took him along Bluff Cove, a favorite spot for surfers who were willing to deal with rocks on the beach. The white cliffs were largely diatomaceous earth, which had the advantage if you lived near them of killing a wide variety of insects. For whatever reason, the chalky dirt was totally harmless to animals and people, but toxic to critters with exoskeletons. So, for example, there were zero ants on his property. The verdant green hill sloped down at a steep angle around Bluff Cove and the native shrubs were long gone after the remaking of the hill in the early part of the previous century. There were wild roses and even wild peacocks strutting around in the eucalyptus groves. Ethel Barrymore used to live in one of the big homes near the cliff edge.

It was just going on six when he pulled into the parking lot. The sun was flattening out on the horizon before disappearing, the colors beautiful like a Japanese teacup his grandmother had. He walked out the pier to find Casa Adobado, which looked like any Mexican restaurant. Rich and Mel were not there yet, so he walked over to the hostess and told her they would need a table for three, he thought.

"No problem," she said, "just tell me when your party are all here."

"Is there a Ricardo Espinosa working here by any chance?"

"Yes, would you like to sit in his area?"

"Sure," he said. A waiter.

Rich and Mel walked in, but no kids.

"I see you opted for a restful evening," Denis said. He kissed Melanie on the cheek and admired her outfit. "Pretty blouse, very becoming." She smiled.

He walked back over to the hostess and said, "We're all here."

She grabbed some menus and walked toward the dining room. "This way," she said as she walked past them.

She seated them by a window, but the last of the sunset was gone, so it was just dark blue outside, with a hint of horizon defined by a slightly lighter-colored shade of indigo where the sun had been. A tall, slim Mexican man with the broad nose of a Mayan, but extraordinarily even features and perfect skin walked over to the table.

"My name is Ricardo and I will be serving you this evening. I see you have your menus. Can I get you a drink?" He motioned to a busboy, who quickly brought some tortilla chips and salsa to the table. Ricardo's voice was deep and friendly, and he had no perceptible accent.

"You from around here?" Denis asked.

"Originally from Indio," he said, "but there's no work out there and I like the beach better than the desert."

"I think you know a friend of ours, Elissa Rosa. She told us to come here and ask for you."

Rich and Mel looked up and at the waiter, and then at Denis, who did not break his gaze with Ricardo.

"Yes, Mrs. Rosa comes here often. I will try to make your dinner extra special."

"My name is Denis, and this is my son, Richard, and his wife, Melanie."

The young man registered the names and looked briefly up at the ceiling then back at Denis. He shifted from one foot to the other and moved closer to Rich and Mel, away from Denis.

"Can I get you a drink?" No break in his composure.

"I'll have a Dos Equis, the darker kind."

"Same for me," Rich said, and Melanie added her order for the same.

"Right back," Ricardo said.

A few minutes later a different waiter arrived with the beers.

"Where's Ricardo?" Denis asked.

"He had to leave. My name is Jose and I will be helping you. I will be back to get your dinner orders in a couple of minutes."

Denis looked at Rich, who just looked puzzled.

"What was all that about?"

"Nothing. He was a friend of your mom's, apparently. I found his phone number in the desk and looked at the phone bill. She called him several times in a row, and she called this restaurant, too."

"So you're trying to check up on Mom, even after she's dead?" Rich asked, his voice rising in pitch and volume as the question finished.

"Not exactly. I admit that I wonder who might have drugged her and pushed her under the water to drown, but that's a police matter. I don't care much what her taste in young studs was. And however much you might think otherwise, her behavior in that department was not news to me. Discretion was not her strong suit."

He explained that Ricardo evidently recognized either their first names, or possibly their faces from the family photos in the house. He also knew that Denis knew who he was and it spooked him. So he ran. No point chasing after him, not now at least.

"Just so you know, there were five other names in the desk, too, all Hispanic."

"Well, she had good taste," Melanie said. "That guy looked like a television hunk."

Rich looked at her sharply.

"Not my type, Rich. I stand by my man." She winked at him and obviously stroked his leg under the table.

"OK, everybody calm down," Denis said. "I sprang this on you, but I did not intend it to go like this. I just wanted to see him and see what he looked like. I didn't want to punch him or scare him. And for what it's worth, he doesn't look like someone who would have killed someone, although I'm not sure what a killer looks like, to tell the truth."

They all sank back down in their chairs and signaled to Jose, who came and took their dinner orders.

"Mom had some fairly big tabs at this restaurant recently. I was just curious, that's all. Tell me about the boys and let's leave Ricardo be and enjoy the food."

It took some effort for each of them, but the atmosphere for the rest of the meal was light and superficial. Mel told little stories about each of the boys and her pride in them beamed out.

When he got home, Denis went to the computer and pulled up the Amex card records. Her card was on his account. There were numerous charges at Casa Adobado, and either they were for large parties or she was getting things that were not on the menu, because her tabs were at least double what dinner had been for the three of them that evening; they had had a couple of beers each, and green corn tamales for dessert. He found the detectives' cards and, on impulse, dialed Sue Mason.

Chapter Six

"You said I could call if I had any questions. I'm sorry to call you off-hours like this. Would you prefer I call you tomorrow instead?"

She said it was OK, she was just watching TV.

"I just wanted to know if you have any leads on what happened, that's all."

She told him that the coroner's report was that death was caused by drowning, but that there was not sufficient evidence to indicate that it was a homicide instead of an accidental overdose, so the death was marked "inconclusive." In other words, there would have to be further evidence to prove it either way. The case would remain open, but they might not pursue it unless the DNA they had collected showed up in a state or FBI database.

"She had boyfriends, you know. Young guys, and I think mostly Chicano. If she brought them up here, they might have got the impression she was rich, although she wasn't. I'm pretty sure I know who one of them was and I have names of several others."

She asked if he had been trying to investigate the situation on his own.

"I looked through her things, which I have to do anyway, and some things jumped out at me. I found this one name and phone number, and she had called his number a bunch of times. He's a waiter and I went to the restaurant where he works. I think he recognized me and my son and his wife, and took off."

"Took off?"

"Well, he took our drinks order and I told him that Elissa had suggested we try the restaurant. Then I introduced us by our first names only, but that was enough. He left and a different waiter took over."

"How old is he?"

"Around late twenties, I think."

"Good-looking?"

"Yes."

"She was what they call a cougar, you know, an older woman who likes younger men."

He sucked in his breath. "Yes, I know about that, it's been that way for a long time. Maybe he was selling her drugs. He probably thought she was rich, like I said."

Detective Mason offered to drive over so they could talk face to face. He looked at the clock: it was ten fifteen. "Maybe in the morning?" he asked. They agreed she would stop over in the morning at eight and he would be sure to have some coffee brewed.

He couldn't resist the pool since the air outside was not chilly, although there was a fogbank sitting offshore as there was almost every night. He had been living in New York for nearly ten years and there was no opportunity to swim there unless he was invited to someone's beach club. He took off his clothes, dived into the deep end, and swam several lengths of breast stroke, coming up panting. The water felt wonderful on his skin. *Nothing gets rid of stress better than exercise.* He pulled himself up and out of the water, holding the chrome railing above the ladder on the side of the pool, grabbed a towel and started to dry off.

A trick of the light made it seem as though there was someone sitting in the hot tub, but he squinted and there was no one there. He picked up his glasses from the wicker table by one of the lounge chairs and looked at the hot tub again. There was a cloud of steam hovering over it like a ghost and picking up the light from the pool.

"Elissa," he said. "No hard feelings, truly. I am going to try to find out how this happened to you, that's all. If someone hurt you, I want to know, and I want the police to know."

No response. The breeze swept up over the edge of the cliff and dispersed the column of steam. He turned off the heat, pulled the cover over the hot tub, and went indoors.

She had taken much of his art collection down. *It's probably all in the wine room and the garage.* She had left a painting by an English artist named Bradford, a big acrylic and oil canvas that had innumerable toys and childhood characters in it--a man on a blue horse, a red-uniformed soldier with a hat like a London Bobby, and a pink and brown airplane on fire and crashing downward. He had always liked it and seeing it over the sofa was like meeting an old friend. *Why do people hang things over the sofa so they can't see them? Oh well.*

He had a nip of brandy and went to bed.

Sue Mason showed up at eight, good as her word. She was more familiar in her attitude, but still a bit distant, as a police officer should be. He poured her some coffee and offered milk or sugar, but she wanted it black. He put a little milk in his cup to cool it down. They walked into the living room and she looked at the red soldier, cocked her head.

"Like it?" he asked.

"Yes, it looks like a dream a little boy might have."

"I think that's the idea. When I bought it there was a companion piece that was all ballerinas and dolls, pastel colors, and maybe even some sweets in it as I recall. It was a long time ago, and I didn't much like the girly painting, but this one spoke to me. It was in a gallery in downtown LA, near Skid Row. I think the painter was deported, to tell the truth--he had overstayed his visa or something. I got a real deal on the piece, though for the life of me I don't remember the cost. It's an eye-grabber, though."

She asked him to tell her again about the incident at the restaurant so he went over the light search he had done of Elissa's handbag and desk, and showed her the phone bill where he had circled the repeat phone numbers that he didn't recognize.

"Look, detective, everyone knows that Elissa liked men, and that she screwed around. It was connected to why I moved to New York, and I was pretty upset at the time. Most people assumed I had been unfaithful to her and had been thrown out, but that was not the case. I left rather than confront the fact that she had at least one boyfriend she was seeing pretty regularly. Prosaically, he was the next-door neighbor's gardener. I told him I was aware of it and he stopped coming around, but I think when I moved out they went right back to it. He was married, too, and I think when I left she moved to younger and younger guys. She was a pretty woman, even at her age, and in shape, too. I got used to it, and she generally behaved when I was visiting to see the kids and grandkids. We actually learned to get along pretty well, considering."

She looked at the phone bills and said, "These that you circled are Espinosa's phone?"

"Yes, that is his number. If you call it you will get his voicemail, or at least I did."

She took out her smartphone and dialed the number.

"Mr. Espinosa? This is Detective Sue Mason from the LA County Sheriff's Department. If you don't mind, I'd like to ask you a few questions... It's about Elissa Rosa... Well, I think it would be best if I came to your place rather than talking about it on the phone. Would that be OK?... A suspect in what? Yes, she is dead. She drowned... No, he did not... No, you are not... Just give me your address and I will be there in about an hour." She wrote it down as he dictated it and held the pad so that Denis could not see it. "OK, about ten thirty then. Thanks."

"I'm going to talk to him and I think it would be best if you did not bother him anymore," she said.

"Are you going to try to find out who did this?"

She said that the implication of the coroner's report was that there was a good chance Elissa had drowned after self-administering a drug.

"That's it? Case closed?" he said softly.

"No case is closed unless there is a clear answer to the question of how it happened. There is no clear answer here and the case is still open," she said in as friendly a manner as she could. "Mr. Rosa, it's normal to be upset, and we are still waiting for some tests of items we took from the home, the vodka bottle, the prescription bottles and pills, her clothing, the sheets that had been taken off her bed, the clothes she had been wearing from the hamper, and the glass tumbler sitting by the bed.

"But you have to understand that there was no evidence of any kind of violence, not even any evidence that there was another person here. We dusted everything for fingerprints--doorknobs, windows, the chrome handrail into the hot tub... The nature of these things is that lots of people touch them, though, and although we will run all the fingerprints we collected, I kinda think it is unlikely that anything helpful will show up.

"Now if you have knowledge of things you are not sharing, you ought to tell us whatever you think or suspect, because this is an open case and we will be trying to find out the truth to the extent it is possible. I'll ask you again. Was anything missing at all?"

He shook his head. "I have no way of knowing, because I was not living here, but if something is missing, it is not something that a thief would take. The televisions and electronics are here, Elissa's smartphone, what looks to be all of her jewelry, her car, her handbag, her checkbook, her credit cards. Everything is here, as far as I can tell. Are you going to ask him if he was here that night?"

"Mr. Rosa," she said. "Everyone has a legitimate expectation of privacy, including Mr. Espinosa. I am going to ask him what he knows, where he was the night of Mrs. Rosa's death, and the other things you would imagine I will ask him. But unless there is reason to believe that he was involved, the answers he gives me will not be public. In other words, I am not going to tell you what he tells me unless there is something that doesn't match up. And to be fair, I am not going to tell him what you have told me either. No one is suspected of a crime here, remember that."

He stared at her, trying to take her measure. "Do you think Elissa killed herself by taking that drug and getting into the hot tub so she would drown?"

She closed her writing pad and clicked the top of her ballpoint pen to retract the point. She looked at him and said, "No, I do not think that. Do I think she might have done it accidentally? She could have. When you have this job, you see a lot more unlikely things than a civilian would guess. But no, I doubt she accidentally overdosed herself. That's a personal statement, not official. I think she was probably in the hot tub with someone else, likely a man, probably a sexual partner. I suspect he poured her a drink and when she slipped under the water he washed the glasses, put them away, and left. I think she knew him, he knew the house, and he left nothing but wet footprints. I think he was someone who had been here before, possibly many times. If it's warranted, we will ask the neighbors who the regular visitors were to the house, but I can almost guarantee you that this waiter is not the guy who did this. He is too young, too helpful. He probably left when he figured out who you were because he did not want to have a scene and get fired. If he had been involved, he would have been pissing his pants when I told him I wanted to come over to his place."

She was on his side, that was what she had just said. She wanted to find out who did it, too.

"Look," she said, "I don't make the rules. I need something to go on, and if you give me something to go on that's not just a jealous husband's anger at someone he never met, I'll look into it. In fact, I am going to leave now and look into Mr. Espinosa, even though I don't have any real reason to think he had anything to do with it. Just call me, OK? Call me if you find anything. You're on the right track with the phone numbers, I think, but you need to be more systematic looking at things, credit card statements, phone bills, and remember that the items she bought in the last few weeks may not have shown up on her credit card statements yet. If you want, I will come over and bring Ron with me, and we can go over the credit card statements, the phone bills, whatever you think is worthwhile. But we can't just come over here and spend a whole day wondering what happened. Got it?"

"Is there any harm in my continuing to talk to other people?" he asked.

"Not unless you violate someone else's rights," she said. "It's a free country. But we don't take kindly to vigilantes, if you have any ideas along those lines."

"Hardly," he said. "I am a senior citizen and would not bounce back quickly from getting punched out."

"A senior citizen?"

"Sixty-eight."

"You're kidding."

"I don't kid about my age. It's not funny. I have a bad right knee, a small hernia in my groin, and the remains of a blood clot in my left leg. I can't count the number of skin cancers I have had removed, and about a quarter of my teeth are crowned. I can't drink a martini without my hand shaking. And I am a widower. First time I've said that. A widower."

She stood and picked up her pad, put her jacket on and moved toward the door. He walked her outside to the curb and noted that she was in a car with no markings on it and a normal-looking license plate. They shook hands and she left.

A widower. He'd been living as a widower for years, now that he thought about it. Never had any interest in holding hands with anyone other than Elissa. Not that he pined for her, because he had thought he was well rid of her until she died. Marriage had not worked for him, and he was once burned twice careful.

He closed the door behind him and went out by the pool and stared at the ocean. It was a changeable view, but always the same. The sun came and went. Clouds came and went. Fog. Rain. Wind. Steam phantoms.

Chapter Seven

He took the car keys, Elissa's car keys, off the key rack and went out to the garage, opened the door and backed her car out onto the driveway. It needed a wash, and no reason why he should keep a rental if he could drive her Jaguar. The sun was warm, and he was dressed for carwashing--in bathing trunks. He picked up some liquid dish soap and dragged a hose out from the spigot by the front door, picked up a plastic bucket and threw a big sponge in it. He found the vacuum cleaner in the hall closet and an extension cord, and took those out to clean the floor mats, etc. The car was a convertible so he put the top down to make it easier to clean inside.

The center console was full of old stuff. He took it all out, put it in a paper bag, vacuumed inside, and then opened the glove box, which was as full of bits and pieces of stuff as the center console. *Well, the car is thirteen years old. It was here when I was living here, so it's amazing it is in as good a condition as it is.* As he looked closer, the glove box was not as crammed with junk as he thought. Half of it was full of the owner's manual in a fancy leather cover that looked as though it had never been opened. There was a Jaguar owner keychain and phone numbers to call for Jaguar service. The car was bought when Jaguar was owned by Ford Motor Company. Now it was owned by an Indian company, Tata Motors. The Commonwealth was taking over the mother country.

He put the stuff from the glove box (apart from the owner's manual) into the paper bag with the detritus from the center console. He vacuumed the seats and under them too, and took the plastic mats out to wash them separately. There were some pieces of paper that had been trapped under the mats and he threw those into the bag, too. The back seat, vestigial as it was, had on it some obvious trash like granola wrappers and a couple of old baseball caps, but nothing else of note. He popped the trunk. It was full of bits and pieces of things, too: more baseball caps, a couple of beach towels that he threw into the garage toward the washing machine, a box of alcohol swabs like the ones he used to clean his leg before he injected himself with Lovenox, and a lot of odds and ends. There was a Band-Aid-looking single plastic package with a brown patch in it that said "Duragesic CII" on it. He took that and put it in the garage where it would not be out in the sun. "Duragesic" sounded like a pain medication, like "analgesic" made into a brand name.

He knew a bit about that because his mother had been treated with OxyContin patches to control the pain she had from an operation for colon cancer. She was in hospice care so they didn't worry about addiction, just tried to keep her out of pain. As he recalled, OxyContin patches had looked different, though, pinker and larger and more like a Band-Aid.

He finished vacuuming, took a damp sponge, and cleaned off the dashboard and the tops of the seats. The leather was in pretty good condition considering the age of the car, but he'd have to put some leather cream on it when he could get to the store and buy some. Then he put the top up and the windows, and started to soap up the outside. It was very dusty and if you'd brushed up against it, you'd have gotten dirty, but there was no mud or bird shit or the sorts of things that were hard to get off.

He went into the garage, opened the cabinets on the side, and poked around to find a chamois cloth. There was one, but it was stiff and dirty, so he threw it in the big sink next to the washing machine and turned the water on. When it was wet, it softened up and he wrung it out a few times, re-wet it and repeated the wringing. Pretty soon it was close to chamois-colored again and he took the cloth outside, dried the car off, and then buffed it with some old towels.

He noticed one of the tires was low. *I should drive it up the Yarmouth hill and check the pressure all around at the 76 station.* When he was finished, he took the cleaning stuff, put it beside the door into the house, and then coiled the hose up by the front steps. He drove the car back into the garage and closed the garage door. He then took the paper bag and the Duragesic CII thing to the bedroom.

First he looked up Duragesic CII, which turned out to be an opium-based prescription painkiller, not, as far as he could tell, that much different from the OxyContin his mother had used. Mom medicated herself with scotch, too, and alternated between diarrhea and constipation. OK, leave that one alone for a bit. He dumped the contents of the paper bag out on the bed and sorted through them.

Most of it was just trash--junk. There were some dirty coins and a lot of something that looked like mashed-up granola bars. There were a couple of socks that didn't match and a colorful scarf that looked like it would be OK if someone washed it. There were some bits of paper, mostly cash register receipts, and the dates were old, some going back a year or more. There was an American Express receipt from a restaurant he didn't know. He kept that and decided to check it on the statements. But the rest of the bagful of junk was just trash. He put it back in the bag, rolled down the top and threw it in the kitchen garbage can.

He took the bedspread off the bed, grabbed it by the corners and walked it over to the sliding door, went outside and shook it hard, spread it out on the lounge chair outside the door so it could get some sun on it, freshen it up. The whole house smelled a little stale anyway. It was probably because he had forgotten the way things smelled at the beach-- that slightly stale smell that comes from the morning fog and keeping the house closed a lot to avoid using the air conditioning. There was a buildup of a slightly musty smell that made cooking smells linger a little longer and Elissa's cologne hover over the pillows at night.

He opened the bureau, went out to the garage, and picked up some empty boxes that he'd seen sitting there. He put Elissa's clothing into the boxes: the top drawers mostly underwear and scarves, then sweaters and pullover T-shirts, finally the woolens in the bottom drawers. Those things filled up one box. He looked into the closet and knew right away he would need a lot more boxes. He didn't know where to start. The entire walk-in closet was full of clothing: two hanging bars on one side and one on the other, ten feet deep. In the center, there was a rack that must have held fifty pairs of shoes. Maggie, Melanie, and Christie would have to help with this. They would know where to take things to give them away. He did, however, go through all the pockets and came up with some money, several phone numbers with no indication of whose they were, some matchbooks advertising collectible stamps and nothing written inside, a small bottle of verbena cologne from L'Occitane, and two gold foil-wrapped magnum-sized condoms, both in the same coat pocket. *Good for her. Big is big.*

Then in the back pocket of a pair of skinny jeans there was a business card for a cosmetic surgeon named Walter Hill in Westwood, not a hop-skip-jump from Rocky Point. He went over to the computer, pulled up the Visa card with the high balance, and looked up the charges. Sure enough, there was a $4,500 fee to Dr. Hill in August and one for $3,800 in April.

He called the phone number and got a female voice which answered with a string of last names.

"Hi there," Denis said with a grin on his face that he hoped carried over the phone line. "I'm calling for my wife, who is a patient of Dr. Hill."

"Oh, OK, let me put you through to Susie then."

"Hi, Susie. My wife is Elissa Rosa and she is a patient of Dr. Hill."

"What can I do for you?" she said.

"Well, Elissa told me she had been to see Dr. Hill a couple of times this year and she spoke very highly of him. Far be it from me to inquire about what she saw him for, because I have been in Europe for the last year, but I thought I would offer to pay off any outstanding balance she might have since August."

"We sent her a statement about two weeks ago," Susie said.

"I can't find it here. Maybe you could just tell me what is owing."

"Sure, I'll look it up and email it to you if you'll give me your email."

"Or you can just call me back, same phone number she gave you."

"I think it will be easier if I send it to your email, if that's OK."

"Sure," he said, "it's DRosa at gmail dot com."

"OK, as soon as I can get to it, I'll send it to you."

Interesting, must not be very much money or she would be all over it.

He Googled Dr. Hill to see what would pop up. He seemed to specialize in body work rather than facial work. Sculpting, he called it. Boobs? The autopsy hadn't turned up anything like that, or at least they hadn't mentioned it. And the girls in the family would know anyway, because they would have noticed if Elissa suddenly got all perky-titted. Besides, there were two payments, so most likely two different procedures.

A little telephone-type bell rang to let him know there was mail on his account. Sure enough, Susie had sent him a statement .April was a "labioplasty" and August was a "vaginoplasty." Definitely a query for the Internet. Both were surgical procedures for tightening the vagina. Well, that was something he might have preferred not to know. When you said, oh look, she's had a lot of work done, you meant an obvious Botox-flattened forehead, or melon-shaped boobs on a woman with a wattled neck, or that thick-lipped look that makes a woman look like she had reconstructive surgery after an apartment fire. But there was apparently reconstructive surgery that was not so apparent.

Well, she had three babies and they were all big ones; Rich was over nine pounds. Of course Rich was thirty-four now, so if there had been a problem, even Denis would have known, because when Rich was born, Maggie was a twinkle in his eye, as they used to say. And frankly, they continued to have a normal, though declining, sexual relationship for about ten years after Maggie was born. When Maggie was about five, they went to see a psychologist to talk about Paul, who seemed unable to get his homework done and was in danger of being held back in fifth grade. Dr. Whatsis, Denis couldn't remember his name, had tried to broaden his relationship with them by asking if he could counsel the parents, who seemed not to be very affectionate with each other. That could be part of the problem since Paul was an eldest child and would be aware of the problem between them.

"Actually, Dr. Whatsis," Denis remembered saying, "we're not super-interested in talking to you about our relationship," some animosity poking its head out over his voice. Dr. Whatsis asked him directly if he couldn't "rip off a quick fuck" when his wife was horny. Well, the answer was no, he was kinda played out on quick fucks, but he didn't answer the question, he just got up and left.

"Typical," Elissa had said.

Maybe, but he was not interested in resurrecting his sex life with her. She wanted things that were not attractive to him and there was no point going into them. But she probably got them from someone over the last few years, especially with a bionic pussy.

Maybe I should have surgery to improve my genitals. A longer penis? Aargh, how would you do that? Maybe vacuum pumping? Bigger balls? Plastic walnuts in my sack? Wouldn't the scar be pretty obvious if there was an extension planted in my cock? Not a pleasant thought. She had her vagina tightened. Maybe she had complaints from some of her young cavaliers?

Most plastic surgery was self-motivated. That is, most bigger tits were basically erotic more to the woman than to her partners. Look at me, I'm sexy. That's wrong, his political conscience said. How little he knew. The lengths people would go to in order to be desirable. *Men do that sort of thing, too.* One of his oldest friends in New York was a gay man in a committed relationship and he had undergone liposuction to keep his suit size what it was when he was in college. That meant a doctor waved a high-tech vacuum cleaner around in his love handles and sucked out human flesh and blood that his bone marrow had to replace, but he lost a couple of inches from his waistline. Probably cost $5,000 per inch lost and a lot of pain in recovery.

Denis had a small hernia in his groin and he had asked his gastro guy, as they say, his gastrointestinal doctor, about fixing it because it kinda puffed out under what they called the bikini line.

"Does it hurt?" he asked.

"No," Denis said.

"Then leave it alone. The recovery from hernia surgery is a bitch." He told Denis that some very large percentage of men his age had a small hernia and most of them never got any worse. Not a superbig comfort when part of your groin sticks out an inch, even though it is not painful. Of course, the only people who saw it were the guys at the gym in the steam room or the showers. Even so. Probably Elissa did not have herself tightened so the girls in the steam room would be impressed.

This isn't leading anyplace. Like a teenager breaking up with a girlfriend. She had surgery because she thought it would help her. Her business, not mine. Still, it made him wonder whether it was worthwhile.

Suddenly he wondered if Detective Mason had taken a DNA sample from young Espinosa. A Q-tip in the cheek was all it took, at least on television. Then they could see if the DNA in Elissa's newly tightened vagina was a match. What would that prove? It would at least prove that they had had sex, and that it had been that same night, the night she died.

He had a vision of an attorney arguing that Elissa was a hot-pants party girl, a superannuated cougar who would do anything to seduce a good-looking, young Mexican waiter. Not good.

Detective Mason thought Espinosa had nothing to do with it. Denis was inclined to think that Detective Mason was pretty smart.

It dawned on him that he had not told her about finding the Duragesic CII in the trunk. He was pretty sure from what he had read on the Internet that it was a controlled substance and not something that you left in your trunk. He would tell her about Dr. Hill and the vaginoplasty, too. He did not want to call her while she was interviewing that waiter. He pulled out his phone and sent her a text message: "Call me. I have some stuff for you."

He stared at his phone, touched the app for his contacts and looked up Rosa, Paul, touched the number and the phone started to ring.

"Hi, Dad."

"Paul, hi. I've been cleaning up around here and wondered if you felt like maybe having lunch or something."

"The stock market closes at one here," he said. "So I could leave then, in about a half-hour. Want me to come out to Rocky Point? Or do you want to meet someplace?"

"You tell me, kiddo. No idea what's good and what's new here. What I really want is just to see you and catch up."

"There's a family-type Italian place in The Plaza now, called Romano. Not very original, I guess, like naming a restaurant 'Parmesan,' I guess. But the food is pretty good and they're quick. I can't really take the afternoon off, so it would be good for me if we went someplace where it doesn't take a long time to get fed."

"Cool. I can meet you there at what, one forty-five?"

"That works. It's over next to where the old post office was, if you remember."

"I know where that is, right off The Plaza."

To some people, The Plaza looked like a movie set because it was so clean, so perfectly put together, and so obviously upper class. To Denis, it was where he went when he ditched school in tenth grade, where he had lime rickeys after school, and where his friend Stephen's father had a bakery where they could swipe chocolate éclairs. His first experience with credit had been in The Plaza, at a bookstore, where they offered to bill him for books he wanted. He was mowing lawns and working after school at a small market in Lunada Bay, so he had some income, and his parents were not trying to tell him what to do with his paychecks. Even so, he had a hard time keeping up with the monthly bills from The Shorebird and learned a hard lesson about his eyes being bigger than his stomach.

He arrived at The Plaza early, found a parking place in the center near the fountain, and wandered around. The drugstore where they used to have a soda fountain was now a CVS. Although it was recessed behind the Roman colonnade and was not allowed to have any obtrusive signage, you could see it was a chain drugstore from a block away. *Well, there are very few independent pharmacies anymore.* He seldom saw one in New York. Most of them were Duane Reade or Rite Aid.

There was a woman getting out of a parked car who looked like Elissa. He noticed as he got older that he saw people who looked like other people. The surprising part was when the people who reminded him of other people were really quite different--fatter or a different race-- but they had the same set of face or something, maybe the same quizzical look. The woman who looked like Elissa walked like her. She was too far away to see, and she was wearing a scarf so he couldn't see her hair. And then she was gone.

He found Romano, a plain-looking place with blown-up photos of Roman street scenes, not the tourist sights, but places that would make you smile if you had seen them. The pyramid near Testaccio, Santa Maria in Trastevere, the basilica of St. Bartholomew on the Isola Tiburina, Santa Sabina. *Good sign. maybe these people are really Italian.*

Paul was not there yet, but he had said he couldn't leave until after the market closed. Denis took a small table next to the window and ordered a glass of Montepulciano d'Abruzzo. He could see the cars on PV Drive through the thicket of eucalyptus trees and bottlebrushes across the street, and remembered taking the bus from here to the high school before the local high school was built near Rocky Point.

He was halfway through his wine when Paul arrived, smiling.

"Market up?" Denis asked.

"Not down anyway," Paul said. "These days not down is almost as good as up. I see you've settled in here."

"I love the eucalyptus trees. You get used to the smell of them because you live here all the time. All I have are those two paintings in New York, and paintings don't smell. And the bottlebrushes draw the hummingbirds, too, so it's like a double feature. Thanks for taking time out of a workday, I know how that is."

They both ordered vegetarian, better for lunch anyway; besides, Denis had brought them up to go light on animal protein. Nothing better for lunch than pasta with red sauce and Denis liked his arrabiata very spicy so it burned going down. Paul was a marinara type guy.

They talked about the girls, school, the state of the housing market.

"Which brings me to the question of what you're planning to do with the house, Dad."

"Well, to tell the truth, I'm not totally sure, but it probably has to be sold. I don't have the resources to continue to keep it up and it's worth enough to change all our lives if we sell it. But I don't know. I was brought up in that house, it has a lot of memories. It's just a house, though, stucco and wood. The memories will be with me whether I own the house or not. I have been talking to a realtor here in The Plaza and it looks to me like it would list at over $6 million. My whole net worth is less than $1 million other than the house and most of it couldn't be turned into cash without a lot of luck and commissions.

"I have spent a lot of money over the years on art, and there's the ranchland in Texas, but that's hemmed in by other people in the family, no right of way, so I could never develop it, even though it has some theoretical value--and it may have natural gas under the surface somewhere. But if I ever am able to retire, I have to just forget whatever the business is worth, because no one wants to buy it--I have tried that, and I know for sure."

That hit Paul like a ton of bricks, though he didn't say much.

"I grew up there, too, Dad. And I wanted my girls and the other grandkids to be able to do at least part of their growing up there, too."

"Were you thinking it would be yours one day?"

"Not really," he said, "just that it would be hard to think of someone I don't even know living in my bedroom, that's all."

"Just to be clear, if I gave it to you, you would then have to sell it to pay the taxes, because the taxes on a gift like that would run upwards of $2 million. That's why I have never given the ranchland to any of you--that, and the fact that none of you has ever seen it, or probably cares much either.

"On another subject, I talked to that detective, Sue Mason, and she was going to interview the waiter at that Mexican restaurant whose name and number I found in your mother's handbag. But she doesn't think he had anything to do with what happened. I got kind of mixed messages from her. She said she does not think Mom killed herself, either accidentally or on purpose, but she said there was nothing to indicate that there was another person there. Of course, they're still waiting for some of the lab tests."

"It's hard for me to believe that Mom would have taken a drug anything like Ecstasy at all, but for sure not while she was alone," Paul said slowly. "It's just not what things like that are about. People might take a pill to get rid of feeling depressed or whatever, but not a club drug like that. She must have had someone with her, and she either took it on purpose, or whoever was with her gave it to her in her drink."

Denis nodded, although as he said, he had spent very little time with Elissa in the last few years and was not able to say what she would do or would not do. He told Paul about the surgery Dr. Hill had done.

"And you know she had just had sex, too. Unprotected sex. The coroner found evidence that she was with a guy."

Paul stared at him, then put his fist under his chin and looked out the window at the trees. Not the sort of thing you wanted to hear about your mother.

"Look, Paul, this is getting heavier than we need to get. There's nothing we can do right now and the case is still open with the Sheriff's Department. Why don't we plan to do something with the girls this weekend? Want to go over to Catalina for the day? They're about the right age for that."

Paul smiled a bit, a controlled smile, but not forced, and said he would talk to Christie about it, but yes, that sounded like a good thing, as long as they could make it all about the kids that day and leave the problems on the mainland.

"Deal," Denis said and held out his hand.

"I love you, Dad," Paul said, "but I have to get back to the office. Call you when I get home about Catalina."

Chapter Eight

Paul called at six to say that they were a go for Catalina, but it would have to be Saturday, not Sunday, because the girls were invited to a pool party at the neighbor's and it was a birthday for another little girl.

"Good," Denis said, "maybe we can buy the gift in Catalina, something you couldn't get on the mainland."

Paul would go online and get the boat schedule and reserve the tickets.

Denis found a baseball game on TV and watched that for a while, but it was low scoring and the teams were not really in contention, so he lost interest and lay down to read one of the books he had brought. He read about a page and drifted off, woke suddenly to find it dark outside. What time must it be? He looked at the digital clock by the bed: it said nine seventeen. He slung his feet over the side of the bed and rubbed his eyes. *Can't go to sleep this early, won't be able to sleep all night.* He lumbered to his feet and walked out into the dark hallway, flicking on the bedroom light as he left the room.

He thought he could hear someone in the kitchen, so he headed that way, but there was no one there, nor anywhere else for that matter, just the wind, which sometimes whipped up over the cliff as the marine layer was moving in. He went outside and there was a huge fogbank rolling toward him, a meteorological phenomenon that most people never got to see. He could smell it: the dampness, the saltiness. He could hear the waves hitting the rocks below and he walked over to the edge of the cliff and looked down.

The waves were phosphorescent as they broke, creating vaguely green, lighted, fluffy moving lines across the dark water, one after another. *A red tide.* That would mean the mussels would be inedible for a while. It was chilly, and he went back inside. He wasn't really hungry, but he found a tin of Planters mixed nuts and pulled the top off that and took a handful. Very salty. He grabbed the new bottle of vodka that he'd picked up at the liquor store up the hill and twisted the cap off. A little looking and he found a martini shaker, poured some vodka into it with some ice, and shook it briskly. The martini glasses were dusty, but he rinsed one out and dried it, poured some olive juice in it with a couple of green olives and red pimientos, and filled it nearly to the brim.

He found a CD of Rameau harpsichord music and started it, sat down with his drink in the big sectional sofa. He took a good swig of the drink and waited for a few minutes. No drug. *Superstition is a funny thing.* The vodka tasted sharp and salty. He advanced the CD to the gavotte, which had a series of fiendish variations that would work up a sweat on the most confident concert artist. It had been a trying few days and he had seldom been able to relax. Tomorrow he would see the two detectives and get some more information on the drugs from the medicine chest. He had to remember to take them the Duragesic CII skin patch he had found in the trunk.

The fog was so thick it felt as though the house had been cut loose from the mainland and was floating out into the ocean like a flying boat on its way to neverland. Take a right at the first star and then straight on till morning.

And suddenly Elissa was there, gauzy and diaphanous, as though she were coalescing from the corners of the room into a phantasm. She was unaware of him, or so it seemed. She was wandering like Lady Macbeth in her sleep, her eyes focused on something very far away. She was naked, her breasts slightly sagging and her shoulders defiantly squared back. She was the same substance as the fog, expanding and contracting, bigger and smaller, looking for something, now on the ceiling, now on the floor. She looked directly at him, but nothing registered in her eyes, as though she were a movie image projected on a column of steam, waving and undulating, now transparent, now solid.

She walked down the hallway and left a wet trail on the beige-colored carpet. He followed her silently. She went to the bedroom and disappeared into the closet. He opened the doors and she was reaching for the attic access panel in the ceiling of the closet. He couldn't reach it, but she evaporated upward and was gone. He got a chair, pushed the panel open, but he could see nothing but some dusty old boxes. He ran to the kitchen and found the flashlight, went back to the closet and shined the light into the attic space. There was something there: a small brown paper bag. He took it and climbed back down from the chair. The bag was full of Duragesic CII skin patches.

He snorted and woke himself up. He was on the sofa, not in the bedroom, and disoriented. *She was here, right here.*

He ran down the hall and into the bedroom, dragged a chair over to the closet and looked up. There was no attic access panel there. *A dream, just a dream.* But even a dream can mean something.

He took a hot shower, looked out the window while he drank some peppermint tea, and then climbed into bed, not at all sure he wanted to go back to that same dream he had earlier.

She was waiting like a kite stuck on a phone line, swaying back and forth in front of the sliding door into the bedroom. He reached out to her, but she didn't see him, maybe didn't see anything. She puffed up like a blowfish and blew away toward the back yard. He got up and walked through the kitchen to the door leading to the pool. She was sitting in the hot tub with her back to him, but she was flesh colored and not as insubstantial as she had been before. A shadowy figure walked by him and through the glass into the back yard like a thought, unimpeded by physicality, and Denis found that he could walk through the glass the same way. Denis hovered over the hot tub like a weightless voyeur and watched the other person, a man whom he could not see well, hand her a drink. She was cherry red at the top of her chest from the hot water.

She looked directly at Denis, raised her tumbler in a toast, drank it to the bottom, and then put it on the cement by the tub. The shadowy man picked it up and flew back into the kitchen with it, put it in the dishwasher and disappeared. Elissa slid under the water and he could see her hair floating above her body, just her hair flat on the surface, and the lights in the hot tub creating black shadows in the green water where she was drowning. He wondered if the drug caused her to inhale her lungs full of water right away, or whether she sputtered and choked, but he couldn't see what was going on.

He forcibly woke himself up in a sweat, and sat up in bed. There was nothing outside, just the fog.

"OK, you. I don't know where this is coming from, but leave me alone." He fell back onto the pillow and slept soundly until morning. He woke up stiff and unrested, but got up and walked over to the window. The fog was still there, but it had thinned out enough that he could see the water below. He did some pushups to see if he could get rid of the pain in his neck and it seemed to help.

He was the only one there, so there was no one to talk to and no human voice to respond to. He made some coffee and the sound of the hissing as the water shot through the ground coffee sounded louder than it could possibly have been. He started to whistle a Beatles song and then hummed it, "Lucy in the sky with diamonds, ahhhhahhh." The coffee started to wake him up and to make the dreams seem sillier than they had been when he was still groggy.

Was it too early to call Detective Mason? The clock said eight fifteen. Maybe he would just leave a message for her to call him.

She answered.

"Oh, Detective Mason. It's Denis Rosa, I was just going to leave a message, sorry if I bothered you so early."

"It's not early. What can I do for you?"

He told her he wondered about the results of the tests on the medicines and the fingerprints, anything else that was left in the way of information.

"And I found something in the trunk of the car that I forgot to tell you about. It's a skin patch with some strong pain medication in it called Duragesic CII. I looked it up and it's stronger than morphine. I have it if you want it and basically have no idea how to get rid of it if you don't, I guess burn it? And there was one other thing. I found out going over the checkbooks that she had some plastic surgery this year, and it was, well, it was on her, um, genitals."

"You mean she had herself tightened up?"

Denis was unnerved. It had surprised him, but this woman knew exactly what he was talking about, and seemed to think it was run-of-the-mill. "Yeah, I guess."

"Not common, but not unusual for a woman of means," she said. "It could also explain the pain medication. Imagine have a few stitches in your scrotum, you might want more than an Advil."

"Oh, well, I am just trying to get myself straight about what happened, and I was only trying to help, so I went through the trunk of the car when I washed it. I guess I'm going to sell it if there's anyone who would want it."

"I'll stop by later and bring the reports with me. We can go over them. To tell you the truth, they arrived on my desk late yesterday and I haven't looked at them yet."

He told her he had no plans to go out, so he would be there all day, whenever it was good for her.

"Later in the afternoon, most likely," she said.

Well, I wonder if I am chasing after things that aren't there. Maybe I ought to just get on with what I am here for and try to put some of this behind me. He kept seeing some version of that dream where Elissa slid into the water and her hair was all he could see with the Jacuzzi turned on. Just her hair.

He thought back and a newsreel of days flashed across his memory. Swim meet days where he was a timekeeper. Little league days where he was the oldest dad, and not by a little. He was forty when the other dads were thirty, and then he was forty-five when there were still dads who were thirty. He thought of the family at that condo on Big Island when Elissa's handbag was stolen by someone at the pool. He thought about ballet recitals, and having to put Paul's baby feet into those awful white shoes with a bar between them to hold them in place because he was born with his knees turned toward each other. He still had bad knees, but that was what the pediatrician told them to do, to try to get his knees to correct before he started to walk. Maggie with scarlet fever, and he volunteered to take a shot first because she was crying. Rich sticking a fish-hook in his hand and having the ER doc remove it and stitch it up. Rich with his ear pierced and the little gold stud sucked inside his earlobe because it got infected and swelled up. Paul in a cell at the police station because he took a dungeons and dragons sword to school and the teachers thought it was a weapon.

They had a fairly normal childhood. He was the one who pulled the rug out from under them, because he cooled off sexually, or just got bored, and his wife decided to go elsewhere to get what she wanted. The kids were grown then, mostly. Maggie was in high school, and generally everyone sympathized with him because Elissa never tried to hide what she was up to. And when Maggie went off to school, he moved out. He never said he was moving out for good, he just did it.

And now that she was dead, he was thinking that someone killed her. Maybe the truth was that she killed herself, not on purpose, but by having no purpose in what she was doing, and that he had set her on that road all those years before.

He made a tuna sandwich for lunch, and whipped up a sour cream coffee cake with cinnamon swirls and pecans in it. It was one of the simplest things to make, but seemed complicated to people who ate it. He started to feel a bit calmer and began to look around to see what he had to get done in order to get the house sold.

The phone rang and it was Jim Kearny.

"Well, we don't even have the house listed and I have a bid," Kearny said. "And it's at $6.5 million, which is higher than we were going to list it at."

"Interesting," Denis said. "I wonder if that means it would get bid up higher if more people knew about it."

"I guess I would say that's pretty likely."

"Look, Jim, I'm thinking of going back to New York. What would you want me to do to the house to put it in shape to show to people?"

He said that houses show better when there is furniture in them. They don't have to look homey and lived-in, but having some furniture in them puts some perspective on the size of the rooms, the height of the ceilings, etc. It would also be good to improve the curbside appeal, ask the gardener to keep flowers blooming in the front yard. In southern California, you can landscape with fresh flowers all year, so someone could come and set out fresh pansies when it was cool. The flowers would make the first impression better.

"What about the art?"

"The paintings? I think they make the place look much more interesting, and they certainly give character to the rooms. But the truth is that anyone who buys the house is most likely going to gut it and remodel it. You don't pay that kind of money for an older house and then just move your couch in and start watching TV. New homes in that price range have home theaters and solar panels all over the roof. Heck, they might put a retractable top on the pool that doubles as a dance floor. Hard to say. So what they would be looking at would be shell space. Long and short of it is that if you can leave some furniture in it, that would be best, but you can move everything else out."

That made it simpler. He would have someone come over and pack everything up and put it in storage. He should ask the kids over and find out from them what they wanted from the house, and give those things to them. He would also tell them that when he sold the house he would set up educational trusts for all the kids to pay for whatever schooling they wanted or needed. And then somebody, some foreigner, would remodel the house to the point where no one would ever know they had lived there. Sobering thought, since he had lived there since he was twelve, which was fifty-six years earlier.

Why did he feel sadder about the house than about Elissa?

The doorbell rang.

Detective Mason. He invited her into the kitchen and they sat at the table. Would she like a piece of cake? It was straight out of the oven. Of course she would. And he put some coffee on.

She took things in order. First of all, the meds in the cabinet were in fact prescribed for her over the course of the year by a physician, Dr. Hill at UCLA Medical Center. They were a variety of painkillers and mood medicines that are commonly prescribed for patients who have had certain types of surgical procedures done. Apparently, from the labeling and the number of pills left in the bottles, Mrs. Rosa did not take many of the pills. A couple were filled at the Medical Center and the rest at a local pharmacy. They talked to Dr. Hill's office and found that they had also given Mrs. Rosa some OxyContin patches, one of which he had apparently found in the trunk of the car. Dr. Hill's office handed her the OxyContin patches, which were adhesive and intended to be applied transdermally--in other words, she would stick one of the patches on her abdomen and it would dispense the painkiller automatically over a period of hours.

The fingerprint search came up with three sets of fingerprints on the vodka bottle: Mrs. Rosa, Mr. Rosa, and Maggie Rosa Schmidt. Although someone else may have touched the bottle, there were no other fingerprints. The glass by the bedside had only Mrs. Rosa's prints on it. They had a DNA sample from the semen found in Mrs. Rosa and it did not match the DNA of the waiter, Ricardo Espinosa. It also did not match any DNA in the state files or the FBI files.

Since the coroner's report said that her death by drowning was inconclusive as to the possible involvement of a third party, the case would remain open, but it was unlikely that they would put a lot more time into the investigation.

She ate a bite of the coffee cake with the dessert fork he had put by the plate, and sipped the coffee.

"You made this?" she asked.

"Yes, I like to cook, and I like to bake even more. Helps me deal with stress."

"It's good."

"It seems fancier than it really is, but thanks. Ever since I was a kid in my grandmother's kitchen, I have found baking an almost magical experience. You mix up ingredients, wave a wand over them, and they turn into a cake or muffins or a pie. It is almost incomprehensible to me, like a spell that a witch casts, and as long as you have the spell, you can do it over and over again. And it's true what the old commercial said, 'nothin' says lovin' like something from the oven.'"

She smiled broadly and looked at him in the eyes. "You're an unusual man."

"I like you, too," he said. "I like that you can get down to business quickly, but you're still a regular person, not a hard-ass."

"Oh, I am a hard-ass. You just haven't seen that side of me," she crinkled up into a mask of amusement.

He cut a piece of coffee cake and picked it up with his fingers, took a bite. The cinnamon and brown sugar crunched as he bit through it and he thought pecans one of the guilty pleasures of life. "You wouldn't, by any chance, consider going to dinner with me one evening?"

"You mean on business? Or on a date?"

"A date, keeping in mind that I have not been on a date in literally decades, so my idea of a date is pretty close to verifiably antique."

She smiled and nodded, "We could do that." Her white blouse and tan slacks were all business, but her eyes cast down were not.

"I'm taking Paul and Christie and the girls to Catalina on Saturday, probably not back until later. Would you be free on Friday evening? I guess that's tomorrow," he said.

She smiled, cocked her head to the left and said, "Sure."

"If you're brave enough, I'd like to cook," he said.

She smiled.

"I make a pretty good cioppino if you're OK with shellfish. Usually make it very spicy with some garlic bread to dip in the sauce."

"Works for me," she said. They agreed that she would show up at six thirty.

"Can I call you Sue instead of Detective?"

She waved and nodded as she walked down the sidewalk to her car.

Chapter Nine

Sue Mason was married when she was twenty-two, had a son when she was twenty-three, and divorced when the boy, Matt, was about six months old. Matt was now thirty-two and had been living in West Hollywood with his husband. She still hoped for grandkids, but obviously that would be as nontraditional as her gay son's apparently happy civil union. She was going on twenty-five years with the Sheriff's Department and had decided that would be a decision point about retirement.

She had dated over the years, but nothing serious. Most of the people she spent time with were cops of one sort or another, and she knew better than to get serious about a cop. She had a good degree in economics and some graduate credits, and figured she would be able to parlay twenty-five years in law enforcement into a management job in a security company, or maybe even allow her to consider teaching.

Always a good-looking woman, Sue was one of those fortunate women who seemed to look better as she got older. Her skin cleared up, her posture actually improved with all the gym workouts, and her lean body mass was in the ideal range. Nothing important had sagged. So she didn't look like Natalie Wood or Elizabeth Taylor, even though she was a brunette.

Oh well, she could run faster than women her age, jump higher, and do a crossword puzzle faster. She had a son and a son-in-law whom she idolized (and it was reciprocated), and it had never bothered her that her son was playing with a guy in bed. Go figure, she was as straight as a modern American woman can be, given how many vampirish women are on magazine covers with their bodies exposed, clearly to be admired more by women than men, because, simply, men don't buy magazines. Women buy magazines.

So, OK, she admired beautiful women and it helped her understand how Matt got all hot and bothered with his obviously attractive and always smiling guy, Josh.

She had decided to wear a silk print sheath, not a fashion runway dress, but kinda clingy in a way that made her feel like she was showing off a bit--not too much. She wouldn't be embarrassed if her mother looked down from heaven and saw her in her three-inch heels and semi-skintight mid-thigh frock. She surveyed herself in the full-length mirror. *Yes, I can throw a mean right hook, but I can shake my booty with the best of them, too.*

And she liked Denis Rosa, had thought he was, well, admirable, from the first time she saw him. And he was still taller than she was even with her fuck-me, open-toed, red, fake lizardskin shoes on. She never used cologne or perfume when she was on duty. There were too many people who were allergic, as the brass had told her when she came in one day smelling of cinnamon. But she had a woman's intuition, especially after eating the cake, that Denis Rosa was not allergic to cinnamon, and she dabbed a dot of Red behind each ear, right on the arteries in her neck, that would make the smell radiate lightly if he got close enough to notice.

She decided that she was tarted up more than she ought to be, and so she picked out a too-large and slightly scuffed shoulder bag that would accommodate her service revolver without making an unseemly bulge. Heck, she was only going to dinner on Rocky Point anyway. The likelihood of encountering a bank heist on a Friday night at the end of the westernmost tip of southern California was low. Even so, rules were rules, and she threw her ID and some basics in with her make-up bag: handcuffs, an evidence kit, latex gloves, an extra clip of ammunition, and a purse-sized container of pepper spray. She looked at herself in the mirror. *OK, so laugh at me, I'd buy her a drink.* She smiled broadly, showing her good teeth and low gums. *Grrrrr,--pounce, kitty!*

She went down the narrow staircase to the garage and flicked the switch to open the garage door. She looked at the Prius. *I should have had it washed.* But what the heck, it was going to be foggy out on Rocky Point anyway, so it would be speckled with a snakelike dust pattern in the morning whether she had it waxed or not. It was a sensible car for a normally sensible woman.

She backed out of the driveway and drove two blocks to the light on Pacific Coast Highway, crossed to the coveted beach side of the highway, and drove down to the Strand. There was still a seawall along the beach at this point, as though they were expecting a tsunami. OK, it was pretty, too, with royal palms up and down the beach, no more native here than they were in Florida. And stinky-smelling nasturtiums growing at the top and down the sides of the old cement bastions. But she skirted the wall and drove up the slight incline to Hollywood Riviera and then across the astonishingly obvious city line with PVE--a line that was announced by a wall of eucalyptus trees on both sides of the broad boulevard.

As she drove out PV Drive, she thought about growing up in Hawthorne, inland from where she lived now in Redondo Beach. It used to be called "greaser" territory in the 1960s, referring to the boys who lowered their old Chevy cars to the point where they scraped on the ground and sent sparks flying as they drove, and who put wads of thick, white hair oil on their slicked-up pompadours. That was opposed to the "surfers" with bleached blond hair who lived in the beach cities. Greasers were assumed to be darker race and surfers were assumed to be--what?-- Danish? Almost none of them were naturally blond, but most of them were northern European, so their hair bleached out to white without turning red. In the old days, there were no Latinos in PVE, for sure, and probably none west of PCH.

Well, she was Irish, or mostly Irish, some bits and pieces of other immigrant groups blended in. Her grandmother could cook Italian, but her eyes were green, her hair was vaguely brownish but dark, and she barely had to shave her legs at all, because there was almost nothing there to shave. Her husband had been Chicano, and Matt had thick, wavy black hair and a slightly oily, olive-colored complexion, with her green eyes and enviable, slightly almond-shaped eyes.

She drove around Bluff Cove as the dark was descending and noted the phosphorescent tide slicing across the bay with neon-lighted wave lines. *How beautiful, they'll be putting signs up on the beach not to eat the mussels.* She drove along the cliffline on Paseo del Mar, carried on without stopping at a stop sign until she got to Rocky Point Road, and turned right onto the little blunt-nosed point with its circular road. The houses were not ostentatiously large, and the lots were fairly small, at least from the front, but there was the distinct look of wealth. No cars parked on the street in spite of the fact that there were no parking restrictions. Woo hoo.

She parked in the driveway of Denis's house and walked up the sidewalk to the front door, looking in the open front window at the lights in the living room and, just beyond, in the kitchen. She rang the bell.

No footsteps. No answer. She stepped off and looked in the front window. Everything looked normal. She checked her watch, six forty-five, not early. She rang the bell again, heard the ding-dong sound as it rang inside. She knocked with her knuckles on the door, wondering if he would hear that easier than the bell.

Nothing.

She walked around to the gate on the side of the house and stood on her toes to look over the fence. Nothing, lights, normal. She pulled the wire handle to release the gate and walked around toward the back. When she got to the pool, she saw him hanging there.

"Jesus Christ!" she yelled and ran toward the figure hanging by his wrists from the eve of the house.

His bathing suit had been pulled down so that it hung around his knees and he had four big plastic patches on his back and buttocks, and a big, dark-colored pillowcase over his head. His toes touched the ground, but only barely. She instinctively reached for his carotid artery, almost a stretch for her, but easy. There was a pulse. She ran through the open door into the kitchen and grabbed a knife, sprinted back to the pool and sawed at the rope holding him up until his body collapsed onto her back, and then she lowered him to the deck. She grabbed for her smartphone and called it in, then felt again for a pulse. He was alive. She turned him on his side and ran into the house to grab something to cover him because he was gray from the chill. She pulled the bedspread off the bed and ran back out and tucked it around him. She heard the sirens.

What the hell...he couldn't have done this himself. She rubbed his shoulders and patted his face gently to see if he would come to. Nothing. Was there anyone in the house?

She ran out to the front of the house as the paramedics arrived and waved them through the side gate. They found the body and went to work, and she grabbed her bag and her service revolver, and ran into the house. She went from room to room and found no one, nothing amiss. She went into the garage to find the door to the side yard yawning open, but nothing else was wrong. She ran through the door to the side yard on the other side of the house. The gate was open. She ran out the front, but there was no one in sight on either side of the house, or on the road. She thought back and remembered that the street was completely vacant, no cars parked on the street anywhere. She ran back through the house and found the paramedics strapping Denis onto a board with a green oxygen tank at his head and a mask over his face.

She flashed her badge and asked them about him.

"His lungs were on the verge of quitting, but he is breathing now. And he was covered with fentanyl patches, which would have made it impossible for him to struggle or resist. He was probably on cloud nine, but that much would have killed him because the patches are time-release, and would have kept pumping the drug into him until everything just stopped working."

"Fentanyl?"

"It's a painkiller," the paramedic said. Two noisy police cars screeched into the driveway and the officers came crashing through the side gate.

She knelt by Denis's side to see if there was any hint of consciousness. He had an oxygen mask on and his color was coming back, but he was out.

"When I got here," she said to the cops, "I found him hanging from that hook with his hands tied together and attached to the hook with that rope on the ground. He was virtually suspended in the air, but his toes were touching the ground. He was unconscious when I found him. I cut him down and covered him with that bedspread, called it in. These guys got here first. I checked through the house. No one I could find, but I didn't do a very thorough job because I didn't want to leave him alone out here."

"If you don't mind my asking, how did you happen to wander into the back yard and find him?"

She explained that she had been assigned to the investigation of his wife's death a week earlier and that the Sheriff's Department had been on the verge of deciding that she had died accidentally.

"And yes, I was here to have dinner. He invited me. He was getting ready to go back to New York and wanted to make dinner for me. And I was glad to be asked." The look she gave them dared them to push that line of questioning further.

The paramedics rolled the folding gurney across the grass and to the gate with Denis strapped onto it. They had bagged the four patches they pulled off Denis and were taking them with them to the ER for analysis.

"No way he did this to himself," she said. "It would have taken at least two strong guys to string him up like that." She decided to follow the paramedics to Harbor General, and suddenly felt underdressed or overdressed, depending on which point of view you took. She wished she had a raincoat with her.

While they were loading Denis into the ambulance, she looked up "fentanyl" on her smartphone. One of the brands was Duragesic CII, which was what that patch was that Denis had found in the trunk of his wife's car. That had been given to her by her surgeon up at UCLA, or that was what Sue had been told.

She dialed Ron Furman.

"Furman."

"Ron, it's Sue. Got a situation here. I am just following an ambulance over to Harbor General with Denis Rosa in it, again. This time it looks like someone tried to kill him, looks like someone tied him up and plastered him with transdermal patches with a painkiller in them."

"Fuck."

"Yeah. Listen, can you look up a drug for me? F-E-N-T-A-N-Y-L. I can't get much on my phone. According to Wikipedia, it has all kinds of brand names associated with it, including that Duragesic that Rosa found in the trunk of Mrs. Rosa's car. Can you see how commonly it is prescribed for post-surgical pain? I am going to be off the air while I'm driving, but if you can come over to Harbor General, I'll be there."

"Ten-four," he said.

"Ron, I was going to have dinner with him. Rosa. A date, more or less. I found him when I got here. Just so you know."

He made a noise like an exaggerated exhale.

Harbor-UCLA Medical Center was a sprawling campus that started off as a county hospital and was still commonly called Harbor General, but it had become an outpost of the UCLA School of Medicine some years back. It was a major teaching hospital and had a level one trauma center and emergency room. It was located at the foot of the hill that PVE was on, but on the inland side, in Torrance.

She stuck a Cyclops light on her roof, but did not have a siren, so she was not able to keep up with the ambulance as they raced away, but she made good time. Ron was already there when she trotted into the ambulance entrance.

"Ooh-la-la," he said.

"Can it," she said, and flashed him a can-it kind of look. "Yeah, I told you it was gonna be like a date. Didn't turn out that way, though. I wouldn't have worn these shoes if I knew this was going to happen."

He had some notes on fentanyl. Yes, it was one of the painkillers that was commonly used for post-surgical patients. It had fewer side effects than morphine, and basically was several times stronger. It was commonly administered in transdermal, time-release patches.

"Some people," he said, "chew the patches to get the drug. High danger of overdosing that way. Mostly kids do that."

She told him that Rosa had the patches stuck on his back and his buttocks, and from the fact that his swim trunks were pulled down around his thighs, it may have been done after they had hoisted him up onto the hook that was fixed into the beam on the edge of the roof overhang.

"I can't understand how they would have gotten him to hold still for that. Maybe just threats, said they were going to tie him up there so he wouldn't get in their way, pretending to be a robbery? Maybe he would have let them tie him up like that so they wouldn't hurt him. No idea, but he is a big guy, over six feet, I'd say, and it would not be easy to wrestle with him while you were trying to hoist him up so you could tie his hands, like this." She demonstrated by stretching her hands as high over her head as she could reach and putting the wrists together.

The ER doctors would not let them in the area where they were treating him.

"He's not conscious anyway, nothing you could get from him. He may come around fairly soon, depends on how much of the drug his body absorbed. It looks like one of his shoulders may have dislocated, but then popped back into place later. Are you the officer who found him?" he asked Sue.

"Yes, Doctor. Sue Mason." She had her badge on a lanyard around her neck.

"Can you tell me how you found him?"

She told him the whole thing: that his toes were barely touching the ground, his head was hanging forward, and his legs were slack. She had cut the rope and caught him on her back as he slumped.

"Crucifixion, or what they sometimes call 'Palestinian hanging' for whatever reason. There was that notorious picture of an Iraqi prisoner in Baghdad in an American prison being tortured the same way," the doctor said. "Basically he would have suffocated if he had been left there. He was probably standing on his toes when they tied him up, but his body would not have been able to hold that position, and the more weight that was put on his arms, the less able he would be to hoist himself up to breathe."

"And the drug patches?"

"They would have made him either unconscious or semiconscious pretty fast if there were four of them. Fentanyl is a very strong painkiller. He would have been out in a matter of minutes."

"Is he going to be all right?"

"We think so, yes. Hard to tell how much of the drug his body took up, but from the patches themselves that the guys brought in, it appears that they had not been on him for more than, maybe, ten to fifteen minutes. He wasn't gagged, was he?"

"No."

"I wonder why he didn't yell," the doctor said, "make noise, alert the neighbors."

"We're hoping he'll be able to tell us that, and the rest, too," Furman said.

Crucifixion. That's a new one. Killing him by suffocating him with his own body weight. How many people would know that was even possible? Why not just jab him with a drug and put him under and then kill him? Seemed like a drug kill, a revenge kill.

She took a stick of gum out of her bag and folded it up, put it in her mouth. The spearmint taste made her realize that her mouth was dry. She was standing with her arms crossed staring at the parking lot through the ambulance bay, trying to remember what had happened in detail. No, he wasn't gagged. Was there anything lying on the ground? She couldn't summon up a picture in her mind. Oh well, there were crime scene guys there; they would find anything.

Ron Furman tapped her on the shoulder and she turned to him. He was offering her a pasteboard cup of coffee. She took it, gratefully, and sipped at it.

"Might as well relax, I guess," he said. "You want to talk to me about this?"

They sat down outdoors on an adobe brick planter box along the sidewalk leading to the ER waiting room.

"He said he was going back to New York after I told him we basically had nothing to go on and he asked me if I would have dinner with him. He's older than I am, but I think he's good-looking, and we already knew he was civilized. He seemed very sad, but OK. I told him yes, I would like to have dinner, and he said he would cook something. Seafood, he said. Shellfish. I couldn't tell you when I cooked a real dinner, and I thought well, I can kick back with this nice man. Who knows? We might even like each other. That's all there is to it. I haven't dressed up in months, so I put on a dress. Jesus, when did I last wear a dress? Long time."

"But there wasn't anything going on, right?"

"Nothing going on. I'm not saying that there would not have been something going on if he'd made dinner and poured me a glass of wine.

But when I got there he was, well, you heard the doctor, crucified next to the pool. Even with his shorts around his knees, that's not very sexy. There was no blood. Attempted murder, but no blood. No blood with the wife, either."

About an hour later, one of the ER nurses told them that Mr. Rosa was starting to come around and they could come in for a few minutes. As they were being led into the warren of cloth-hung ER cubicles, the doctor they had spoken to earlier met them. He told them that Mr. Rosa was probably going to be OK, but that there was more to this than was apparent at first. There was a site on his neck that had a needle mark. They were attempting to find out what had been injected, but so far the lab had no results. They had immobilized his left arm because the left shoulder had indeed been dislocated, either in a struggle, or just from hanging by his arms as he lost consciousness. Either was possible.

Chapter Ten

The room was spinning and he wanted it to stop. It seemed like he had been whirling in circles for days. Lights. Swirling lights that made him feel like he would throw up, but he couldn't move. He would yell, help me, help me, then it would be dark again for a time.

"He's been vocalizing," the resident said. "Just noises, but he is trying to say something. His eyes flicker a bit. I think he is coming back up from wherever he's been, probably having a hard time. His blood is showing LSD as well as the fentanyl. That would not be what was in the injection, but perhaps it was put in his mouth. It would absorb through the mucosa very quickly. If the fentanyl is letting go of him, he has to travel through the acid trip to get back to us."

He took Denis's good arm and held the hand, careful not to put pressure on the bandages on his wrists, and patted him gently on the cheek. "Mr. Rosa, can you hear me? It's OK now. You're safe. Denis? You're safe now. We will take care of you. Can you open your eyes?"

The eyes fluttered, but did not open.

"You're hearing me, Denis. That's good. Very good. You're going to be all right now, just come to my voice and we will be able to help you."

Sue stepped forward. "Let me try," she said.

"Denis. It's me, Sue Mason. Can you hear me? I can see you, you're here in the hospital and it's safe here. You can come back. There," she said, "he squeezed my hand. Denis, Denis. If you can hear me, open your eyes."

His eyelids moved and both were open the tiniest slit possible. He made a sound, low-pitched and round, not a word, just a sound.

"Oh, that's good, Denis. You can hear me. That's fine. Can you come toward my voice?" She held his hand and stroked his forehead. "It's safe here. I'm here. You want to see your children, don't you? Your grandchildren? Rich and Melanie, isn't that right? Rich and Melanie?" She wished she could remember the names of the others.

He made another noise and it sounded more like a word, maybe a word of two syllables. Ah-uh, ah-uh.

"I'm going to stay here with you, Denis, and we are going to call Rich and Melanie and they will come to see you, too."

She turned to her partner. "We need to get in touch with the family. I know we have their phone numbers." He nodded, and stepped out.

He gradually came up from the deep blackness he had been in, through the psychedelic wind that wanted to spin him around and throw him off a parapet, and finally into a bed with people bending over and talking to him. He knew the woman, just not sure who she was. They were asking if he could hear them; he tried to answer, but it didn't work. Words too hard. Lights too bright. Pain. "Squeeze my hand," she said, and he did.

Maggie's voice. "Dad, it's me. Can you open your eyes?"

He opened his eyes enough to see her, then shut them because it was too bright. He said her name, but it didn't sound right. The room seemed to be rocking back and forth and his head hurt and his arm hurt, or his back. Yes, his back hurt.

Maggie held his hand and rubbed his upper arm. There was a catheter in his forearm and two bags of liquid dripping into him. She didn't feel like crying, but she was frightened. He was her father, and from what they said, someone had tried to kill him, like someone had killed her mother.

The hospital admitted him and moved him to a single room. He made constant progress. By morning he was able to form clear words, and to string them into responses to questions. Maggie, Paul, and Rich stayed there all night, waiting for him to be his old self again.

Sue Mason and Ron Furman headed back to their office in Lomita and called Captain John Martinez of the PVE police department to report to him what they knew, and to see what assistance they could provide to the small, but proud department. Their investigative staff consisted of Captain Martinez and one detective, and the entire population of the city was less than fourteen thousand, so it was common for Sheriff's Department personnel to be dispatched in the four municipal areas of the PV Peninsula: the Olmstead-designed PVE; the highly exclusive and gated city of Rolling Hills with its horse properties and whitewashed fences; and the two newer, largely master-developed cities of Rolling Hills Estates and Rancho Palos Verdes.

Two PVE officers had been detailed to participate with the Sheriff's Department in the crime scene investigation at the Rosa house on Rocky Point, but the forensic investigation was spearheaded by the Sheriff's Department, which had state-of-the-art labs, as well as the ability to draw upon other local departments for personnel if needed.

The PV Peninsula had historically been largely farmland, and although its scenic coastline was one of the most breathtaking south of Malibu, there had been a major problem with the land in a large area of the peninsula, as early homes in the area then called Portuguese Bend began in the late 1950s to slide--slowly but with no pause--into the ocean, and roads cracked and separated, water pipes burst, buried utility cables snapped, and the homeowners were left with no one to sue, since homeowners' insurance does not cover land slippage. It cast a pall over oceanside development in the area even after geologists mapped out the edges of the slide area, where the layers of topsoil were situated on top of a steep and slippery diatomaceous earth hillside. Whenever the diatomaceous earth got wet, the land slid, burdened as it was with homes, swimming pools, roads, etc.

The long and the short was that the newer cities of Rancho Palos Verdes and Rolling Hills Estates were late to develop after the newspapers detailed hundreds of expensive homes plunging into the ocean in the blue waters of the former Portuguese Bend Club back in the 1960s. When development came to those areas, it was denser than in the extravagantly wealthy areas of PVE and Rolling Hills, both of which were consistently on lists of the one hundred richest cities in the country.

Homes in Rolling Hills were on plots of land ranging from the smallest at two acres to gentleman-rancher spreads of ten times that much land.

The PVE police department was simply not equipped to investigate a gruesome and puzzling pair of crimes like the apparent murder of Elissa Rosa, and the attempted murder of her husband a week and a half later, both crimes using drugs in fiendish ways that scared newspaper readers and television watchers all over LA County. Reporters were referred solely to the Sheriff's Department for information, but there were reporters and television units sporadically prowling around Rocky Point every day. One television station took video of the house from a helicopter, but when it revealed nothing, there was no repeat.

The Harbor-UCLA Public Relations Department published status reports on Denis Rosa's progress twice a day, and the good news was that he was recovering from the attempt on his life, although he was not going to be released from the hospital right away. The truth was that no one -- not the family, not the Sheriff, not the PVE police--wanted Denis Rosa to go home to the house on the cliff, at least not alone, and so, although he regained his strength, and his memory had started to come back in bits and pieces, he stayed in a hospital room with a twenty-four-hour police guard.

Sue and Ron were working in a situation room in the Lomita office where they were stationed and they were online to the PVE police, who were in charge of maintaining the integrity of the crime scene. The two of them showed up at three o'clock on the day that Denis woke up more or less fully, to question him about what happened.

The hospital personnel and the family members had been strictly instructed to say nothing to him about what happened. They were to tell him that he came in with these injuries, and that was all they knew.

Sue told him she was going to record their conversation and asked Denis to tell them what he remembered about that evening.

"I was working on dinner, cleaning some shellfish, and I heard something outside. I was just wearing a bathing suit because I was planning to jump in the pool before you arrived. I went outside to see what was going on."

"What kind of noise?"

"Well, I thought it sounded like people arguing, but when I got outside, there was no one there. That's pretty much all I remember, although there are some things that couldn't be real, just mainly dreams I guess. My arm, my shoulder, it was dislocated they told me. Did I fall?"

"Mr. Rosa, it seems that someone tried to kill you, and they very nearly succeeded."

"Kill me? Me? Whatever for?"

"We don't really know, but it seems like it may have something to do with your wife's death in the same back yard a few days before. I have to tell you that the news media have a lot of the details of what happened, and there are a lot of stories in the papers and on TV. One of the reasons we have a guard outside your door is to make sure that reporters don't try to get to you."

They told him how Sue had found him, and what had happened after that.

"Palestinian hanging? What the fuck? Crucified?" he said. "Crucified?"

"Not exactly, but the effect is the same. When the Romans crucified someone--and apparently they did it a lot to make public examples of people like slaves who ran away--the person on the cross died of asphyxiation because their arms were unable to support their body's need to fill their lungs with air. When you are suspended by your arms, you have to pull up to breathe, and eventually you can't do that. But whoever strung you up on a hook in the back yard also put a lot of drugs into you, which would have shortened the process quite a bit, because you were deeply unconscious from painkillers that were administered to you. You have an injection site on the side of your neck, and you had patches of a painkiller dotted over your back. You were apparently given a heavy dose of LSD with it, which would be the reason you have recollections of things that seem like dreams."

He stared at her and said nothing.

"Mr. Rosa?"

His eyes were focused elsewhere and he said, "I think there were two or three men in the yard, dressed in black, and one of them ran toward me and grabbed me, but I couldn't see his face. He hit me I think, in the chest, maybe with something he had in his hand. But that's it. I remember being in a dark place, like a well, and trying to scream, but it was like one of those dreams where you can't make a noise come out."

The resident who was in the room said, "That's enough for now, Mr. Rosa. Relax and I will lower your bed a little. Here's some juice." He waved the two detectives away and they left.

"Someone tried to kill me?" he asked the resident.

"That's what they tell me, but you're safe here, you're safe now."

"I want to see my kids," he said. "Are they here?"

"I'll check, but I think they are, yes. "He pushed a button and moments later a middle-aged nurse came in.

"Yes, doctor?"

"Would you stay here with Mr. Rosa while I check to see if his family are here?

"Certainly, doctor." She turned to Denis with a warm smile and reached out to him, took his good hand, and said, "We'll be right here." She had an authoritative voice, and he relaxed.

"Someone tried to kill me. That's what they said."

"Well, they're not going to kill you while I'm here, so you stop worrying about that. We're pretty fierce here with people who try to kill our patients." She smiled again, and rubbed the inside of his wrist.

"What's your name?" he asked her.

"Rosie," she said. "I'm Rosie and you're Mr. Rosa, so we're going to be good friends."

The door opened, and Rich, Paul, and Maggie came in.

"Kiddos," he said, and held his arm out to them, letting go of Rosie, who stepped away and went to sit in the armchair by the bed.

"Were you here for a long time?" he asked.

"No biggie," Paul said. "You feeling better?"

"My arm hurts, or my back, I don't know which. They say my arm was dislocated. And they say someone tried to kill me." He looked from face to face. "But it didn't work, I guess." He smiled. "You guys look good enough to eat. Give your dad a kiss."

Maggie started to cry noisily and the boys both started to ooze tears simultaneously, wiping at their cheeks with their sleeves.

"Oh, Dad," Rich said, "we were so worried, and it's so wonderful to hear your voice."

"I bet I was a mess before. Were you here? I thought I remembered Maggie talking to me."

Maggie snuffled and choked on her voice when she tried to talk, but grabbed his hand and said something that clearly meant I love you, Dad, even though it sounded like she was saying it underwater, and at the same time a big bubble of snot inflated in her right nostril and then popped.

Chapter Eleven

"Rosie the Riveter," he said when she walked in. She smiled and checked his catheter and drip.

"My uncle used to call me that," she said. "Pretty flowers. Those from your kids?"

"Well, the card said they're from my grandkids."

She took his blood pressure and stuck a small probe in his ear. "One hundred seventeen over eighty, not bad for an old guy who got beat up," she said.

"My problem is I'm soft in the head," he said. "Got some big holes in my memory bank."

She fluffed his pillow and said she would be back to give him a bath.

"No, you won't," he said. "I can take a bath myself, or I can just stink."

She smiled and did not say, "We'll see about that," but he knew that was what she was thinking.

He was having flashes of memory, but they were like single frames from a filmstrip, and they didn't make sense. He was beginning to be fairly sure that there were three guys in the pool area when he went outside. He first remembered they were all dressed in black, but then he realized that they weren't. One had a T-shirt with a logo on it, but he couldn't see enough of it, and one was a lot shorter than the other two, and was wearing faded jeans.

"Make a sound and I'll kill you." That was all he remembered them saying, and it was the man behind him who said it. No accent that he could hear, a low-pitched voice, almost but not quite whispering, like a growl. Then someone stuck something in his neck and he blacked out. The next thing he remembered was the lights, the whirling lights that went on and on and on like the teacup ride at Disneyland, making him sick like he would throw up.

The detectives kept coming around and asking him more questions, and sometimes that would help him remember some other little shard of something--like a flashlight, one of them had a flashlight. He could see the beam when he was being held by the man behind him, who had his arms behind him and bent upward so he couldn't move.

"Did they steal anything?" he asked them.

The house was not trashed, and it did not appear that they had looked through the drawers, although the hall closet was ajar and there were some bits of dust and some paint flakes on the coats hanging in the closet. It looked as though they had pushed open the attic panel in the closet. Of course they were dusting everything for fingerprints, but it appeared that the men had been wearing gloves. One of the dining room chairs was in the hallway by the closet and it had traces of a dusty footprint on it.

"Where were you when the man grabbed your arms from behind you?" Sue asked.

"Just outside the kitchen. He must have been crouching beneath the window because when I looked through the window there was no one there. That's why I went outside."

"Good," she said. "Good. In fact, there were some footprints in the flowers beneath the window and some dried mudprints on the deck."

"What were you doing in the kitchen when you heard the noise outside?"

"I was cleaning the mussels and clams I got at Whole Foods because I was going to make cioppino," he said. "That's why I could see out the window because I was scrubbing them in the sink. But the outside light wasn't on."

"What did you keep in the attic?"

"Nothing. I mean, not nothing, I just have no idea. I had forgotten that attic was even there. I have been living in New York. I remember it being where my parents kept the Christmas decorations when I was a kid, but that's about it. It's hard to get into. I had a dream about the attic last week, though, Elissa was showing me something in the attic, but it was in the wrong place."

"The attic was in the wrong place?"

"No, the access to the attic was in the wrong place. Just a weird dream. Strange, though, because I would have sold the house without remembering to even look in the attic."

"We had a look up there and there were some old boxes that had been there for a long time. There were some strings of lights and a tree stand in one of the boxes. Mostly they were of no interest, old school papers and some debating trophies. But there was one area where a box had been dragged through the dust, and we're guessing they took that. But you have no idea what it could have been?"

"Sorry. I didn't really live there, you know. Elissa lived there. She had some good jewelry. Did you check that?"

They had looked at the bedroom and the jewelry, and it did not appear that anything was missing. There was a dinner ring that appeared to have a very large uncut emerald in it and it would have been gone if the intruders had been after jewelry.

"That was my mother's ring," Denis said. "I gave it to Elissa when Mom died, but I don't think she ever wore it. It was too large, and women don't wear those big dinner rings anymore, or that's what she told me when I asked her about it."

Rosie was having him walk up and down the hallway, back and forth, back and forth. At first he felt he might fall, but he was in good shape, had always been athletic, and the more he walked up and down the hall, the more his natural stride came back. She took the sling off his arm and asked him to move his hand. It was stiff, and he could feel the soreness all the way up to his shoulder. He could not raise his arm in front of him, not even to open the door.

That afternoon, they took him in a wheelchair to the rehab department and they started to manipulate his arm. It frightened him because it hurt, but the more they moved it, the more he realized that he might be able to move it himself. There was hope he would get back to normal, back to the way he was before someone tried to kill him. Crucify him. Drug him and leave him hanging like a side of beef until he died from not being able to breathe. Persons unknown. Reasons unknown. Probably the same people who had killed Elissa, murdered her, drowned her in her own back yard. It made him feel like he had to stand next to a structural wall and watch the door to make sure he saw everything. *Macbeth hath murdered sleep. How will I ever blink, much less sleep?*

"Rosie, when are they going to send me home?" he asked her when the orderly wheeled him back to his floor and he saw her at the nurse's station. She took the wheelchair from the orderly and pushed him into his room, past the young police guard at the door.

"Well, I would say you're probably about ready to be discharged now," she said, "but I kinda think they want to be sure you'll be able to take the pressure of being on your own again. You went through some pretty hairy stuff, Denis."

He knew he would feel pretty freaky going back to Rocky Point by himself. Maybe he should just go back to New York, where he could feel safe. No one would attack him in his apartment on the thirty-fourth floor of a concierge building, where the neighbors would hear a scuffle and yelling, and he had an intercom to the front desk. But that wouldn't work, because until the police found who had done this, he would never feel safe again. He had heard of people whose houses had been burglarized, how violated they felt, and how they had trouble sleeping.

For the first time since he left New York, he had the fluttery feeling in his stomach, as though he were on the edge of a panic attack, like he would feel light-headed and pass out.

"I need to talk to Detective Mason," he said to Rosie. "Maybe she'll have something to tell me."

Rosie fastened the blood pressure cuff around his bicep and pumped it up. His blood pressure was sky-high. She wrinkled her forehead and wrote in the file.

"What?" he asked.

"One ninety-five over one twenty. Let me help you into bed. You have to take control of yourself and calm down," she said. "You are doing this to yourself."

She put her hand under his head as he leaned back, sweating, and hefted his feet onto the bed, eased his slippers off. She sat down next to him and took his hand.

"Now breathe in deeply and then breathe out evenly, not all at once. Don't hold your breath, just concentrate on what it sounds like to breathe. Close your eyes or focus on the wall. Listen to the breath coming into your lungs and then listen to the sound as you exhale. Breathe. Oxygen is what will help you calm down. Breathe out." She felt for the pulse on his wrist. It was slowing down.

"I'm going to check in at the nursing station now. You going to be OK?"

He nodded. "It comes and goes. I really want to talk to Sue Mason."

He found the sudden fluttering in his stomach frightening. He had never been in a position where a boogeyman could pop out and hurt him. He had worked all his life, supported his family, and made some kind of contribution to society. There were lots of stresses, but nothing that scared him like this. Nothing that made him afraid of the dark.

While Denis was hyperventilating, Sue Mason and Ron Furman were going back over all the information they had on Rocky Point. Physical evidence was in short supply. Some shoeprints, indications of something being removed from near the attic access panel, a bottle of vodka with GHB in it, several bottles of unused painkillers from the medicine cabinet in the master bathroom, a fentanyl patch from the trunk of the car, some common white rope that could be bought anywhere, the inconclusive autopsy report on Elissa Rosa (the body now cremated), the DNA signature of the sperm from Mrs. Rosa's body, and the bloodwork and examination of Denis Rosa.

Other than that, Denis Rosa had told them that he had found the numbers of several of what he presumed were sexual partners of his dead wife. One of those, Ricardo Espinosa, had given a sample of DNA that did not match the sperm. But there were some other names that Denis had found and those needed to be followed up. The PVE police had interviewed the neighbors and had found one who thought there was a black SUV parked down the street the night that Denis Rosa was attacked.

None of the neighbors reported any noise or commotion of any type that night until the police arrived. Several of the neighbors were aware that Mrs. Rosa entertained men fairly regularly, and that they were usually a good deal younger. None of the neighbors had met any of the young men, but the general impression was that they tended to look Mexican.

There was the surgery that Mrs. Rosa had at the UCLA Medical Center not quite a year earlier, the surgeon being Dr. Hill, whose nurse had given her the prescriptions for painkillers that were filled but apparently not used, and a couple of fentanyl patches, at least one of which was found unopened in the trunk of her car.

Other than continuing to interview neighbors, Denis Rosa was probably their best potential for more information. They would also interview the staff at Casa Adobado on the pier at King Harbor, since Mr. Espinosa had said Mrs. Rosa was a regular there. Perhaps they could find someone there who could either tell them other places that she might have frequented, or who could identify people who had been with her when she had dinner or drinks there.

"We either need to take Denis Rosa on a field trip back to the house or find out whether they can discharge him. We need to see how much of what happened he can reconstruct when he gets back there, and if he still has the names and phone numbers of the men he found when he was looking through the phone bills or the charge cards or whatever," Ron said.

So, just as Denis Rosa was hoping Sue Mason would show up, she did.

The hospital was not ready to discharge Denis, but they were fine with the two detectives taking him out for a few hours to help with the investigation. The resident talked to Denis with no one else in the room other than Rosie and asked him how he felt about getting dressed and going out with the detectives. He said he felt OK, had no trouble walking, and did not think he would have a panic attack if he was with two detectives. The resident put his arm into a loose sling and Rosie removed the catheter from his good arm, wrapping new gauze around his wrists. Maggie had brought over some clothing and he was able to get dressed. He asked if they could stop and get some real food on the way. Big smiles all around.

They put Denis in the back seat of the unmarked car, a newish, burgundy-colored Chevy Malibu with plenty of leg room, and Sue scooted forward to give him even more.

"We want to take you back to the house and see if you can help us piece some things together," she said. "No stress, no pressure. We just need you to show us where you were, what you remember, and maybe being there will bring some memories back that you haven't been able to access. Also, we need to ask you to find the list of men you mentioned who might have dated your wife. You said you had called some phone numbers, but you did not give us the list."

He asked if they could stop in The Plaza and go to Romano, the Italian restaurant, so he could get some pasta. Seeing the sun and smelling the outside air, he was famished.

"You know," he said, "it makes me feel kinda queasy to think of going back to the house. I was thinking I would go back to New York when they check me out."

Ron said he thought it would be hard on the investigation if he were not there, and that they would do everything they could to make sure he was safe and had nothing to worry about. He asked Denis if he could stay with one of his children.

"I thought about that," Denis said, "but there's no way it could work. They all have kids, their houses are small, and they all work, all three husbands and all three wives. The kids are all in school. The last thing they need is for me to be hanging around like some kind of apparition. I either have to stay in a hotel or I have to stay at the house. But if I stay at the house, I need protection. Maybe not because someone would try to hurt me, but because I would lose my mind worrying about it."

They drove up Hawthorne Boulevard to the crest of the hill and when they came up over the top onto Granvia Altamira, they could see all the way to Malibu and the hulk of Catalina off to the left.

"Oh my God, it is so beautiful here," Denis said. "It makes me want to cry remembering when I was a teenager and one of my friends lived right over there," he said, pointing to a wrought-iron gate surrounded by dense shrubbery. "I think it is some rock singer who lives there now, but then it was just a castle or a movie set for us. There was actually a pipe organ in the living room and an old speak-easy in the basement, with a bowling alley. And they had a gas pump in the driveway."

They wound down through the red-tiled homes above Malaga Cove and past La Venta Inn, which was one of the oldest buildings on the peninsula and constantly booked for weddings. From there it was only a minute before they pulled under the Spanish Renaissance herringbone brick archway that was the back portal to The Plaza. Denis studied his surroundings. *It looks so normal.* They parked and went into Romano, where he and Paul had eaten just a few days earlier. They sat next to the window.

"So what are you thinking is the next step?" he asked, looking at Sue while he talked.

Ron answered. He said that as time passed, it became more and more difficult to find clues, and they were concerned that they move as quickly as possible to figure out what had happened, both to Elissa and to him.

"I can't stay there by myself. I would go straight to the airport and take the first plane back to New York. I'm not afraid to go there with you, but I am not going to be there by myself. The last time I was there by myself, it didn't turn out well."

"One thing at a time," Furman said, "one thing at a time." And he waved to the waiter.

Denis ordered penne with vodka sauce, but asked them to leave out the bacon. The detectives agreed and told the waiter to make it three of the same. Much to his surprise, Denis's hand began to shake when he picked up his water glass.

"Let me get you a straw," Sue said, and smiled. "No biggie." She got up and walked over to the register and came back with a straw.

No wonder I wanted to make dinner for her.

He loaded his plate with cheese and the pasta tasted wonderful after a few days of nutritious, but unsalted, bland hospital food--and it was easy to eat with his left hand. He pulled his arm out of the sling to keep it from getting stiff and cramping, and held the water glass with his right hand while he bent over to sip the water from the straw. Ron paid the bill and said they could thank LA County for lunch. And then they were off toward Rocky Point.

"It's the westernmost point on the mainland south of Malibu," he said. "That's Resort Point over there, and Lunada Bay is one of three prized surfing spots in the area for surfers who can deal with the rocks. I never surfed here, but I did surf in Bluff Cove, the next bay up." He smiled, remembering the days of surfing on a heavy wooden longboard, listening to Jan and Dean on the car radio.

"We were one of the first houses out here, and my Dad paid about $40,000 for the house in 1956. Now the realtor tells me we should list it for nearly $7 million. Same house, just older. And we put in the swimming pool."

They pulled up in front of the house and he shivered when he saw the yellow plastic crime scene tape.

"You gonna be OK?" Sue asked.

"Catch me if I'm not," he said, and put a grin on. "I don't have a key, I just remembered."

"I do," Sue said. "I took it off the kitchen counter while the paramedics were packing you up to transport you. We have used it to get in several times. For a while, there was white powder all over from fingerprinting, but the cleaning crew has been here and it should be OK now."

It looked like the house of seven gables to him, only Hepzibah Pyncheon had drowned in the hot tub instead of gagging on her own blood from the family curse. They got out of the car and walked up the front walk. The next-door neighbor stepped out and waved. Denis waved back, smiled.

Sue handed him the key and he unlocked the door. It smelled as it had smelled when he came from New York--musty and closed-up.

"It's a beautiful house," Ron said.

"It's outdated," Denis said. "Whoever buys it is likely to tear it down and start over, they tell me."

The fireplace was faced with PV stone, big, irregular pieces of chalky white stone quarried over in Rolling Hills, laid together like a dry-stone fence in New England, but held together by mortar in this earthquake-prone area. There was a blackstone hearth to sit on when there was a fire burning. His mind ran back to see himself putting a homemade yule log in, with pine boughs, red ribbons, and holly. *You can't get PV stone anymore, but that wouldn't stop someone from tearing down the house.*

"What first?" he asked.

They wanted him to show them what he remembered of the night he was attacked. He showed them where he was standing, cleaning the shellfish for dinner, when he heard what he thought were people talking or arguing, and then he walked slowly over to the sliding glass door and unlocked it, slid it open.

"Was the door locked when you opened it?" Sue asked.

"Um, yes, I think it was. I lock it reflexively. We always had animals when I was a kid and you didn't want them tracking mud into the house. The pool wasn't there then. Anyway, yes, I think it was locked." They were both making notes.

"Did you turn on the outdoor light?" Ron asked.

"I don't remember turning it on, but I could have. No, I didn't, because when I went outside, it was very dark. No, wait, I did turn it on, but the light was out, because when I went out, I turned to look at the light to see if it was flickering or whatever. I couldn't see it." He pointed to the spotlight over the kitchen window. He went in and flicked the switch and the light turned on.

"How long had you been in the kitchen?"

"Well, not long, because I had just got out of the shower. My hair was wet and I was wearing my shorts." He could see himself coming to the kitchen sink where the mussels were in a wire basket there.

"You know, I heard the noise in the bathroom, not when I was in the kitchen. That's why I came out here. But then there was no noise when I got here, so I went over to the sink and ran the water over the mussels to keep them wet."

"The master bathroom, right over there on the other end of the pool, right?"

"Yes, but I couldn't see outside because the window is opaque, you can't see through it."

"So when you stepped out the door, you turned to look at the light to see why it wasn't working, and then what?"

"Someone grabbed me and twisted my arms and told me if I made any noise he would kill me." He could feel the man behind him. "He was shorter than me, but strong. He was right up next to me and his knees were below my knees. I could feel them. And then I saw the two other guys. They were wearing caps and Lone Ranger masks."

"Caps?"

"Like baseball caps."

"Logos on them?"

"Not on the caps, but one of the guys had a picture of a pizza on his shirt, or maybe a wheel."

"Tall? Short?"

"Ordinary. One of them went by me toward the house, and then I felt something stick into my neck and I felt like I was going to faint, and then I don't remember anything. Some voices, but not real words, not making any sense."

They asked him if he was standing about where he was standing that night, and he said yes.

"OK, let's try something different," Ron said. "Show us where you found the names of the guys you thought might have been fooling around with your wife."

"I need a drink of water. I need to sit down." Denis plopped into a chair at the kitchen table and looked up at them."I'm OK, I just, this just creeps me out."

They sat down at the table with him and Sue handed him a glass of tap water from the kitchen faucet.

"They wanted to kill me. I had no idea who they even were and they wanted to kill me. You know?"

He looked around and said, "I'm not scared because you're here, but I can't stay here by myself. They could come back."

He drained the glass of water, then said, "OK, the desk. I was looking through the desk when I made that list of names." He pushed himself up and walked toward the master bedroom. He walked through the bedroom into the bathroom. "See, here are the clothes I had been wearing before I took the shower," he said, pointing to the back of the bathroom door.

He walked over to the desk, opened the center drawer and pulled out a slip of paper with several phone numbers on it. "These are the phone numbers I decided were most likely to be guys she was seeing, based on the telephone bills." He opened the file drawer and pulled out a folder with telephone bills in it. "I circled the calls to these people on the last few months of bills. I called the numbers, and as I recall, of the six, three had messages that had names, and the others didn't. One of them, maybe this one, was disconnected." He gave the telephone bills and the list to Sue Mason.

"And one of these is Ricardo Espinosa?" she asked.

"Um, no. I found his number on a receipt from the restaurant and I thought I gave it to you when you were going to see him."

"I don't think you did," she said.

"Then maybe it is in the living room," he said, and walked into the front room with the big fireplace. He walked over to the end table by the sofa. "Here it is," he said. "Sorry." He handed it to her.

"So you did not leave a message for any of these people and none of them would know you had rung their phones, right? The only one you contacted was Espinosa?"

"Right. And the surgeon, Dr. Hill. Not him, but his receptionist, or his bookkeeper, I guess."

They locked up the house and left to take Denis back to the hospital. On the way, Sue turned to him and said, "Look, I know this might not be what you had in mind, but my son and his husband", she paused for emphasis, "are just moving out of their apartment in Hermosa Beach. They're pretty normal guys, and both gym rats, kinda buffed up. Maybe I could ask them to stay with you for a bit and make sure you are not alone in the house."

He stared at her. "When can I meet them?"

Chapter Twelve

The next day he announced to the resident that he intended to leave as soon as they could get their paperwork together. He was not taking any medications, and he didn't see any point staying at the hospital any longer. He sent a text from his phone to Paul, Rich, and Maggie, to let them know he was going to be checking out of the hospital, and that one of the detectives had arranged for someone to stay with him at the house so he would not be alone.

"You could stay with us," came Rich's reply

"And who would have to move out of their room for me to do that?"

"It doesn't matter."

He thanked Rich and the others. But he was too old to be anyone's roommate and anyway, he preferred to be at the house he grew up in, even considering what had happened. Until they found out who had attacked him, he would be taking extra steps to make sure he was safe, and would be meeting a security company at the house to install alarms, motion detectors, and spotlights.

"Who is it that's gonna stay with you, Dad?"

"Well, I haven't met them yet, but one of them is the son of one of the detectives, Sue Mason."

"And the other one?"

"Um, a friend of his, I guess you would say. Actually, I think they consider themselves married. And they have a pair of German shepherds, too. Once they get moved in, I think we should have dinner at the house, and you can all meet each other."

Paul said he wanted to drive Denis to Rocky Point and maybe that way he could meet the houseguests.

"Fine with me," Denis said, "we can meet them at the same time."

When they pulled up in front of the house, there was a silver-gray Ford Escape sitting in front and a man in a suit was leaning against the curbside. A cop? They pulled in the driveway and as they got out of the car, the man walked toward them. He was about six feet tall, youngish, built like a soccer player, and walked with an athletic bounce. He held his hand out to Denis.

"You must be Mr. Rosa," he said. "I'm Matt Mason."

"Oh, hi," Denis said. "I guess I was expecting two guys and two dogs. Nice to meet you. Come on in. I really appreciate your help. This is my son, Paul. Paul, Matt." Firm handshake, could be a stockbroker from the open smile and direct gaze. *I think I can see some of Sue Mason in him, but only from certain angles.*

Matt turned around and shaded his eyes from the sun, looked up the street. "There they are," he said, pointing to a man with two German shepherds on leashes, the dogs sniffing every plant along the curb. He waved over his head. "That's Josh. And the dogs are Frick and Frack. They look pretty much alike, so we named them that when they were puppies."

"Big dogs," Denis said, looking doubtfully in their direction.

"They have very good manners," Matt said. "You can't have big dogs with bad manners, doesn't work. And these guys are smart, too. They learn fast."

Josh ambled up to the three men standing in the driveway and handed the leashes to Matt, stuck his hand out. Not as tall as Matt, almost barrel-chested, but his suit jacket was well-tailored and made him look slim.

"Hi, I'm Josh Underwood, Matt's partner." Up close, Josh was strikingly good-looking, with sparkling blue eyes and a suspiciously even tan. "Boys," he said, "down." The two dogs sank to their haunches like their feet had been swept out from under them. "Good," Josh said, ruffling the fur on their heads one at a time.

Denis smiled at everyone. "Let's go inside. I doubt there's any food we would want to eat, since I've been, um, away for a bit--but there's always plenty of wine, and I think there are Pellegrino orange drinks in the fridge, too." The cleanup crew had taken down all the yellow crime scene tape.

"I sure do appreciate you guys volunteering to hang out here. I guess your mom told you I'm a little spooked after what happened and it will keep me sane to have you here. Otherwise, I would have to get in the car and hide someplace where the bad guys couldn't find me. Are the dogs barkers? I mean, I like dogs that bark if there's anything outside."

"They're not barkers, no," Josh said. "But they'll tell us if there is something wrong. A cold nose is just as good an alarm as a bark in the middle of the night."

"Can they stay out by the pool at night?"

"They could, but they are better in the house .If they're out by the pool they can't tell you if someone is sneaking around on the other side of the house. Believe me, they know if a fly lands on a windowsill. Now we need to introduce you to the dogs, and you need to let them know you want to be friends with them. Give them your open palm to smell, that's the best thing, and when they have smelled you, give them a nice pat on the head, or a scratch behind the ears."

The two dogs looked like a pair of Shetland ponies to Denis, and he had visions of them climbing on the furniture, not that it would make any difference, but he was not particularly a dog person.

"Frick, here." One dog came and sat in front of Josh.

"Frack, here." The other dog obediently came and sat in front of him too.

"Now, Denis, if you would come over here."

Denis walked over to them, sank down on one knee, and gave them each a hand to sniff, then rolled the hands over onto their heads, gave them a good pet. "Good boys," he said. "Do they get cookies?" The dogs' ears perked up.

"They only get treats when they do something to earn them. We don't want people to be able to make friends by holding out a treat. Let's take them for a walk around the house, maybe if you go with us you can show us around at the same time."

"Oh, right. I need to show you the bedrooms so you can decide where you want to camp out. It is a four-bedroom house and two of the bedrooms have twin beds. You guys probably want the one we think of as the guest bedroom. It has a queen-size bed."

"Well, that's appropriate," Matt said, "queen-size for queens."

Denis looked at him blankly then realized that was a joke. "Oh, right, well, I meant--"

"I just thought we should get that out of the way. I know Sue told you about us, that we want to get married whenever it's legal, but there are just four guys here, and the longer it goes unsaid, the more difficult it is," Josh said. Matt walked over to him and put one hand on either side of Josh's head, pulled Josh toward him, and kissed him, a real kiss; a lingering kiss.

Paul said nothing, just looked at Denis. Denis smiled at him, patted him on the back. "It's cool, Paul. It's cool. And great dogs, right?"

"When are you gonna move in?"

Matt said they had some luggage in the car, and, "Ready when you are, CB."

Paul shook hands with Matt and Josh and said to Denis that it was time for him to get back to the office. Denis walked him out, hugged him and told him again that it was OK. "Nice guys, you gotta admit they're nice guys. And the dogs are great. I will be able to sleep better with the dogs in the house."

As Paul was getting into his car, an ADT truck pulled up.

"Mr. Rosa?"

"We've been expecting you. Come on in and I'll show you around. We want motion sensors around the house and lights that go on automatically if the motion sensors are set off. We were robbed a few days back and we need to feel safe here."

"We can get you all safe and sound, no problem."

Denis took the two workmen up to the door, and just as he was opening it, Matt Mason stepped up. "We need to see your identification," he said. The two man produced laminated cards. Matt took them, pulled out his smartphone, and called ADT, verifying that the two men who were here were indeed the men who had been sent, complete with physical descriptions.

"I wouldn't have thought to do that," Denis said.

"My mom's a detective," Matt said. "You pick things up."

Denis walked the two men around the house and they made notes. He showed them the master bedroom, which he wanted to be extra secure, and the fence gates.

"Do you want us to electrify the fence?" one of the men asked.

"I don't want you to do anything that requires a permit or a city inspector before you do it, and nothing that could hurt any of the kids in the neighborhood either. And there are two dogs in the house, nothing that can hurt them."

They settled on a series of steps that would take a few days, but they would put the first layer of security devices in place today, including a direct line to the ADT dispatching station from a handheld phone that would stay with Denis.

"So if something happens that bothers you, you just press the O for Operator on this phone and we will pick up right away. There is a clamp on it for your belt. You can put it under your pillow when you sleep and take it with you into the bathroom when you are having a shower. It's not waterproof, but it is water resistant."

The two men got to work, and Denis said to Matt and Josh, "I wonder if I am going overboard on this. It's just that when someone tries to kill you, and you don't know who or why, it's scary."

"No such thing," Josh said. "And both of us will be here 24/7. We're working on a website project and no reason we have to be anywhere else. If you want some privacy, just let us know and we'll go for a walk or something."

"You guys are great," Denis said. "We need to go to the market and get some supplies. Anything you don't eat?"

"We're easy. More vegetarian, but we can make do with almost any kind of menu. Usually not a lot of sweets or fats."

They went to a Ralph's Market on top of the hill and bought a lot more groceries than Denis had anticipated, but it all fit into the back of the SUV. The dogs stayed at home, with the door to the pool area open so they could go outside. The ADT workmen were there, too. When they returned, all was as it had been when they left. They carried the groceries into the kitchen, and Denis started putting things away and throwing out old food that might have gone bad: bread, and the shrimps in the fridge that had been bought for the cioppino he had not made because those men tried to kill him.

He had inherited from his mother a deep insecurity about food. She had grown up during the Depression and she couldn't stand not to have a pantry that was so jammed with food that it would simply not hold one more can, jar, or box of corn meal. When the pantry was completely full, she could breathe easier. He felt the same. As long as there was a lot of food in the house, he could relax. He was not the sort of person who could go shopping on the way home and get everything he needed to make dinner. He had to have six kinds of pasta in the cupboard, five types of rice, ten cans of beans, dried lentils and dried black-eyed peas, enough garlic to last three weeks, a basket of potatoes and onions and shallots, a case of crushed tomatoes, bottles of roasted peppers, tins of anchovies and bottles of capers, several bottles of olive oil, fresh horseradish, lots of fruit, and plenty of baking ingredients, including a couple of pounds of butter, sour milk, and sour cream. He liked to open the pantry and have twenty things stare at him saying, "Make me for dinner." One of the ultimate luxuries in life was having your pick of things to eat, and if you weren't a ninny, it was not even expensive, especially since you were going to eat it all anyway.

When he and Matt and Josh had unloaded the groceries, he had to leave some of the things they had bought on the countertop because he could not fit them under the counter, in the pantry, or even in the corners behind the food processor and the toaster.

He called Paul and asked if he and Christie would like to come over for penne arrabiata and salad. He would whip up something for dessert, too, and get out a couple of bottles of good wine, which was stored in a room that was originally envisioned as a den, but had become a multipurpose storage room that held, among other things, twenty or so cases of red wine, the extra chairs for the dining table if all the leaves were put in at Christmas, several shelves of useless vinyl recordings for which there was no turntable anymore, some rolled-up oriental carpets, and a variety of paintings that Elissa had stacked against a wall because she didn't want them hanging in the house after he moved out.

Paul and Christie showed up at seven. Denis was peeling garlic, gingerly using his right hand to slice the garlic cloves. He asked Paul to pour some drinks. Christie said, "Here let me," and took over the garlic slicing, much to Denis's relief.

Josh and Matt walked into the room, followed by a very quiet Frick and Frack, who, on a whispered command, dropped to a "lie down" position well outside the boundaries of the open-plan kitchen. Christie finished the garlic, grabbed a dishtowel to wipe off her hands, and walked over to the dogs.

"They are Frick and Frack, and I'm Matt. That handsome hunk over there is my boyfriend, Josh Underwood."

Christie beamed at Matt, held out her hand to shake, and then walked over to Josh and did the same.

"Frick and Frack," she said, "what cute names for such big dogs!" The canine ears pricked up when the names were said, but the dogs didn't stir. "Can I pet them?"

"Of course, although they may lick you. Be prepared."

"They wouldn't be dogs if they didn't lick," she said, looking at the animals. She squatted down and ran her hand down from the crown of his head to the middle of Frick's back. He raised his nose and sniffed her hand and she held it for him to smell, then petted him again. Then she repeated the actions with Frack.

"They're perfect gentlemen," she said. "I wish you could train our dog, Angus, who has no manners at all, and still pees in the front hallway when he gets excited."

"So," Paul started tentatively, "how does it happen that you guys are free to move in here with Dad? Great timing from our point of view, of course."

Josh explained that their landlord was not particularly happy about having the two dogs in the apartment where they were living in Hermosa Beach, just up the coast and near some of the most famous surfing beaches in the area.

"We run a web design service, and we work online, so it's not particularly important to us to go to an office. When Mom called, I thought well, who wouldn't want to stay in PVE for a while in a house on the cliff? Also, it gives us time to look for a new place, maybe one to buy this time, instead of just a rental. We left all our stuff in the apartment because the rent is paid and no one will care, but if we find something we like, we're on month-to-month because the lease is expired now."

"Can I pour you a drink?" Paul asked.

"Vodka tonic with lime if you have it," Matt said, "and a sarsaparilla for my better half over there. He's a teetotaler. Like having a built-in designated driver."

"Or a party pooper," Denis chimed in. "Give him one of those orange sodas from the fridge. I want to propose a toast." Paul complied quickly, and Denis said, "To my friends, Matt and Josh, thanks for keeping me from jumping off the cliff, and long may they wave!"

"Here, here," Christie said, and upended her scotch. She slid back into the kitchen, picked up the knife, and said, "OK, boss, what else can I slice up?"

"Get half a dozen of those roma tomatoes in the vegetable bin and slice them kinda roughly, but into fairly small pieces, like the size of the top part of my thumb," he said, holding his hand up and bending his thumb. "And while you're at it, you could open two of those small tins of anchovies because I'll never get them open with my gimpy arm."

"They're great," she said, "the guys and the dogs. Hizzoner over there was worried that somehow it might not be OK," gesturing toward Paul, who was flipping the channels of the television looking for something. "He's a hard case sometimes, but it's easy to see these guys are gold."

"I figured if Paul said it was OK, the others would be OK, too."

Denis put the pasta on to cook, then heated the oil and scraped in the garlic and the two tins of anchovies, cooking them until the anchovies melted into the oil. As the penne rigate cooked, he added the fresh tomatoes, a couple of teaspoons of crushed red pepper, half a bottle of capers, a couple of dozen black olives chopped up, and a dash of cheap grappa. He simmered it until the pasta was ready, then poured everything into a pasta bowl and tossed it. Like a magician, he pulled two baguettes of garlic bread out of the oven and handed it all to Christie to put on the table. The fridge held the steamed and chilled tops of four big leeks, and a cereal bowl full of fresh vinaigrette with horseradish and shallots.

They sat down to eat at the dining room table and linked hands for a moment to remember the ones who were no longer with them.

Both of the dogs got up at the same moment and ran to the glass door leading to the pool. They paced up and down, but then sat back down where they had been before.

"Probably an animal in the yard," Josh said. "They'll get used to that."

"There is supposed to be a motion detector in the back yard that would turn on spotlights if there were someone there," Denis said. "I suppose it could be not hooked up yet, or that it could allow for a neighbor's cat or a possum or an owl, but not a vampire."

Paul looked up at him quizzically.

"Just seeing if you were listening." Denis smiled and turned his attention to the pasta bowl. "There's fresh Parmesan cheese here if you want. In Italy they wouldn't use it, but we're not in Italy, so do as you please."

Chapter Thirteen

He woke up the next morning to the smell of coffee brewing. He put on a bathrobe and walked out to the kitchen.

"I hope I didn't wake you rattling around," Matt said.

"No, you didn't. The coffee smells delicious." He took a mug from the stand and poured it full.

"I have to take the boys for a walk," Matt said. "Josh is in there, just so you know, working on our website project. Door's open. You won't bother him if you walk in."

"No, I'll walk around the block with you. It's cool out so I need to put on clothes, though. Give me a couple of minutes?"

They each took a leash and went out the front door to find a black-and-white parked in front of the house next door. They walked on by, and walked around the long, irregular oval that formed Rocky Point Road, about a mile and a half in circumference. The dogs never pulled on the leashes, but, being dogs, they wanted to sniff everything they went by, so the walk took nearly half an hour. They had taken plastic baggies and cleaned up after Frick and Frack, and when they rounded the bend and could see the house ahead, the police car was gone. Albert Hanszen, the neighbor, was standing fully dressed with his arms crossed in his front yard. He waved and walked toward them.

"Hi, Denis," he said. "I haven't seen you since you got back, but wanted to say how sorry I am about what happened to Elissa. The TV news was reporting on the men who attacked you. Guess it must be a little tense after that. If there's anything we can do, I hope you'll let us know."

"Thanks, Al. Say hi to Matt Mason. Matt and his buddy, Josh, are going to be staying with me for a while, and these fine fellows are Frick and Frack. They're not barkers, so they shouldn't bother you, but they are guard dogs, more or less, so they help me sleep better. What was the cop car here for?"

"I think there were some kids horsing around last night, left muddy footprints all over the flower garden. Not the first time it's happened, and I think I know which kids. I see them climbing around on the cliff sometimes. Gayle called the police this morning and of course they came right over, especially since we're right next door to you. I don't think it was anything to worry about."

"Appreciate your offer, Al," Denis said. "One of these evenings you and Susie should stop over for a drink. I'm thinking about putting the house on the market, by the way, so I apologize in advance if people park along the street."

"You've been here longer than anyone on the point," Al said. "You're like one of the pioneers. We sure would hate to see you move away."

Denis shrugged his shoulders deprecatingly and said, "Well, give my love to Susie." They walked on home and Matt detoured along the side of the house that bordered the Hanszen home. No muddy footprints, and nothing disturbed. They walked slowly around the parts of the house that were on the streetside of the fence. Nothing unusual, and the dogs sniffed everything like they did all the way around the block, but did not seem to find anything out of the ordinary. Matt slipped their leashes off, pulled a tennis ball out of his pocket, and said "Frick", throwing the ball across the yard. Frick ran to get the ball and Frack heeled next to Matt's left leg. Frick brought the ball back and Matt rubbed his muzzle with "Good boy, Good boy." Then the same for Frack. The two dogs followed Matt as closely as if they were still on the leash. They went back indoors and Matt gave them each a piece of jerky from a bowl on the counter in the kitchen.

"If it's OK with you, I'm going to take the dogs in the pool and teach them how to get out. They need to know how to get out of the pool by using the stairs at the shallow end. Otherwise they would end up drowning if they were in the pool."

Denis offered to go in the pool with the dogs, but Matt preferred that he do it by himself, since it was a learning experience--a new trick. He took the tennis ball, stripped off his shirt, and pulled off his jeans revealing a Speedo-like bathing suit underneath. The gym training showed all over him, every muscle in his arms and legs displaying definition, and he had a flat stomach too. He threw the ball in the pool and both dogs jumped in the water after it. He walked to the shallow end of the pool and told them to bring him the ball. The dogs swam naturally and got to the shallow end, but could not get out. Matt walked to the corner of the pool where there was an angled series of steps, stepped into the water, and stood on the first step. The dogs swam over to him and found the bottom of the second step. Matt turned and walked out of the pool and the dogs followed. He threw the ball back in the pool and walked to the deep end. They swam to him, but of course could not find the steps. So he walked back to the shallow end and stood on the first step again; the dogs got out of the pool and shook themselves off. He threw the ball again, standing in the middle of the poolside. One of the dogs grabbed the ball, swam to the shallow end, got out of the pool, and brought the ball to Matt.

Denis looked on admiringly. *Damn, I want dogs like that. If I had dogs like that, I would like dogs again.*

Matt continued to horse around with the dogs by the pool and threw the ball again and again. The dogs learned to swim to the shallow end and get out. Then Matt dived into the pool himself and the dogs yelped and jumped in after him. They played like kids for a few minutes, and then they all got out using the steps. He squatted down and hugged the wet animals. He toweled the dogs off and told them to stay outside, opening the sliding door and letting himself in. The dogs sat still. He cracked the door and said, "Go play," and the dogs took off running around the pool on a tear, chasing each other and chasing the ball.

"They'll forget how to get out of the pool, but eventually they'll learn and then they won't forget," he said. "I'm gonna go see how Josh is getting along."

Denis called Rich, left a message, "Not important, kiddo. Dad. Give me a call when you can." Same with Maggie. Everyone was at work. As he hung up, the phone rang. It was Sue Mason.

"Hi, Sue. You looking for Matt?"

"No, looking for you. If you're available, I'd like to swing by, have a couple of questions, and a couple of photos to show you."

Denis said he would fix some lunch if that was OK.

"Well, as I recall, you owe me a dinner," she said. "But I'll collect on that another time. If you want to make something simple, that would be great."

"The boys are here, and I gotta tell you, those dogs are great. I want to steal them."

"Not stealable," she said. "They're bonded to Josh and Matt."

"See you when I see you," Denis said.

The two detectives had, it turned out, combed over the telephone and credit card bills and had come up with a couple of additional names on top of the four that Denis had found. Unsurprisingly, all of them were Hispanic names. They had been to interview three of the men already. All three were in their twenties, all were good-looking, all spoke good English, and all had jobs in restaurants.

"She must have had a good come-on line," Denis said, turning the corners of his mouth down.

"Well, for a reasonably good-looking woman, the best come-on line is nothing at all, just eye contact. Men are usually ready to say hello if a woman looks interested. But yes, she may have initiated a conversation with them. The three men we have talked to so far are all bartenders, so it's not hard to imagine a conversation starting almost spontaneously between a single woman and a bartender. And that old thing about single women not sitting at the bar has been out the window for decades, if you're thinking about that."

Denis asked if any of the men had dated Elissa. They had only gotten a complete answer from one of the men on that. Yes, he said, he banged her a few times, and she helped him with his school fees. Where did he bang her? Big house up in PVE by the ocean. When had he last seen her? Over the summer sometime, not since school started at the end of August.

The other two both remembered her at the bar when they showed her picture, but neither one recalled ever seeing that woman outside the restaurants where they worked. "We told them that we had records of calls to their personal phones and both of them said they gave out their smartphone numbers pretty freely. One pulled out his phone and typed in Rosa, and up popped Elissa's number, no photo, just a silhouette, and no address, just the number."

"If you didn't show me the picture, I woulda had no idea who this lady was," the one bartender had said. "She did call me a few times, I think, but that was when I was at the bar. Lotta people don't want to come in if the place isn't busy and they call to find out what time they should come over when there will be a lot of people here."

"Where does that put us?" Denis asked.

"Not much further along than we were before, but we know more about her. She went to bars and she liked to be there when it was busy. Maybe she felt like that would make her less conspicuous talking to younger men. She apparently didn't object to slipping a good-looking guy some bills, too. But none of that is unusual, and none of that tells us anything that's helpful about how she died."

Denis suggested that a bartender could have brought a bottle of vodka with him that was already spiked with GHB and poured the drink without contaminating anything in the kitchen on Rocky Point. That would mean that if he rinsed out the glass, there would be no evidence.

"Yes," Sue said, "that's true, but if he had a little bottle of GHB, he could empty it into the vodka she had there already and it would have the same effect."

"But something happened, didn't it? I mean something happened that caused those men to come after me. The way I look at it, it could only have been a few things. I could have upset someone at the surgeon's office in Westwood. I could have upset someone, maybe even a customer, at the Mexican restaurant on the pier in Redondo Beach. Or I could just have been in the wrong place at the wrong time when they came to retrieve whatever they took from the attic through the access panel in the closet. In any case, they were prepared for me, because they had at least three kinds of drugs, right? So they weren't just breaking and entering, especially since they didn't take anything that a burglar would take, and they found something in the attic instead."

Denis was chopping garlic and rapini, and he threw some pasta in a pot when the water boiled. He put the garlic, the greens, and some oil in a skillet with some red pepper flakes and put it on a burner absent-mindedly.

"How long?" she asked.

"What? Oh, twelve minutes," he said. "We can eat at the counter here." He put two plates out with silverware while they were talking.

"Mom! I didn't know you were here." It was Matt. "I smelled the food and just wondered what it was."

"Oh, sorry, Matt. I should just throw some more on the stove. It's real easy, just vegetables and pasta. Do you want some?"

Matt walked over to his mother and kissed her on the cheek. "Not right now, thanks. You have something you're working on and so do Josh and I. We're working on a new shopping-cart approach for this website. Or hey, as long as you're here, maybe we'll rush out and do some errands. You gonna be here for a while?"

"An hour, I'd say."

"Outahere then." He yelped at Josh, and the two of them dashed out the front door. "Leaving the boys with you!" The dogs wandered into the television room in tandem, as though they were having a conversation, then went over to the sliding glass doors and lay down in the sunlight with their heads on their paws.

"You know, this pasta you made is delicious. You can cook this for me any time you want," she cooed.

He paused with his fork in midair, and put it back on his plate. "There's no way to say this but to just say it. I hope we can try to pick up where we left off when you found me hanging around by the pool. I felt old and used up when I was in the hospital, and not at all the kind of guy who ought to be interested in a smart chickie like you. But I feel better now and like the guy says in the movie--gimme da ball, gimme da ball." He did not make a move of any kind, just looked at her. She put down her fork and touched his hand with her hand.

"Deal," she said. "Deal."

They finished the rest of the lunch without saying a word, then he stood up and took the plates and put them in the sink.

"Where were we?" he said.

"Well," she said, "I thought you were going to kiss me."

His face blazed red; he could feel it on his cheeks and ears and all over his neck. Without a whisper of a pause, he put his hand behind her head and pulled her toward him. After he kissed her, she rested her head on his shoulder. He put his arms around her shoulders lightly, then squeezed, then opened his arms and put his hands on her shoulders, looked at her straight on. He smiled, then stepped back and finished putting the dishes in the sink.

"Does this get in the way of trying to figure out what happened?" he asked, looking down at the sink and rinsing the dishes.

"Never kissed a cop before?" she asked lightly.

He grinned. "Not that I can recall, though there was a cop who gave me a warning instead of a ticket one time and I told Elissa I could have kissed him."

"No," she said, "it will not get in the way of anything, and we will not take this any further until we know what's next. But now we know something we did not know before, about each other."

Her smartphone buzzed on the counter.

"Mason." She looked out the window and listened. "I'll be there as fast as I can." She turned to Denis.

"Ricardo Espinosa just called to confess to being with Elissa the night she died."

"I thought the DNA didn't match."

"It doesn't. I have to get over to Lomita, he is on his way to the station. Can we finish the talk we were having later? Your summary is right about what we know, but Espinosa's statement is new information and our first chance to talk to him will be at the station."

Right then the front door opened and Matt and Josh walked in with some dry-cleaning and a couple of cloth shopping bags, both of which looked full.

"Thanks, Sue," Josh said. "As you can see, we needed to pick up a few things."

"I want you to stay close to Denis," she said. "We have just received some new information on the case here, and the last time that happened was when Denis was attacked. I am going to ask the PVE police to keep an eye on this house, but they don't have a lot of personnel, so it's going to be up to you. I frankly don't expect anything to happen because the man providing the information is on his way to Lomita to give us a statement, but you can't be too careful. Under some circumstances, he could go with me to Lomita, but that would not be the best thing given the situation with this man."

She left, and they heard her car peel out of the driveway. She turned on the siren as she drove around the curve away from the house.

"I don't know a lot of what happened," Denis said to the two young men. "A waiter whom I had located, and who was most likely involved with my wife, called in and told someone at your mom's office, maybe Ron Furman--I don't know--that he was here in the house the night my wife died. The book is still open on her death, because the coroner said that although it was obvious that she drowned, the cause of the drowning was inconclusive. So what this guy has to say could help us-- your mom, the Sheriff's Department--figure out what happened. I don't know if you know, but my wife and I had been separated for ten years, and in that time I have been living in New York. I only came out here when someone called to tell me that Elissa had died."

They were standing there with their shopping bags and their dry-cleaning.

"Here, Matt, give me the bags and I will put them in the other room, said Josh." Denis, I hope this means we'll all find out something about what happened to you, more than to Mrs. Rosa. I'm going to check the windows and doors, and have a look at the alarm control panel."

Denis said he had no intention of holing up in the house. *But I'm glad the dogs are there.* He thought about Espinosa, a good-looking young man, and friendly, at least friendly in the way waiters are friendly. *Didn't look like a killer.* Sue had been fairly certain that he was not involved. *Well, I guess he was involved in some way or other, but we don't know yet.*

He looked out the window at the hot tub. "That's where she died, in the Jacuzzi. This seems like I shouldn't say it, but there is something else we know. Elissa had had sex the night that she died and there was some semen that the coroner took a sample of. When I told Sue and Ron that I had found out that Elissa had called this guy, Espinosa, Sue went over to talk to him, and she took a DNA sample from his cheek. Anyway, it was not a match. I don't know what that means, but he was not the guy who had been in bed with her, at least not that night. She was kind of a party gal, though."

He stared at the hot tub and tried to imagine Elissa sitting there with her glass of vodka, and Espinosa lingering at the edge, or maybe sitting in the tub with her. But what about the other guy? Where would he have been? Maybe he left? Hard to sort out.

He decided then and there that he would fill in the hot tub, plant something there so that you could never tell it had been there at all, maybe a couple of palm trees. The pool area could use a couple of palm trees anyway. His mother had complained that Rocky Point never really got hot, even in the summer. She had grown up near San Antonio where hot was hot and not just eighty. Rocky Point stuck out into the ocean and was surrounded on three sides by the Pacific Ocean. She had refused to even consider putting in a pool.

The pool was Denis's idea when he inherited the place. He had slowly revamped the floor plan of the house, enlarged the bathrooms, combined two smaller bedrooms to create a larger single bedroom with its own bath for the boys to share, and put in the pool. It was warm enough for him to swim. The hot tub came along a few years before he moved to New York, part of Elissa's idea to entertain more often. Pool parties, and in the evening when the clouds drifted in over the cliffs, hot tub soaks after dinner, originally not even risqué, but maybe later...well, who knows?

Sue arrived at the Lomita station after Espinosa where he was waiting in an interrogation room with a two-way mirror. Ron took her into the viewing area and they looked at him. *Yes, that's the man I spoke with, the one I took the cheek swab from.*

What he told them was that he had been seeing Elissa off and on for several months.

"I wouldn't say we were dating, but we were friends, and yes, we did have sex," he said. "We met when she came into the restaurant and I was working at the bar, and she invited me out to the house in PVE, great place, and we had a couple of drinks, and then we were in bed. I was afraid she would get pregnant, but then she told me how old she was, and I relaxed. But I have a girlfriend, and Elissa knew we were exactly what we were, just getting together to talk and screw, have a few drinks maybe."

Was she taking drugs of any kind? He looked puzzled. "No, she was a borderline lush, but I never saw her take any pills, and most of those pills are no good with vodka, you know."

And how did he happen to be there the night Mrs. Rosa died?

"I called her smartphone and she didn't answer, so I just drove out there. Figured I would call her again on the regular house phone when I was near the house. But the house phone went to voicemail right away, too. So I pulled up in front of the house and decided to knock on the door. But before I could, somebody came out of the side gate and walked away. I thought, oh, she has guests, so maybe I should just leave."

But he didn't leave. He sat there in his car for a while and there was nothing going on in the house, so he rang the front doorbell. There was no answer, and after a bit, because there were lights in the house, he looked over the fence toward the back yard.

"I thought maybe if she was sitting outside she wouldn't hear the doorbell and it didn't seem like there was anyone else there. I couldn't see anything, so I let myself in through the gate and walked back to the pool. I saw her under the water in the Jacuzzi and I panicked. I ran back to the car and went home. A few days later, Mr. Rosa was in the restaurant and I thought maybe he was going to punch me out or something. I hadn't ever seen any of her family before and I was spooked, because I knew she was dead. Nobody stays underwater like that if they're alive."

"Why didn't you call someone? Or pull her out of the water and try to give her first aid?" Ron asked.

"I don't know. I knew she was dead, she was just there under the water, and I panicked. I'm Chicano you know, and that's not a Chicano part of town, and if I was caught there I would be in jail, man. And I would lose my job and have a record."

They asked him about the man he saw leaving when he was

parked out front.

"I couldn't see him much. Looked like he was in a hurry and he walked off down the street like he lived here. He was too far away to see his face, but I think he was maybe about the height of the fence, because I couldn't see him until he opened the gate. That's about it. He wasn't running, but he was in a hurry."

Would he recognize him if he saw the man again?

"I never got a look at him. Honest. If he killed her, I would help if I could, but I didn't see him."

"You said there was nothing going on in the house. You could see inside?"

"Well, not exactly because the curtains were closed--you know, those thin curtains that are behind the regular curtains. But there was nobody walking around, and no music or anything."

"Could you see into the kitchen at all?"

He didn't think he could have seen into the kitchen even if the curtains were open. "But mostly when I went over there, I went into the house through the garage, because I would follow her home after work."

They asked if he knew of any other men who were dating Mrs. Rosa.

"I knew she was seeing other guys," he said." She was pretty clear about that. And she liked Latino guys, you know, kinda hunky, sexy guys. She came into the restaurant with one guy a few months ago. I thought it was strange that she would bring her date to my bar, but she was all friendly like, and they sat at one of the booths and talked."

"She didn't introduce you?"

"No."

"Do you remember him?"

"Yeah, I do. I kept looking at him because I thought it was strange, like I said. Yeah, I would remember him."

They called in a sketch artist, and sent Espinosa to work with him.

"What do you think?" Ron asked her.

"I think the same thing I thought when I talked to him before," she said. "I think he is worried, but not scared, and I doubt he would be a good liar. Of course you can't take that to the bank."

"And the fact that he didn't call anyone when he saw Mrs. Rosa at the bottom of the hot tub?"

"That's not good, but I believe him when he said he panicked. And we both know there was someone else with her that night, maybe the man Espinosa saw leaving by the side gate."

They agreed that they would do some more background work on Espinosa.

"And if it wasn't Espinosa, the next logical person would be someone connected to the surgeon, or someone else at the restaurant where Espinosa works, because those are the only people Denis called and left a message for. He said he called some of the numbers from the telephone bill, but did not leave any messages."

"But those calls would show up as missed calls on a caller ID," Ron said, "message or no message."

Chapter Fourteen

Denis called Paul and said he was thinking of going over to Catalina, thought maybe he would offer them a rain check, but Christie and the girls had plans. Paul offered to see if they could change, but Denis said not to worry, they would do it another time. He called Rich. It was Friday and he was thinking maybe they would like to go to Catalina in the morning.

"You've got a bum arm, Dad," Rich said. "You sure you're up to it? You still in a sling?"

"C'mon, Rich, there's nothing strenuous about taking a boat over to Catalina and wandering around with the kids. I'd have to be a lefty at skee-ball, but I'm not all that good as a righty. And I keep the sling on sometimes, but not all the time. I'm getting the use of the arm back. I can eat tacos and chips with my left hand, but my right hand is functional enough for the dinner table now. I have a hard time raising my arm above chest height, and if I have to carry anything, I'd carry it on the left. But other than that, it would be good for me to spend some time with really smart people like your boys."

They agreed that Rich and Mel would pick him up at the house Saturday morning at seven so they could get to the dock and get in line by eight for the nine o'clock Catalina Express from Berth 95 in San Pedro.

"No, wait a minute. Get to the house by six thirty, because I want you to meet my new roommates, Matt and Josh. And the boys can meet the dogs, Frick and Frack. Great animals, almost human. Or in the case of these animals, you might say humans are almost up to the level of these dogs."

"If you have coffee ready, you're on," Rich said.

As the day wore on, he began to wonder what had transpired at the Lomita sheriff's station, what it was that Espinosa had told them. No call from Sue, so that meant either that they were still talking to him, or that he told them something that she had to keep to herself.

He went online to check some stock trades that he had asked his broker to take care of a couple of weeks before. Nothing big, he was not a rich man, but the trades were important to him. He was close to being able to pay off the last of his credit cards, based largely on the strength of his 401(k) plan, which he was plenty old enough to dip into without penalty. Not that it was all that important if he was going to sell the house, because the numbers would be different. But the house was something his father had done, not something he had done. He had built a business on his own, and when the economy fell off the table, so did his business. He lived off the credit cards for about three years, managing to pay the people who were working with him and keep their insurance policies paid up. It seemed odd that if he sold the house, he wouldn't have to worry anymore about money. But the trades had been made, and he wired money to MasterCard to take his last big balance down to under $1,000. It was like taking a cake out of the oven, all brown and sweet-smelling with vanilla, that sort of sense of accomplishment.

He dug through the books in the living room and found an old Paul Theroux travel book about a walking trip around England and Scotland along the water's edge. He took it into the bedroom, stretched out on the bed, and started to read. It started in London, and then headed out the Thames estuary to Southend, a has-been Victorian resort town more notable for drabness and grime than anything else. And he drifted off to sleep.

There was some screaming outside, a raucous piercing sound coming from more than one voice. He ran outside and the pool wasn't there, just grass, and he looked up at the roof to see two big birds on one of the eves, a peacock and a peahen. They were yelling at Old Duke, the black lab, who was jumping up at them, but not coming within six feet of the roofline. He floated over to Old Duke and looked up at the peacock, who spread his tail.

He woke up smiling. He remembered when the peacocks had taken up residence on the roof when he was a teenager. Their screaming nearly drove his mother nuts, or so she said, and it was loud, no getting around that, but there were empty lots on either side of the house at that time, so the only neighbors who were really annoyed were the Baumgardners across the street. But the peacocks were not going away; they had found a crevice in the roof where two gables came together and they had built a nest. Odd that they were wild peacocks, had something to do with one of the big old estates up the hill, where someone had raised peacocks that later went wild. One of the extras of living in PVE.

The sun was lower in the sky than it had been, so he had probably fallen asleep for a half-hour or so, and he felt refreshed. He turned over and realized his shoulder was really sore from having slept on the wrong side. He wandered down the hallway toward where Matt and Josh were staying, but veered toward the living room when their door was closed. Hate California, it's cold and it's damp, that's why the lady is a tramp, he hummed.

It was a pretty room. He had always liked it. The PV stone fireplace had a dated look, like an old sitcom set, but it was solid-looking, and the slate hearth was a really nice place to sit when there was a fire because the chimney drew well and there was no smoke that escaped into the room. Having a fire in the fireplace was a good thing living on a point poking out into the water, because it tended to get chilly and damp at night, especially in the cooler months.

When he was about thirteen, he had built a fire in a little cave in the side of the cliff below the house and got in Dutch with his mom because the smoke drifted up the cliff and into the house and she thought the house was on fire. That cave, or indented ledge really, was only about ten feet below the precipice, and almost completely invisible if you stood on the cliffside, so it was an ideal private clubhouse for Denis--and when they were teenagers, for Denis and a couple of his friends who wanted to sneak cigarettes. But he never built another fire there because his father promised him a good tanning if he ever scared his mom like that again.

The Red Soldier painting was perfect in the living room, but he made a mental note to go through the canvases stacked in the storage room because he liked to see more art on the walls than just the occasional picture. He liked those Victorian gallery walls that had paintings from floor to ceiling, like Gertrude Stein's family's home in Paris that the Metropolitan Museum in New York had recreated a few years back as a special exhibit.

The doorbell rang. He looked out the living room window to see who was at the door and saw Sue Mason.

"Well, welcome, fancy meeting you here," he said, planting himself where she would have to virtually brush up against him to get into the house. She reached out, caressed his cheek, and slipped by him.

"We should talk," she said.

She told him about the interview with Espinosa and what he had seen the night that Elissa had died.

"So you think maybe the guy who was leaving when Espinosa got there had killed her?"

It was a possibility, she said. Of course if Elissa was at the bottom of the pool and he had seen her, the man before him, whoever he was, could have come across the same sight and fled the same way. So the question was, did Denis know anyone up the block to the right who might have been on close enough terms with Elissa to wander over in the evening?

"To tell you the truth, I don't really even know who lives around here anymore," he said. "A lot of these houses have been sold, or even sold several times, in the last few years, and of course each time someone new moves in, they are richer than the people who were there before. And then you get to someone like me, and I've been here for way longer than anyone else, and they are all way richer than me. Which just means I would not be likely to know them, that's all. Different social groups, rich, not rich."

She said that Espinosa told them that the man looked like he was walking home. There were plenty of places to park on the street close by if he had wanted to. Espinosa had parked just at the side of the front yard, which is why he saw the man leave. So if he headed off toward the right, he could live in the next few houses.

"Or he could be going to the passage up to Paseo del Mar, which is between the two houses at the curve up there where the road bends left," Denis said. "But I'd have to ask the neighbors I do know to even find out who still lives in the neighborhood. There used to be a family up on the other side of the street, not the cliffside, who had a son who was Rich's age. I'll ask him, because we're all going to Catalina tomorrow. As a matter of fact, why don't you come with us and you can ask them directly if they know anyone in the neighborhood? And, if the dogs can stay here alone, Matt and Josh could come, too, and that way they could get to know Rich and Mel and the kids."

She looked at him and smiled. "One thing at a time, OK?"

Well, that wasn't a no.

The light was changing because the sun was going down, flattening out into the water like a beach ball going flat and spreading pumpkin-colored fire across the sky.

"You on duty, or can I offer you a drink?" he asked.

"Let's say I'm on duty for now, but you can offer me a drink in a bit."

She told him her impressions of Espinosa, including the blot on his story that he had not tried to help Elissa when he saw her at the bottom of the hot tub. "He said she looked dead, and he panicked."

"I had a dream about her in that hot tub, and her hair was floating. It was all I could see of her, her hair on top of the water."

"Dreams sometimes have a lot of truth to them," she said, "but not necessarily a lot of facts. If she sank to the bottom of the water, her hair would go with her to the bottom. And she might look quiet. After a while she floated to the top, of course, because of things that happen in the body after death, and that's how the gardener found her. But she might have been on the bottom when Espinosa and the other guy saw her. I checked that with the coroner."

So if there is someone in the neighborhood who was one of Elissa's gentleman callers, that might change the picture about who was after him, too.

"What about the other names?"

She said her department would be trying to locate the guys whose names and phone numbers they had, and she told him that Espinosa had helped them put together a composite drawing of a young Chicano guy Elissa had brought into the bar at Casa Adobado. She pulled a copy of the drawing out of her handbag and handed it to him. "Look familiar?"

He stared at the sketch and nothing clicked. Never saw him before. He shook his head and put the sketch down, then stood up. "How about that drink?"

"How 'bout dem Yanks?" came a voice from behind him. It was Matt.

"Huh? Yanks?"

"It's a line from a play," Matt said. "It was meant to be funny. Kinda like walking into a tense room and saying 'Tennis anyone?' Hi, Mom."

She smiled. "That's my boy," she said.

The dogs ambled in after Matt, stretching after a nap.

"So," Denis said, "I have a proposal. My son, Rich, and his wife and kids and I are going to Catalina tomorrow for the day. I think it would be great if Sue and you guys went with us. I doubt the dogs would be allowed on the boat from San Pedro, but we could ask. Can they stay here if we're going to be gone all day?"

Matt went and fetched Josh, and they all sat down in the living room and talked. Yes, they would all go to Catalina together, and yes, the dogs could stay alone. "They usually stay home alone all day when Josh and I are working in offices," Matt said.

"I thought you were going to pour me a drink," Sue said.

"What's your pleasure?" he asked. She said a dry vodka martini with olives if he had the makings.

"Sounds good to me. I think I'll have the same. Guys?"

Matt said he would have a glass of red if there was a bottle open and Josh said he would love a sparkling water on the rocks with lime. Matt kept looking back and forth between Sue and Denis, and smiling.

"Don't look so smug, Matso," Sue said, showing him the back of her hand. He grinned.

Sue walked into the kitchen where Denis was wondering how to carry the drinks back to the living room with his one and a half good arms.

"I'll take those," Sue said, picking up the two martinis. "Matt, come get your drinks." Matt appeared, and picked up the sparkling water and the red wine.

"The wine is a pinot noir," Denis said. "There's a lot of that around since that is what Elissa liked best, but there is a whole roomful of wine down the hall, don't know if you've seen it. A lot of that is stuff I bought, Italians and southwestern French wines, Malbecs and Garnachas from Spain, dirtier and rougher than the Pinots. And the best part is that most of them are more than ten years old because I bought them before I moved back east."

"Here," he said to Sue, "I need your hands." He handed her two avocadoes. "Can you cut them and scoop them out into that bowl, please?" Then he dumped some hot sauce in the bowl, some kosher salt, and threw some cilantro on a cutting board, chopping it with a rocking motion with his gimpy right hand. Same with a bunch of scallions. He cut and squeezed a lemon in the bowl and threw a generous spoonful of mayonnaise in. When Sue dumped the avocado in, he said, "Mix it up some, not a lot, but some." He grabbed a bag of Tostitos and went into the living room. She brought in the avocado dip and he opened the chips.

"Amen. Dig in," Denis said. "Anybody want seasick pills for morning? If you think you might get seasick, you need to take them ahead of time. If you wait until you're feeling woozy, they won't help," Denis said. No takers. "I know Mel will take one, and she will probably want the boys to take a half. They have four boys, eldest is nine, so it's fun trying to keep up with them."

They spent a quiet evening together. Denis made some chicken hash in a surprisingly short period of time with a roast chicken he had bought at the market, and they sat passively watching a television drama about doctors trying to figure out how to get a young drug addict to talk to his parents about his problems. Josh and Matt cuddled up on the floor with the cushions from two overstuffed chairs, and Josh started to snore.

"Oops, that's my sign to tuck him in," Matt said, and shook his partner. They toddled off, and then Matt came back with the dogs and took them out the front door.

"Well," Denis said. "And what are we going to do with you?"

"We're going to walk me out to the car," Sue said. "And then you're going to kiss me and I'm going to kiss you back and you're going to feel me up and try to get me to stay, and I'm going to say no even though my nipples are standing straight up already, and then I'm going to get in my car and leave and be back here at six thirty for some of the coffee you promised."

She was absolutely right.

Denis woke up at six and realized that the dogs were sleeping in his room. They looked up when he got out of bed.

"It's OK, boys, go back to sleep," he said. He took a quick shower, brushed his teeth and ran his Crest dental floss back and forth like a shoeshine boy buffing shoes. He couldn't whistle while he was brushing his teeth, but he would've if he could've. The dogs were up and tail-wagging when he came out and he walked toward the kitchen. They stopped at the glass door, looked at him, looked outside, and wagged their tails. He opened the door and they ran outside. He had put the coffee on before he went to bed, so he pushed the button and it started to brew.

He looked outside and the dogs were paddling around in the pool. He poured some kibble into a pair of bowls. They heard him do it and got out of the pool by using the steps.

Damn.

They finished off the kibble in short order and he toweled them with a pair of beach towels that were slung over the back of one of the lounge chairs.

"You guys are going to unhinge your butts if you wag your tails any harder," he said.

A car pulled up in front and it was Rich and his family.

"Now, boys, be gentle with Grandpa, his shoulder is hurting him," Melanie said, pecking Denis on the cheek.

Denis crouched down and hugged the boys all together while they giggled. He looked at Sammy, the eldest. *Still young enough to hug. Not much longer, though.* Sue drove up and parked on the curb and he introduced her to Rich and Melanie.

"Boys, say hi to Mrs. Mason," he said.

"Good morning, Mrs. Mason," they said all together. The boys shrieked and attacked Frick and Frack, who stood up and allowed themselves to be manhandled, sniffing each child several times.

"Be gentle," Denis said.

They agreed to ride over to San Pedro in two cars. Matt and Josh would take all four boys, and Rich and Mel would take Denis and Sue. When Rich pulled into the parking lot, Matt and Josh were already playing tag with the boys in the waiting area outside the ticket booth for the Catalina Express. They were whooping and yelling and ducking behind parking stanchions and under chains designed to keep people out of places. Mel and Sue stood and smiled like old people at the two younger generations running around like crazed tree monkeys while Rich went with Denis to get the tickets. They came back out with two containers of milk and dosed the boys with half a Dramamine tablet each. Mel took a whole tablet. They had to get in line with about sixty other people and it was chilly, the way it is by the water on a southern California morning. Josh had a laptop with him ("Just in case," he said, "you never know"), and all the adults had smartphones of various kinds. No broadband for the hourlong boat ride, but they could watch for flying fish and dolphins, and if they were lucky, whales.

The sleek white catamaran whizzed across the mostly placid waters of the Catalina Channel. It had comfortable, high-backed seats that did not recline and did not have tray tables built into them. If you wanted a snack, you had to get up, get out and then bring it back and eat it on your lap. All the open spaces were packed with backpacks, bedrolls, rollaboards, some standard suitcases, and a bevy of bicycles, surfboards, golf clubs, and other sporting gear. They were in Avalon almost before it seemed possible, and the boys were about to vaporize from excitement.

Chapter Fifteen

One thing about being in law enforcement was that you were never completely off duty. Sue sat facing the cabin, in the front row of seats that was lined up across the inside of the bow, facing the cabin instead of facing the front. She wasn't consciously being a bodyguard, but she couldn't help scanning the people on the boat to see if there were any faces she recognized, or faces she wanted to be able to recognize because she didn't trust them.

The crew tied the boat up to the dock and placed the passenger ramp for disembarking, *No one knows we're here except the people on this boat, and I can see most of them from where I'm sitting.* She caught herself. *Don't be theatrical, Sue, no one is going to follow you to Catalina.* She still kept scanning, though.

The walk from the boat terminal into town is about two football fields long, and the town of Avalon is about three football fields of waterfront. At the other end is a spit of land with an incongruously large Art Deco-looking building that is called The Casino, although it functions as a movie theater at times, and as a party venue at others. The waterfront is remarkably clean, possibly because there is so little of it. But the overall impression is of a beachfront village of surpassing charm. Unlike the water on the west- and south-facing beaches of the California mainland, the water at Avalon is clear, so you can see the beautiful, bright orange garibaldi fish that are everywhere when you look in the water.

From a parent's point of view, one of the best things about Avalon is that, for the most part, there simply are no cars. There are quite a few golf carts, but even those are not allowed on most of the oceanfront walkway, which is just that--a walkway. Even so, it is a wonderful place to see bodies sunning, because the small size puts the strollers a mere few feet from the beach towels on the sand. Denis watched Matt and Josh surreptitiously, or at least he thought he was being cool, and he did see them eyeing the beach. The kids were ducking in and out of the crowds on the oceanfront walk.

They walked through town and past The Casino to a beach club that sold day passes, and he paid fifty dollars for a tent-like cabana that had several reclining deck chairs facing the rocky beach. Rich and Mel said they wanted to run the boys around for a while, and headed back into town, a good eight minute walk, to find some pizza or tacos or something the boys could eat standing up. Matt and Josh went off to the changing room to put on their bathing suits, and Denis and Sue stretched out like millionaires and signaled to a waiter. "Screwdrivers, mid-morning screwdrivers, with Grey Goose. And some guacamole and chips, if possible," requested Denis.

"Nice to have a few minutes to ourselves," he said. "I watched you watching the crowd on the boat. You're always on duty, aren't you?"

She looked out at the sheen on the water and nodded.

"Was it always that way?"

She shook her head. "But I haven't really dated anyone since Matt's sonofabitch father disappeared, which was before he was born. So," and she turned to look at him, "I am out of practice trying to be a girl when a man wants to be a boy." She smiled and crinkled her eyes, put her hand up to block the sun. He sat up on his chaise and made to kiss her, but Matt and Josh walked up.

"Oh, just in time," Josh said, making a sad clown face. "As you were. We're going in the frigid water to splash around and see if we can manage not to get hypothermia." They were wearing surfer shorts and the sort of rubber booties that divers wear in coral reefs. The beach was rocky, and some rocks, even mostly smooth-rolled ones, would have sharp points.

"Have fun, kids," Sue yelled as they were walking toward the water. "Don't hurry back on our account."

"It's hard to think about going back to New York sitting here with you."

"But you probably will, right?"

"I honestly don't know what I am going to do. If I sell the house, I will clear a pretty large amount of money, and that would probably let me do whatever I want. But I don't want to sell the house, even though I feel creeped out living in it sometimes. You know I grew up in that house, and it has a lot of good memories, but it's hard to see over the barrier of the last two weeks or so, and I know I can't go on looking over my shoulder every five minutes. And I hadn't expected to meet you, so I keep staring at you wondering what you're thinking about all this, too."

"I have all the finesse of a roller-derby bitch," she said. "At least that's what Matt tells me. I think with me, what you see is what you get. If I seem interested, that's because I am interested. I know, better than most people, what kind of spot you're in right now, and I'm not pushing, except as a cop. I want to get to the bottom of all this. It gives me the creeps, too, frankly, and that's not just because I like being around you--it's because there's some dark current under the water here and we don't know what it is.

"No one just happens by, breaks into a house, hangs the owner by his hands and drugs him, and then doesn't steal anything notable."

She looked around reflexively to see if anyone was listening. They were pretty isolated, and Josh and Matt were swimming out toward the floating boundary rope.

"What if the thing that was in the attic was not something that Elissa knew anything about? What if it was something that one of her boyfriends hid there? I mean, anyone she was seeing who wanted to hide something would have to know that, almost anywhere else, she might find it, right?"

Drugs. They both thought there was some kind of drug connection, especially since the bad guys had stuck fentanyl patches all over Denis's back and rear to keep him from being able to get himself free.

"But if the drugs are gone now, maybe that's the end of it?" he said uncertainly.

"Could be, yes, but there may be something else in the house that they want or need, or are afraid of. We didn't see any evidence that they ransacked anything, but they had to be worried that they had left a body hanging outside, so they would have been pretty anxious to get out of there."

Rich, Mel, and the boys came toward them laughing, the boys finishing ice cream cones, with drips all down their shirts.

"Hey, guys, you having fun?"

General consensus among the children that fun was being had.

Denis told Rich quietly that he and Sue would like to have a word privately with Rich and Mel. It wouldn't take long. Would it be OK if Josh and Matt took the kids for twenty minutes or so? Mel answered right away that it was OK with her and Rich shrugged in a husbandish way. Sue got up and walked down toward the water and waved at her son and Josh, summoning them. They talked for a minute and then came loping back up to the cabana.

"Hey, guys, you wanna go see what's on at the movies tonight?"

Unanimous yes. And they were off, the six of them, leaving Rich and Mel with Denis and Sue.

Sue explained to Rich what Espinosa had told them about seeing someone leave the side gate the night that Mrs. Rosa had died. Espinosa said that there were no cars parked on the street anywhere near, and the man he saw leave the property looked like he was walking up the street to the right of the house. Did Rich know anyone who lived up that way?

"There are a lot of new people all around the point," he said, "but there are some of the old-timers left."

He named several families. The Deans, an older man and his wife. They had a son about Rich's age or a couple of years older, so he would be mid-thirties, but Rich thought he moved away a while back. The Parrishes, similar, older couple, big house, swimming pool, but no kids living with them. The Schneiders, three boys, but Mr. Schneider had died and Mrs. Schneider was a bit of a hermit.

"Her boys live somewhere close, but probably not in PVE, I'd guess. I saw Ray's car parked out in front of Mrs. Schneider's house some time ago, I don't know, maybe a few months."

The McCormicks lived up near where the road joined Paseo del

Mar. That was all he could come up with in that direction. "We could ask Maggie if she knows. She was living here more recently than Paul or I were. And there were some families with little kids when Mel and I got married, but I didn't really know them. That house up at the bend of the road on the cliffside with all the little statues and cutesy things in the yard. Paisley, maybe?"

There was a pause while they stared at the water and Rich looked toward The Casino to see if he could spot the boys.

"Are you saying that this guy that was leaving, maybe he killed Mom?"

"No, I am not saying that," Sue said, "although it is one of several possibilities. It is still possible that your mother died accidentally after drinking that vodka with GHB in it. She could have added it herself like some kids do in clubs, where they call it Super-Ecstasy, or someone else could have added it. But if someone else added it, that does not mean that person had to be there when your mother died, and it does not mean that whoever it was would have known she would get into the hot tub to drink it, or, I guess, since there was no glass, that she would drink it and then get in the hot tub. And if the man who was in the back yard was a neighbor, we want to talk to him to find out what he saw, if anything."

They talked about the families that Rich had mentioned, but he didn't really know much. He knew that Mr. Schneider had worked for a chemical company of some kind and Mrs. Parrish had been a teacher, Mr. Parrish maybe a chemical engineer. There was Mr. Burkett who worked in Sacramento, around the other side of the point. He had spent more time at the Parrish house than the others, because their son, Max, was a friend, and their daughter, Bette, was prom queen material. "Max is in the army, I think," Rich said. "He was in Korea the last time I heard."

Sue pulled out her smartphone and checked. She had four bars, pretty good reception. She stood up and excused herself, walked a bit away and called Ron Furman, gave him the families' names and suggested that PVE cops would be the best way to talk to these people, but otherwise maybe Sheriff's investigators. He said he would talk to the PVE liaison and keep her informed.

"Phoned it in, did you?" Denis said when she sat back down. She smiled a cop smile, nodded. "Can we relax now?" She smiled again, a different smile, and nodded again, a friendlier nod.

They lazed around in the sun. It wasn't hot enough to worry about getting burned, but it was warm enough to feel like going to sleep on the comfortable lounge chairs. Denis would have dozed off, but the boys came clambering back, laughing and holding seashells and rocks for their collections.

"What collection?" Rich asked rhetorically. A collection could be two rocks, of course, at that age. Nice that the boys were friends. He and Paul had been friends, but they had never played together except when they were both sick. They had different friends, and were never best buds.

"Boat back leaves at four," Denis said. "Let's go over to the seafood place on the water and have some lunch, and then we can stroll over to the boat dock and be first in line. Boys? Anyone have to go to the bathroom?" All of them did, so he walked over to the restrooms with them and waited outside until they came out in a row.

Denis had sand dabs, a delicacy of Catalina Island. They are small, flat-bottom fish, like a sole, but much smaller, and they are grilled or sautéed virtually whole and boned like a sole. Add some lemon butter and it was a perfect lunch with a dark Dos Equis beer. He smiled at the boys and remembered Avalon from the 1960s. Oddly, it hadn't really changed much. The skee-ball parlor had moved away from the beach to less expensive digs, but other than that, if you changed the fashions, it could be fifty years earlier. Although come to think of it, he hadn't seen any saltwater taffy for sale.

The ride back to San Pedro was quieter because the boys went to sleep in their chairs. Denis put his arm around Sue, and she slumped toward him. He kissed the top of her head.

When they disembarked in San Pedro, the boys were all for riding with Josh and Matt again, but they split it up so that the boys rode with their parents because they were going home, and Denis and Sue rode with Josh and Matt to head back to Rocky Point. The sun was getting low, but there would be plenty of sunlight when they got back to the house.

They parked in the driveway and went in the front door. There was a breeze coming from inside the house when they opened the door and the dogs came bounding into the living room. Josh headed toward the kitchen and yelled back, "The sliding doors are open. Did you leave them open this morning?"

"No," replied Denis.

"Was the gardener here today?" Josh asked as they all walked into the kitchen.

"No," replied Denis again.

"Someone opened the door and let the dogs out. They're wet, so they must have been in the pool," Josh said.

"Somebody either saw us leave, or knew we were going to be gone all day," Denis said.

"Mmm," Sue muttered. "Well, anybody could have seen us leaving this morning. We made quite a stir with our two-car caravan. Come with me, Denis, if you don't mind. Boys, see if you are missing anything."

She walked out the front door directly over to the next-door neighbor's house and rang the bell. Albert Hanszen answered the door.

"Denis?" he said. "Come in." He stepped aside and waved them into the house.

"Detective Mason," Denis said. "I don't think you have met." They nodded at each other.

"Albert, when we just got back from taking Rich and the kids to Catalina for the day, the sliding doors were open in the kitchen and the dogs were running around outside. I wonder if you saw anyone near the house?"

"Well, no, I didn't see anyone, but the dogs were barking to beat the band while I was working in the garden, so I went over and let myself into the back through the gate to see if there was something going on, a fire or something. The dogs were running around inside the house, barking, and I tried the door. It wasn't locked so I opened it and let them out. I didn't go inside because I didn't smell smoke or anything, so I just left them in the yard, figured they wouldn't do any harm. Nice dogs. They calmed down when they got outside, so maybe they just needed to do their business. Sorry, I should have put a note on the door after I did that, so you would know it was me."

Sue asked if the dogs had barked again later.

"They did, yes, but not for long, it was soon after I got home from letting them out, and I was just thinking I would go over and take them for a walk if they kept up that racket when they stopped."

"But you never saw anyone around the Rosa house, even when you were in the back yard?" she asked.

"Well, I wasn't really looking for anyone, I guess," he said, "but no, I didn't see anyone that I can remember. No, I would say I didn't see anyone all day, after I saw you and the kids leave this morning."

"You were up early." Denis said, "either that or we made a lot of noise."

"I don't really sleep very well anymore," he said. "I wake up a lot and I usually just get up early and watch the early show on TV."

They thanked him and headed back.

"I've known him for years," Denis said. "I'm not surprised he did that. He's generally aware of everything that goes on in the neighborhood. He either doesn't work anymore or whatever he does is at home, and he is quite a gardener, so he is always out in the yard. He has beautiful roses in the back, used to bring us bouquets." He smiled. "A little bit of a busybody, but nice. We always invited him for dinner on the holidays, though he usually had other plans."

"I wonder if he could have been the man Espinosa saw walking up the street, although he could have just cut across the lawn if he was going home," she said.

"Albert and I were never best friends, but I've known him for a long time, and I would guess if he had been in the back yard and seen that Elissa was dead, he would have called the cops right away."

Sue was listening. *Most likely.*

They made a thorough search of the house to see if they could find anything missing. Between them, there was no one who had lived in the house for very long, given that Denis had been living in New York, but when they went through the storage room, it did appear that some of the wine cases had been shuffled around because they weren't stacked the way he thought they had been. But no one would break into the house just to rearrange the wine cases, and none of them was worth stealing.

"We need a K9 helper here," Sue said, and dialed a number on her smartphone. "Everybody stay out of this room now. Don't touch anything."

She came back into the living room after she made her call, and told Josh and Matt to take the dogs to a park or down to the beach, and not to come back until she called them. They grabbed the leashes and left with the dogs.

About twenty minutes later, two cars arrived, one from the PVE police and one from the Sheriff's Department marked K9. Sue walked out to meet them and had a brief conversation with the officer who was the dog's handler. She introduced the handler to Denis and asked Denis to wait in the front yard while she and the officer looked through the house. He sat on the planter. Night had fallen and although there were streetlights, it was dark. The two PVE cops set out to look at the outside of the house to see if they could find anything, so he was alone.

"Hey Denis, I heard about what happened. You OK?" It was Jim Parrish, out with his dog. They shook hands and allowed as how they hadn't seen each other in a while.

"Well, you know," Denis offered, "Elissa and I had some issues and I moved back east."

"Elissa had issues with a lot of people," Parrish said.

"How so?"

"She and Mamie McCormick had a set-to up at the Westward Ho Market at the top of Yarmouth Street and had to be pulled apart by the cops. Mamie and Elissa, neither one was pleasant to be around at times."

Denis said he actually barely remembered the McCormicks.

"He was a lawyer for some big hedge fund that got into trouble," Parrish said, "but he did OK I think, at least financially. Had some headaches with the government, but was never indicted for anything .I don't know if she had a job, maybe not, and they didn't have kids, but they are social, give money to downtown arts associations, things like that. Maybe some family money."

"Don't sound like people we would run into if they're that kind of rich. Of course I've been kind of out of the picture for a while, so I don't know a lot about what Elissa was up to."

"Well, if you had been here a year or so ago, you might have had the impression that Elissa and Marcus were old friends, if you know what I mean. I mean, speak kindly of the dead, of course, but there was a time when Marcus and Mamie seemed like they were on the outs, and it looked like for a while he and Elissa might be an item, if you know what I mean. Then there was that nasty scene up the hill, and after that, I think, that was all she wrote on that one."

Dennis nodded. *Interesting.*

"Anyway, you look OK," Parrish said. "I heard someone burglarized your home and you got beaten up, but you look pretty normal to me."

Denis considered telling him what happened, and thought better of it. "I had some trouble with my shoulder, but it feels a lot better now. Listen, Jim, these officers and one inside are doing a look-through after someone was snooping around and I've got to get inside to see what's going on .Let's get together. Why don't you guys come over for a drink one of these evenings?"

Maybe it's closer to home. Parrish and his dog moved on along the road. *Maybe Elissa had ideas about Marcus McCormick. But he would be about the same age as I am, not the young Latino types she was hanging out with.*

"Who was that?" Sue asked as she came out the door.

"Neighbor I haven't seen for years. He told me that there was some kind of altercation between Elissa and one of the neighbors, Mamie McCormick, a few months back, maybe a year. I never heard a thing about it, but then Jim implied that Elissa was seeing the husband on the side or something. Doesn't fit what we know about Elissa, but I guess it's worth checking out, right? His name is Marcus McCormick, and they live in that house with red brick facing by the garage just after you turn left on Rocky Point Road, the first house on the cliffside of the road."

"So if he was here, he could walk home?"

"Oh sure, you can't see the house from here because of the way the road curves, but it's not more than a couple of football fields away."

"The dog smelled narcotics in several places," she said. "Nothing there now, but there have apparently been containers with drugs in them because the dog can smell what was there. Mostly in your wine room or storage room, but also in the closet in the master bedroom. We're cleaning up the dust and anything else that might have left bits of drugs that the dog could smell, and we should be able to tell what kinds of narcotics were being stored in the house. Unfortunately, the dog can't tell us what he is smelling, because he is trained to have the same reaction to a number of different narcotics. Could be marijuana, could be heroin, cocaine or some of the designer drugs."

"Just out of curiosity, can you check about a police report, would be PVE police, on a spat between Elissa and Mamie McCormick? Might give us a lead on the man Espinosa saw leaving the gate the night she died."

She made a call and took him inside to show him where the dog had smelled drugs. The first place they had looked was where the wine cases had been disarranged while they were in Catalina, and that came up positive. There was another positive near the stack of paintings that was leaning against the wall. The area around Elissa's shoe rack was another place, and, interestingly, the pantry in the kitchen. They had taken everything out of the pantry and vacuumed up the shelves and containers into a sterile evidence bag. They had found a small plastic bag with seeds in it, and the dog signaled that the seeds were contraband.

"I'm betting they are marijuana seeds," she said.

"What would that mean?"

"Well, they're illegal to have, but certainly not worth killing for, so it would probably mean they were not part of what we're trying to figure out, most likely."

As it turned out, there had been a police report filed about eight months earlier after Mrs. McCormick slapped Mrs. Rosa at the supermarket. The two women had been restrained by other shoppers and kept separate until the police arrived. Mrs. McCormick accused Mrs. Rosa of having an affair with Mr. McCormick, and Mrs. Rosa denied that. The two women were not cited for creating a disturbance, but the supermarket manager wanted a copy of the police report in case there were any repercussions, so a report was filed. There was very little further information.

"I don't remember much about either one of them, the husband or the wife," Denis said. "Strange. I wonder if Elissa was involved with him. She was certainly involved with other men, so it would not be out of character."

Sue said that the PVE police were going to ask Mr. and Mrs. McCormick to come to the PVE Police Department to answer some questions, and that she would be present when they were interviewed. She said they would most likely be interrogated separately, although that part would be up to the PVE police. It would not be the first time that neighborly infidelity had led to violence, but it was far from a slam-dunk that there was any connection.

It was night; the last sliver of sunlight had long before disappeared from the ocean horizon. It was a clear night and there were stars. The two PVE police officers and the K9 handler were ready to leave, and Sue asked them to call her if they had a time to meet with the McCormicks.

Not long thereafter, Josh and Matt came back with the dogs, who knew from the time they hit the driveway that there had been strangers around, not to mention a strange dog. Frick and Frack had to inspect the entire house, sniffing carefully around the edges of the rooms.

"Well, that was quite a long day," Denis said. "Started early and never really slowed down, did it?" He opened the cupboard and pulled out a lowball glass. "Can I pour drinks for anyone?" Josh and Matt declined and took the dogs for a turn around the pool area.

"I'll have what you're having," Sue said, "but a short one, in case I have to go down to The Plaza to meet the McCormicks. I doubt that's going to happen until tomorrow at this point, though." She stood directly behind him as he poured the drinks and blew on the back of his neck. He turned around to give her the drink and her mouth was about three inches from him. He kissed her lightly, then handed her the glass.

"Cheers." He waited for her to sip her drink, then took a gulp of his. "Every party has a pooper. Sorry. I am thinking about Espinosa seeing someone leave the night that Elissa died, and the possibility that it could have been Marcus McCormick."

"Hmm. Me, too."

"Is there anything we can do?"

"We're going to talk to them, as soon as they can get to the PVE Police Department."

"Why not go and pick them up?"

"For what?"

"Murder."

"You must know how that would look if we did it, and no judge would let us hold them. We would be asking to be fired, and, worse than that, we would be trampling all over the McCormicks' rights. That means we would be making it nearly impossible to bring charges against them later on. No one has any evidence that they are involved at all. The only witness would not be able to identify Mr. McCormick even if that was him that Espinosa saw. We have some unidentified fingerprints from the house, but Mr. McCormick is not in the State of California database. We are checking to see if he is in the federal data base, and he might be, since he is a lawyer. But even if he is, and even if some of the fingerprints are his, it doesn't mean he was here that night--it just means he was here at some point. He's a neighbor, and we know he was here at some point because Mr. Snoopy with the dog told us that he was, and Mrs. McCormick accused your wife of having an affair with him."

"So we wait?"

"Right."

He gestured with his glass toward the bedroom. "Let's wait in there then."

"I don't think the McCormicks will be going to the PVE police until tomorrow," she said.

"Good," he said. "We'll just wait then. In there."

She smiled. "Sounds like a plan," she said.

Chapter Sixteen

Sue's smartphone rang; it was Ron Furman. They had located two of the young men whose phone numbers Denis had found in the telephone and credit card bills. Both of them were in Lomita and one of them was saying that the Rosa house in Rocky Point was a storehouse for a variety of prescription drugs. They had let the two men have a glimpse of each other and that was enough to get both of them talking in separate interrogation rooms.

"They've found Alberto Dominguez and Rob Cruz from the phone bills that you went through," she said, "and they're down at the Lomita station. One of them has some interesting stories to tell and I have to get down there. I guess I'll have to beg for a rain check from you." She gave him a forlorn look that was clearly manufactured, and then cracked a naughty smile and chucked him under the chin. "Be a love and make some strong coffee while I get myself together."

He shuffled off to the kitchen and clattered around a bit making coffee.

"Can you share anything with me about what they are saying?"

"Shouldn't, no."

"Are you coming back?"

"Not this evening. I'll call you when I know what's going on."

She chugged a mug of coffee with milk in it to cool it down, fished her keys out of her bag, and was out the front door. He followed her outside as she was getting into her car. She waved and blew a kiss, and backed out.

He looked up and down the street, went back into the house,

turned on the outside lights, and walked into the television room. Josh and Matt came back in with the dogs who had taken a dip in the pool and were smelling of wet dog in spite of having been toweled off.

"Sue had to go down to Lomita," he said.

"I guessed," Matt said. "Remember, I grew up with that."

Dominguez and Cruz had been kept in separate interview rooms and, although they had been observed through a two-way mirror, they had not been interviewed beyond what Dominguez had blurted out when the officers accosted him, "Some guy out there in PVE had a stash and he was dealing, man."

Both men were bartenders at respectable, but not fancy restaurants in the South Bay. Both were under thirty, and tall and lean. Neither was particularly handsome, but with a smile in a bar, they would have been engaging. Dominguez had numerous geometric or tribal tattoos on his arms and one that peeked out from his collar in the back. All his tattoos were done by a professional tattoo artist; they did not look like prison tattoos.

"They recognized each other when we walked them in, but they have not had a chance to talk," Ron said, "and we have not questioned them about each other. I wanted you to be able to observe their answers since you know the house a lot better than anyone else on the force."

She took up her position in the observation room, and Ron and a uniformed officer went into Dominguez's room. He stiffened up.

Was he Alberto Dominguez? Yes .Did he live at 221 23rd Street with his sister, Imelda? Yes. They asked for his smartphone number and it matched the phone bill from the Rosa house. They had pulled his arrest record and there was nothing serious, nothing recent. He had been arrested for trespass a couple of times and he had violated a restraining order that required him to stay away from his father after his mother and father separated, but those offenses were more than five years in the past and all were booked as misdemeanors. He was found to have less than two ounces of marijuana when he was stopped for a traffic infraction two years earlier, but no charges were filed, and it appeared that the reasoning behind this was that it would cause him to lose his bartending job. He had served one hundred hours of community service as an orderly in a local hospital and gotten good marks from the hospital transportation department. He had dropped out of high school, but had taken GED tests and been granted an equivalency high school graduation diploma. He had taken some courses at El Camino College, a two-year junior college in the area.

"Nice ink," Furman said when they walked in.

Dominguez's eyes followed them as they walked in and sat down, but he said nothing.

"You know why you're here?"

He shook his head tentatively.

"You know this lady?" Furman said, and the uniformed officer showed him a picture of Elissa Rosa. He looked at the picture briefly and shook his head again.

"Have another look."

He looked at the picture again, and then looked away.

"Maybe she came into the bar where I work."

"Maybe?"

"She did, she came into the bar where I work."

"And that's the extent of what you know about her?"

He nodded.

"Did you fuck her?"

He looked startled and clenched his hands together in front of him.

"It's not a crime if you fucked her, you know."

"I don't remember," he said.

"That's a good one. How many older women you fuck if you can't remember whether you fucked this one? Twenty? Fifty?" Furman's tone of voice was still calm, but the speed of his questions was faster and his eyes were boring into Dominguez.

"Maybe I fucked her. Maybe she wanted me to fuck her in the back of her car."

"But not at her house?"

"Maybe."

"She pay you?" He didn't answer, just looked at Furman and then at the mirror.

"She back there looking at me?"

"She's dead."

"Dead?" He looked around like a caged animal, and then shrugged his shoulders. "OK, look, I fucked her a few times, and she gave me some money to help with my classes, but that's all, man. I didn't want to have anything to do with her because she was a rich lady and I didn't want to get in trouble. I don't ever want to get in trouble. I gotta take care of my sister and my mom."

Furman flashed him a brief, fake smile. "You want a Coke or something?"

"No."

"I do," Furman said. "Back in a few. Officer Barrio here will stay with you while I'm gone. I have to talk to another guy about the same subject. Oh, I think you know him, right? You saw each other in the station."

"I don't remember."

"You don't remember if you know him? Or you don't remember seeing anyone?"

"I don't remember seeing anyone."

"OK, I just want to be sure I understand your answers, because of course this is a murder investigation. Murder One."

"OK, I know him. We knew each other from high school at Hawthorne High. He's a smart kid, got good grades, scored with all the girls. Lived a couple of blocks from us. But I haven't talked to him in maybe three to four years."

"Oh, OK. Like I said, Officer Barrio will be here with you while I talk to Mr. Cruz. And he's gonna take a DNA sample with a cotton swab." He left and the door slammed. When he got into the observation room, he looked inquiringly at Sue. She said he looked to her like he was telling the truth, at least when he was pushed to do it.

"De que pueblo eres?" he asked the officer after Furman closed the door.

"I don't speak Spanish," Barrio said. "Sorry." He took the DNA swab and put the cotton stick in a glass receptacle.

Dominguez clearly didn't believe that, but he rested his chin on his forearms and didn't make any further comments.

"So?" Furman said to Sue in the observation room.

"Either he's a good liar or he's been coming clean when you push him. But I'd let him stew a while, see what happens."

They went to the room where Cruz was and Sue went into the observation room attached. Robert Cruz was considerably more put together than Alberto had been. Shorter haircut, neater clothing, a close-clipped and trimmed goatee, and otherwise clean-shaven. Altogether better looking. Furman walked in with another uniformed cop.

"Roberto Cruz?"

"Robert."

"Oh, sorry, Robert Cruz, yes, it says that here." They verified his address and age, and asked him if he had ever been arrested.

"Never."

They verified his smartphone number.

"And when was the last time you spoke with Elissa Rosa?"

"Who?"

"Mrs. Elissa Rosa, a woman from PVE whom we believe you are acquainted with."

"If she's who I think, she comes into the bar where I work sometimes."

"But you also talk to her on the phone, according to the phone records."

"You went and got my phone records?" he looked hostile.

"No, we have her phone records and that smartphone you have in your pocket is a frequently called number."

"I need a lawyer?"

"That's up to you, but you're not under arrest, if that's what you're asking. We appreciate your agreeing to answer a few questions but of course we will be keeping a voice recording of this interview," Ron said, with no coloration to the statement.

"Yeah, OK. Yeah, she used to call me."

"Used to?"

"Not for a few weeks now. And she stopped coming into my bar, too. She's a cougar, man, she likes Chicano studs, young ones like me. Told me Latin men have big dicks and she likes big dicks. She wanted to know if I was uncut."

"So you had sex with her?"

"No."

"Come on, no harm in having sex with a woman."

"No. I said no, man, didn't have sex with that lady."

"We're gonna ask you to give us a DNA sample," Furman said, taking out a kit to swab his cheek.

"Why?"

"Somebody killed her, we thought you probably knew that."

No surprise registered on his face as he stared at Furman. "No, I didn't know that, but older women who go around picking up young guys are kinda looking for trouble, aren't they? And what if I don't want to give you a DNA sample?"

Furman just stared at him.

"OK, man. Do what you gotta do." He opened his mouth and Furman swabbed the inside of his cheek.

"So now my DNA's gonna be in the files forever, right?"

Furman nodded. "No biggie if you stay out of trouble, but it would help us identify your body if someone hit you with a car."

Cruz rolled his eyes. "Yeah, sure."

"You're sure about not having sex with her, right? Because there was DNA found when her body was taken to the coroner and we'll be checking."

"Like you said, no crime if I did, right?"

"Right, if that's all you did."

"I want a lawyer. Not gonna talk anymore without a lawyer."

"As I told you, you're not under arrest. You can leave if you want to. We can't provide a lawyer to you free of charge if you're not under arrest."

"Yeah, I fucked her. That's what she wanted, she was all hot for Mexican dick."

"And when would that have been?"

"Couple times."

"Most recently?"

"A little over two weeks ago. Monday or Wednesday. Those are my days off."

"Was this at Mrs. Rosa's home?"

He nodded.

"Nice place, huh?"

He nodded again.

"No condom, eh?"

"She wasn't gonna get pregnant at her age," he said. "And she wanted me to talk dirty to her in Spanish, too."

"She pay you?"

He didn't answer.

"Did she pay you?"

"Not exactly. She used to write big tips, extra big tips, after we would get together."

"And then you pushed her under the water and drowned her, did you? Held her under until she didn't move anymore?"

"No, man. What water? Once I finished, she wanted me to get out, and I did. I never even got undressed. Just opened my fly."

"Interesting. Did she talk to you about other guys?"

"No. She would talk about her husband at the bar sometimes, or her kids, but when she wanted me to fuck her, it had to be kinda hands-off. No kissing or anything, just fuck and go."

"You smoke some grass while you were there?"

"No man, I don't use that stuff, but I'll tell you I could smell it in the air sometimes."

"You ever deal, Robert?"

"I don't use and I don't deal. It was a mistake for me to do what that lady wanted me to do. I did it, but I didn't do anything else to her, and I never dealt drugs in my life. I don't smoke and I don't use. I'm a bartender and I see too much to want to be like that."

"OK, I'm gonna ask you to sit here for a bit and I'll be back. We can get you a Coke or something if you want."

"I'm free to go?"

"We're asking you to stay here for a few minutes, and if you want, we can give you a lift someplace afterward."

"I got my own car and I don't need to get out of a police car when

I go home either."

Furman got up, walked out, and joined Sue. He nodded at her inquisitively.

"Interesting," she said. "I wonder what she said to these young guys to get them to do what they did. I wonder if there were drugs involved, at least with some of them. And we've all known dealers who don't use, so the fact that he says he is clean means nothing. See if you can get a sample of his hair so we can see whether he's been clean for a while."

"And what do you think about him?"

"I think he's pretty cool for someone who might be involved in a murder. Don't know whether he is telling you all he knows or not, but I'd put money on his DNA being a match, which puts him right in the middle of this. And if there's anyone who knows how to spike the vodka, it would be a bartender."

Furman told both young men that they could go and asked them to be available in case there were more questions. Furman asked the captain if they could get a search warrant to inspect phone records on these two guys since both of them admitted to having sex with the dead woman. The captain called an ADA, who said she would talk to one of the judges and see.

As she was driving home, Sue decided on impulse to drive over to King Harbor to Casa Adobado. She freshened her make-up in the rearview mirror and threw a shawl that was in the back seat around her shoulders to ward off the chilly breeze that was blowing in off the water. As fate would have it, Ricardo Espinosa was at the bar.

She took a seat at the bar at the end, and since it was not a busy time, she was nearly alone. Espinosa walked over to her and put a cocktail napkin down in front of her. He was about to ask her for a drink order when he recognized her, and he just looked at her, nodding his head toward the maître d' as if to tell her to be discreet.

"Hi, Ricardo," she said. "I'm not here to cause you any problems." He picked up a glass, scooped some ice into it, and put it in front of her, filling it with ginger ale. "Thanks. I wonder if you recognize either of these names." She wrote on the napkin "Alberto Dominguez" and "Robert

Cruz."

"I know both of them," he said. "Most bartenders freelance for catering companies, so we can get some extra money. Tending bar at a Mexican restaurant, even a busy one, doesn't get you a lot of money. People who have dinner at a Mexican restaurant are just not big tippers, that's all. So I know these guys and other guys I see pretty regularly on catering jobs."

"Catering jobs? Like weddings?"

"Weddings, company functions, sometimes birthdays or graduation parties. Wherever they need waiters or people to serve drinks."

"Are you friendly with either Mr. Dominguez or Mr. Cruz?"

"Not particularly, but they're OK. I don't really know them like friends, just guys I see on catering jobs."

He excused himself and walked down the bar to a customer who was signaling to him. He went to the register and pulled a slip out of it, put it in a black leatherette cover, stuck a pen in it, and put it down in front of the man, then walked back to Sue.

"All three of you slept with the same woman."

He hunched his shoulders down to indicate that he wanted her to speak more softly.

"Sorry," she said. "But it's true, and you know which woman."

"I don't know what to say. Everything comes back to bite you, I guess."

She asked him very quietly if, when he had sex with Mrs. Rosa, there was anything unusual about it.

"Unusual? Well, it was unusual that I did it."

"No, I mean kinky. Was there anything kinky?"

"No, I don't think so. She was usually a little lighted up, but not drunk, and she wanted to feel like she was with someone who liked her. She talked about her husband sometimes, not during, you know, but after." He told her that Elissa Rosa told him she was still in love with her husband, but they could never get back together because of some things that had happened.

"And you took that to mean what?"

"Nothing. Like I said, she tended to be a little tipsy, and she didn't tell me what it was that had happened."

"But she never wanted to do any kind of role-play, or get rough or anything like that?"

"No, not even close. She always wanted me to stay over and go to sleep with her. I never did, because it seemed like I shouldn't, like she would regret it if I did, and I would certainly have regretted it, too. It wasn't a great idea to start off with, but like I told you, she helped me out."

"Thanks," Sue said, smiled, and slapped five dollars down on the bar.

"No charge for the ginger ale."

"I know," she said, turned, and walked away.

"Thanks," he said.

She drove home, had a vodka with orange juice, and pitched herself into her bed with the window cracked to let in the chilly ocean air. She pulled up her grandmother's quilt to her neck, and said to herself that she was not only going to figure this one out, but she was also going to get the guy.

Chapter Seventeen

Denis warmed up a refrigerated, but not frozen, chicken vindaloo that he had picked up at Trader Joe's. It had two long, thin, dried hot peppers on top of the yellow rice, and the spicy chicken was in a different part of the plastic heating tray. How bad could it be? He took it out of the microwave after a five-minute warm-up and it nearly burned his hands so he almost threw it at the marble countertop. He got out one of the blue-and-white bistro plates from the cabinet over the pass-through to the TV room and dumped the rice first and then the chicken and sauce over the top of it. He rummaged around in the door of the fridge, found an old bottle of orange marmalade, and dumped a couple of spoons of the sweet citrus jam on top of the fiery vindaloo sauce since he didn't have any proper chutney.

He poured a good glass of 1989 burgundy, took the plate and the glass into the TV room, and turned on CBS. If there was anything he had in spades, it was good wine--maybe not fancy wine, but goddamned good wine. The TV was all college football, not something he cared about other than his alma mater, which was not playing. He was a big baseball fan, but he knew football itself well, being a red-blooded American, so he ate the chicken mixture and watched the Oregon Ducks kick the crap out of the USC Trojans He found himself smiling as the two teams' totals spread further apart. It was particularly humorous that Trojans could be stomped on by Ducks.

He remembered being at Desert Springs, the big Marriott golf and tennis resort in Palm Desert, and watching two big carp surface and swallow three or four baby ducks who were swimming after their mother across one of the many man-made rivulets, while he was on the way to the spa from the main building. In its way it was horrifying, the way it is to watch a lioness grab an antelope on the Discovery Channel, the little fuzzy ducklings swimming in a prim, Madeline-ish line after their wood duck mom, and then being sucked under the water and visibly swallowed whole by the hungry fish.

Anyway, even with the memory, the vindaloo was surprisingly good.

He thought about Sue off questioning two more bartenders who had probably slept with his wife. He had never really blamed her for what she did, just couldn't be what she wanted or needed any longer than he already had been. It was a mistake to automatically assume that the male was the horny one all the time, even though that was the popular idea. In the end it was partly his fault that someone had fed her the drugs that caused her to fill her lungs with water--after all those years they had spent together. The kids, the grandkids.

He looked out the window at the vague outlines of the point opposite and the blurry patch of light from Avalon Harbor on Catalina twenty-three miles off the coast, and wondered how he could have left it all behind. He and Elissa had decided, not through rational discussion, but through years of petty bickering, that they just could not live together full time anymore. Neither one of them wanted to divorce; there was always the hope that they could put it back together. A hope that was not part of the visible universe, because any fool knows that if you abandon something, it is unlikely it will put itself back together. Humpty Dumpty is Humpty Dumpty, after all, and if you walk out on a marriage, you are basically doing a nonverbal, nonlegal divorce, no matter how you look at it.

And no matter how you look at it, he had not been there to keep someone from killing her. He thought back to the days before they were married, the 1971 earthquake when they met because they both ran outside in their underwear. Times full of giggles and thrills. She was young and pretty, and he was smart and confident that he could do anything. The Superman years. Hard to say where it went wrong, or maybe it didn't--maybe they just got too short of patience with each other.

He found her impossibly addicted to easy answers, shortcuts. Her idea, he had said to her, of how to get rich was to buy as many lottery tickets as she had money to spend. She found shortcuts through the hills that were no shorter than going the "long" way, but sometimes they were interesting. She wanted to cook dinner faster or easier, which is why he had taken over cooking the meal, because he wanted dinner to be one of the high points of the day, not just a hurdle to be jumped over. So in a way she had won that round, because she no longer had to cook dinner, and his concept of the meal was undeniably more adventuresome.

In all the years he knew her, he never knew Elissa to buy anything at the market that she had not cooked before. She would order odd dishes in restaurants and enjoy them, but it never occurred to her to make pureed celery root, or even to use fresh horseradish to spice up some baked fish. So she stayed home all day so she would be able to be there when the kids came home, and then when he got home from work, he cooked and he did homework with Paul, then Rich, then Mags. She watched TV, and she wanted him to be horny and hard when he fell into bed.

That would have been the way he would have told that story. He knew she would have told it differently. She would have said there was no way to please him with anything she did and he looked down his nose at her constantly. And he ignored her opinions because he thought she was silly. He didn't care that she changed her hair color and frequently did not even notice. He didn't care when she lost weight and he really didn't care when she had her nose shortened, but he clearly disapproved in a pinched, intolerant way.

He had written a music column for the PVE newspaper for years and that got them good seats to any concert in LA County he wanted to go to. She liked going out to concerts, but liked going to dinner more. So the trade-off was if they went to hear three Schubert quartets on the other side of LA, they would have dinner at the Pacific Dining Car on 6th Street. For years they had passes to the whole summer of concerts at the Hollywood Bowl, not in the best seats, where the fancy picnics with candelabra were being held, but not the worst seats either. They would camp out at one of the picnic tables on the hillside by the close-in parking lot and have cold chicken or sandwiches and a bottle of wine, maybe some cupcakes.

No point hashing over all that. He knew he had left tire tracks all over her; he had always known that, even when he was doing it. *She was childish, just acting like a teenager having a temper tantrum, and I was acting like an adult.* Maybe it was the other way around. They certainly both ended up hissing and spitting equally at the intersection of tired and angry.

I never stopped loving her. That was why he never had a girlfriend, even though she was playing the field like some Rita Hayworth character in a cheap fifties sob story.

The door of the guest bedroom opened briefly and the dogs came out. They loped down the hall toward him, nuzzled him, and ran over to the sliding door. They needed to pee. He got up and let them out, stood and watched them sniff around the yard and pee on the fence posts. They were feeling frisky and he wasn't, but he tossed a tennis ball for them a few times, then went back in to watch whatever was on TV. Nothing. The news. He whistled and the dogs came obediently inside and walked into the kitchen to lap up some water from the bowl by the pantry door. He locked the door and activated the new security panel inside his bedroom.

"C'mon boys," he said, and they ran in ahead of him and curled up together on the big, nappy bathmat he had put down for them to sleep on between the door and the bed. He pulled out his English travel book, propped the pillows up on the bed, and started to read as the author made his way west along the southern coastline of England, stopping in the Cinque Ports towns of Sandwich and Rye, always on foot to the extent possible. *What a great adventure, to walk all the way around the edges of England, Wales, and Scotland until you get back to the starting place.*

The stars were fading out in the creeping mist of the marine layer flowing over the land like a legion of Transylvanian angels. You half expected to hear trumpets, because the mist, which would turn to fog, amplified sounds just as it obscured vision. Maybe Mrs. Danvers would step in and try to get him to jump off the cliff. He smiled, and went back to the English travelogue.

He knew Elissa was not there, that she was dead, but it seemed as though she was just outside, or just around the corner, just where he couldn't see her.

"It wasn't your fault, Denis," her voice said. "I was angry and I thought I hated you for leaving me, but it wasn't your fault." *It's not an echo, it's her voice, an illusion like a mirage on the sand in the bright desert sun.*

He twisted around to see where the voice was coming from, but there was no one there. *Whew, Ghost of Christmas Past. The party at Fezziwig's.* He got up, walked to the glass doors, and looked out at the pool area. He could imagine her hair on the water like it was in his dream, but he could see the hot tub and there was no hair there. He looked at the mist and tried to make out a figure rising somewhere, but as hard as he looked, it was just the gray-white of mist with the outside spotlights showing through here and there.

"I shouldn't have left," he said out loud.

There was no response, and the unexpectedly loud sound of his own voice took him back to the moment. It also woke the dogs up; they picked up their heads and looked at him, half expecting to be told to do something. But he walked back and said softly, "It's OK, boys." And they put their heads back down on their paws.

The next he knew, it was morning. He heard the rustling of dishes in the kitchen and he looked up to see the dogs standing at the door, tails wagging. He ran his hands through his hair, then swished some mouthwash around and gargled it a little.

Josh was whisking eggs with milk and he could smell coffee, and butter melting in the skillet. Very comforting smells. His shoulder ached a bit; he must have slept on that side too long.

Matt took the leashes down and the dogs wagged their butts until it looked like they would fall off. He hooked them up and walked them through the living room and out the front door. Josh said, "You want an omelette? We're gonna have omelettes. I'm pretty good at them."

"You know, Josh, I am a pretty good cook but I am lousy at omelettes, never have been able to flip them up and over like you're supposed to. If I tried to do that, they would end up on the floor. So mine tend to be thick and not very pretty."

"Hand-eye coordination, like throwing a football," he said.

"Anything Peyton Manning can do, I can do."

"You trying to say you think Peyton Manning can make a good omelette?" Denis said, pouring a mug of coffee. "Oh, my God, this smells great. Nothing like coffee, just hook me up to an IV and pump it directly into my arm." He paused. "You mind if I ask you a personal question?"

"I have a feeling you're gonna ask it anyway, so go ahead."

"Sue said she thinks you guys are gonna get married whenever it's legal here."

"Yeah. I didn't hear a question."

"Oh, I was wondering if you were planning to have a church wedding, that's all. The Glass Chapel is a really cool place to have a wedding. I just thought if you were going to do that, I would like to offer to have the reception here. It's big enough, and with some tents it could be really nice."

Josh looked at him and didn't say anything, just cocked his head.

"Look, if I'm out of line, I'm sorry," Denis said.

Josh put down the skillet, walked over to Denis, who was at least six inches taller, and threw his arms around the older man.

"Thanks. You'll never know how much I appreciate your saying that."

"Well, you'll never know how much I appreciate your, umm, dogs," Denis said, grinning. "Think about it while you make the omelettes. I'm gonna go take a shower."

When he walked back out into the TV room, Sue was there, saying she had already eaten while she poured a mug of coffee. She told Denis with an eye movement that she wanted to talk and took the coffee out onto the pool deck where the sun had already burned off the fog.

"So we interviewed Alberto Dominguez and Robert Cruz last night. Nothing conclusive, but I doubt either one of them had anything directly to do with what happened to Elissa or to you. They both admitted to sleeping with her, as Espinosa did, but there's no reason to think they did her any harm. We took DNA swabs, but it will be a couple of days before we have any results. I can't hang around here, just wanted to touch base. We're going to meet the McCormicks at the PVE police station this morning, in about an hour as a matter of fact."

"Did you find out anything useful?"

"It may have been Cruz's DNA that was found by the coroner, at least from what he said. And there is something about him that doesn't sit right, but I doubt he had anything to do with what happened to her. We did find out that all three of the bartenders knew each other. They all work on their off days as freelance waiters and bartenders for catering services that do weddings, parties, stuff like that, graduations, corporate product unveilings. That could be meaningful, but it's not unlikely that they would know each other anyway. Dominguez and Cruz don't care much for each other. Apparently grew up going to the same schools and never got along."

Denis pointed at her like a teacher. "You know," he said, and paused. "You know, the McCormicks are big party people. When I drove by there the other day, they were unloading a big party tent. I think maybe he was a lawyer for big investors or something, don't really know because they only moved in about the time I was moving to New York."

"Meaning?" Sue said it like a statement.

"Well, I don't know. But I'd lay dollars to donuts that Marcus and Mamie know every caterer for fifty miles. As a matter of fact, I was just talking to Josh about doing something like that here if the two of them decide to get hitched. I can't tell you how much I appreciate their help and their friendly presence these days. Not to mention the dogs, of course, who have taken to sleeping between me and the door, makes me feel a lot safer. I told Josh we could get some tents set up here if they wanted to have a wedding party or whatever, and I thought of that because I saw a rental company unloading tents up the street."

"Interesting," Sue said. "We don't really have anything solid to say that McCormick was the man Espinosa saw that night at your house."

"But he doesn't know that, right?"

"Right, he doesn't know that, but he is a big fish, and if we mess with him, the backlash could be pretty fearsome."

"That's why you make the big bucks, I guess," Denis said, looking up at the roof overhang. "Someone strung me up there and left me for dead. I'd say that is pretty fearsome, too."

"Evidence is not just useful in a trial, you know," she said. "You need it to help sort through what might have happened. So far we have some, but it's not enough to draw any conclusions from."

"I'm just saying it wouldn't surprise me if our bartenders had worked for the McCormicks."

She said she had to scoot, because she was due at the PVE police to meet the McCormicks. She chugged the rest of the coffee and they walked in. She hugged the boys and headed out the front door.

Josh made the omelettes and they had a quiet breakfast. He really did flip them in the pan. Denis looked on. *Like magic, like magic.*

Sue pulled over in front of the McCormick house and had a brief look at the white tent that was being set up in the back of the McCormick home. The pavilion top was easily visible over the side fence. She took out her smartphone and tapped a message on it, then drove off toward The Plaza.

She got there minutes before Marcus and Mamie McCormick arrived and had only a brief chat with Ron, who said he had asked the Lomita station to check the customer logs at the caterers that Dominguez, Espinosa, and Cruz worked with. When the McCormicks were shown into the interview room, Sue and Ron were standing by the door and thanked them for helping out by coming over to talk. They showed their badges, introduced themselves, and said they were teamed with the PVE police on this case.

Marcus McCormick looked like someone who would be in a commercial for expensive wines. He was medium height and slim, with the kind of squared-off features that models have sometimes. He was inspecting the room and everyone in it, and making mental notes. Sue looked at Mamie. *She's a catalog of Prada. Her clothes are not too tight, but they nearly are, and they're slightly odd-looking for a woman in her fifties.* In some ways she had a resemblance to the pictures of Elissa Rosa: similar hair style and honey blonde dye anyway, similar skin coloring.

"I just drove by your house," Sue said, "on my way from the Rosa home. Looks like you're going to have a party." She smiled.

"It's a dinner for one of the museums in West LA, trying to raise money to sponsor an Impressionist show from the Hermitage in St. Petersburg," Marcus said.

"Just curious, but who does the cooking for something like that? Surely you don't just put some grills out and do steaks?" Sue asked.

"No," Mamie said, "there are caterers who do all that. We agree with them on a menu and then they do everything. They do the tents and tables, the centerpieces, the drinks and wine, and the food, down to mints. And best of all, they clean it all up afterward."

"Wow, painless," Sue said.

Ron said that they just needed to ask them a few questions that related back to a public incident with Mrs. Rosa, who had recently drowned in a hot tub in her back yard. The coroner had said that the cause of the drowning was inconclusive, meaning that it could have been an accident, or suicide, or someone else could have been involved, which might make it a homicide.

"We were neighbors for years," Mamie said. "We barely knew each other, but we invited her to some of the evenings when we were entertaining, just because we knew she was living mostly by herself and might like to get out. Then we kinda got on each other's nerves, I guess, and ended up having a loud discussion at the market up the hill. It is embarrassing to say now, but I slapped her right across the face. I was boiling, not proud to say it, but I was steamed. You never live something like that down, I guess." She blushed and her neck turned scarlet red.

Ron mentioned that the police report said that there had been words about an affair between Mrs. Rosa and Mr. McCormick.

"Now wait a minute," Marcus said.

"Well, actually, we were not accusing anyone of anything. We just wanted to know more about the spat because we are obliged to follow up any leads we have when the cause of a death is inconclusive," Ron said.

Marcus blinked in annoyance and sat back in his chair.

"The way I remember it," Mamie said, "I told her to stop making eyes at my husband because she had been at a party at our home and had been drinking, and just threw herself at him. All you had to do was know her to know that Marcus of all people would not be attracted to her. Right, honey?" She looked at him with a rehearsed smile.

"I think this whole catfight was somewhere between stupid and comic," Marcus said. "We've talked about this, and the last thing anyone wants is to be the subject of gossip of that sort. If you're going to accuse me of having an affair, at least make it someone worth having an affair with. And by the way, she never threw herself at me. She was the kind who was interested in the waiters. She liked studs, young Mexican guys with attitude."

"Do you often have guests who drink too much?" Sue asked. "How do you handle that if it's a charity event?"

"You try to get whoever it is to sit down and drink some coffee, and then you get someone to drive them home," Marcus said.

"Who took her home that night?" Ron asked.

"I did," he said. "I wanted to apologize for some offensive things that my wife had said, and after all, she only lived a few houses down the street. No one needed to drive her."

"The police report on the disagreement at the market was dated April 11," Sue said. "How long after the party was that?"

"A couple of days," Mrs. McCormick said. "I'm not sure. It was the first time I had seen her since that night and she gave me one of those looks, and I just lost it. We were trying to be nice to her and she turned out to be a drinker. And not only that, she looked like she'd had a face-lift that went wrong, not exactly like a clown-face, but not what anyone would want to look like."

"Let's let this drop now, Mamie," Marcus said. "She was a pretty woman, in good shape and well dressed. She was a drinker that night, but as we all know, lots of people step over that line sometimes and don't get slapped at the supermarket for it." He clearly was trying to end the conversation.

"Just one other thing then," Ron said. "Do any of these men look familiar to you?" He put down pictures of six Latino men, three of whom were the bartenders they had interviewed.

"Why?" Marcus asked.

"Just look to see if any of them are familiar, that's all. There may be someone there who knew Mrs. Rosa."

"Well, I'm sure I wouldn't know anything about that," Mrs. McCormick said, exhaling noisily.

"If you wouldn't mind looking, it would be helpful to us," Ron said.

Mrs. McCormick pointed to the picture of Robert Cruz, and then to the picture of Ricardo Espinosa.

"They look familiar, but I don't know where I would have seen them."

"I think they're waiters, dear," Marcus McCormick said. He agreed that he recognized those two and one other, Alberto Dominguez. "I think they have worked parties for us, but I couldn't help you with names."

"Oh well, then, maybe she picked them up while she was drunk," Mrs. McCormick said. "Probably would have had to tip them afterward, though."

Ron Furman thanked them and ushered them out.

"She's a piece of work," Ron said when he walked back in.

"I was just thinking he looked like a human IED, ready to spray shrapnel all over the room if someone pushed him too far," she said. "Well, Denis was certainly on target about them. They knew all of our bartenders."

Ron told her that the analysis from the dust picked up after the dogs were there had come back. It was marijuana that was in the master bedroom, but the traces in the wine room were OxyContin and fentanyl.

"Any way to know how much was there?" she asked.

"None at all. All the marijuana traces were the same chemical signature, so it was most likely one batch, not a series of them."

"Did we get anything from the attic where someone had moved a box up there?" she asked.

"I don't think we sampled it because the dog was not up in the attic," he said.

So the lab had concluded from what they had that Mrs. Rosa had some marijuana in her bedroom at some point--not necessarily recently-- and that there had been some painkiller residue found in the wine room representing at least two batches, one of OxyContin and one of fentanyl. It was already in evidence that there had been fentanyl in the car after her surgery, and four fentanyl patches had been found affixed to Mr. Rosa's back when he was found hanging from his wrists.

"We are pretty clear that there were two boxes or containers, one of OxyContin and the other of fentanyl that were moved out of there while the family was in Catalina on Saturday. It was unlikely, the lab said, that just a trace of something had rubbed off, say, from the bottom of someone's shoe. If that were the case, there would have been traces in other parts of the house," Ron said.

At least one of those boxes could have contained some of the weapons used in the attempted homicide of Denis Rosa.

"What about the GHB?" she asked.

"We never found any trace of that other than in the vodka, and of course in Mr. Rosa's stomach when it was pumped out," he said. There were chemicals in Mrs. Rosa's body that indicated there had probably been GHB in her stomach, and because her digestive system had stopped functioning when she drowned, it had been fairly well preserved.

Ron explained that it was likely that either the person who stored the drugs there had spent quite a lot of money acquiring them, or they had been purloined in some fashion. There was a survey going out to pharmacies and hospitals to see if any of those drugs had gone missing, but since they did not know when the drugs were hidden there, the timing was a problem.

"And no drugs in the record for Dominguez, Cruz, or Espinosa?"

"Nothing in the record."

"Have we interviewed the surgeon who operated on Mrs. Rosa?"

They had not. He was in Westwood, not nearby, and there was no indication that there had been any contact, at least by telephone, between the two of them. But the Sheriff's Department could arrange to ask him some questions near UCLA if there was a reason to do that.

They were still waiting for records on the McCormicks, but there were no warrants, not even an unpaid parking ticket.

Chapter Eighteen

Sue and Ron were used to driving, and they were used to traffic, but they were not used to the glacial parking-lot pace of the 405 Freeway. Dr. Walter Hill had agreed right away to meet with them when he learned that Mrs. Rosa had died, but preferred to do that at his office if possible, because he was seeing patients. If they needed him to meet them at a Sheriff's office, he would have to cancel appointments, and two of the appointments that afternoon were with burn victims who needed facial reconstruction. They agreed to meet him at his office at four, when he could take some time out and his office could shuffle some appointments around. He had hospital rounds at five thirty.

They kept thinking the traffic would let up. First they figured it would lighten up after they passed LAX. It didn't. Then they figured it would be better after the junction with the Marina Freeway. No change. The big white Al Jolson memorial was off to their right at southern California's most easily seen cemetery, Hillside Memorial Park, which appeared to abut the freeway itself and then to run up a well-landscaped hill to an Art Deco pavilion that looked for all the world like a modern version of a Roman temple.

"Mammy, how I love ya, how I love ya, my dear ol' Mammy," Ron crooned.

"Hang on to your day job," she grinned, and switched on the AM radio to get another traffic report.

Actually, they had plenty of time, provided they did not want to have lunch before they met the good doctor. It seemed impossible for the cars to go even slower, but the closer they got to the Santa Monica

Freeway, the slower the creep forward. Then there was about a half-mile of respite and they were getting off at Wilshire Boulevard. There were neat, even rows of military burials with little white marble markets on the left side of the street, and a painfully pedestrian rectangle of a federal building on the right.

They turned up Gayley Avenue and found a UCLA parking kiosk, flashed their badges, and were admitted right away.

The UCLA Medical Center is the primary teaching hospital for the enormous UCLA Medical School. Both are currently named after famous movie people (Ronald Reagan Medical Center, David Geffen Medical School), as you might guess, considering where fortunes were made in LA. Both institutions have grown exponentially over the last several decades and have taken over the Westwood Village (or south) end of the UCLA campus. Westwood, which is only about five blocks deep from Wilshire Boulevard, was a sleepy student-dominated "village" for most of its history, but it has now become perhaps the most thickly populated area in southern California. It is swamped with car traffic and, unusually for LA, foot traffic. And as though it were not already crowded enough with the biggest university in southern California and one of the biggest medical facilities, Westwood is a center for chic shopping, theater, and movies, and still manages to provide student services for the thirty thousand or more students. The buildings in the Medical Center are all relatively new--the oldest only date back to about 1955--and they are undistinguished architecturally, unlike some of the slightly more adventuresome buildings on the university campus that stretch along Sunset Boulevard like a patient etherized upon a table.

The Plastic and Reconstructive Surgery Department is in a new area that borders Westwood Boulevard, the main thoroughfare of the nonschool part of the area, and Le Conte Avenue, which forms the theoretical southern boundary of the campus. It is modern and glassy, with nary a bow to the architectural tradition of the area. Fast and functional is the watchword here. It has an anonymously attractive look, of course, and it has soothing patient areas, although the tendency to call patients by numbers given out on arrival is there, just as it is in all big cities.

They were, however, ushered into a conference room and offered coffee as soon as they arrived. Shortly after that, Walter Hill walked in. He was a little taller than average, maybe 5'10", and had the look of a young man in some ways, particularly the way he walked and the way he moved. He was an athlete, and Sue guessed he was in his late thirties.

"I was very sad to hear what happened to Mrs. Rosa," he said. "If there is anything I can do to help you, please know that I will cooperate in every possible way. Unfortunately, I do not know much about Mrs. Rosa's private life. She commuted up here from PVE, which is quite a long drive, but if there is anything I can do, please tell me."

Ron indicated that they appreciated his help, and they would do their best to minimize the demands on his time. But they needed to tell him that Mrs. Rosa's death, which was ruled "inconclusive" as to its cause, could very well be ruled a homicide, and it seemed likely to be connected to an attempt made on Mr. Rosa's life less than a week later in the same house.

"Oh, my," he said. "I didn't even know there was a Mr. Rosa, at least not, what should I say, living with her."

"He was not living with her. When she died," Sue said, "he flew out from New York and was staying in the house, which he owns as part of an inheritance. He grew up in that house."

"I see," Dr. Hill said. "How can I be of help?"

Ron said that although it was a delicate matter, they wondered if Dr. Hill could tell them how Mrs. Rosa came to have the surgeries that she had. How had she been referred? And did she tell him why she chose to have that particular kind of surgery?

He opened a file folder that he had brought with him. "This is Mrs. Rosa's patient file, and I have to say that most of what I know is in this folder. I see a lot of patients and her surgery was some months ago. It is not uncommon, a vaginal rejuvenation, especially for a woman who has had multiple births, as I believe Mrs. Rosa had. Yes," he paused and read in the file, "three children over seven years."

"That term," Sue said, "that term that you used, 'vaginal rejuvenation,' sounds like a marketing term, if you don't mind my saying so."

"Well, I suppose it is. It would be called a vaginoplasty in medical school. As a baby passes through the birth canal and ultimately through the vagina, it stretches the tissue to several times its normal size. After the birth, that tissue contracts, but never back to its original size. For most women, and for their partners, it is not a problem. For Mrs. Rosa, she felt that she needed to be tighter."

He read again. "Yes, she had read about vaginal rejuvenation somewhere and was referred to us by an OB/GYN in Torrance, a Dr. Samuel Smith." He offered them the file and pointed to the referral. "I can give you his contacts if you like."

"How is it done?" Sue asked, pulling back a bit from the table.

"Are you asking what the surgery consists of?"

"Yes."

He pulled out a sheath with film in it. "I can show you," he said.

"Oh, please don't," she said. "I mean, it's not necessary."

Dr. Hill cleared his throat and looked down at his lap for a moment. "Well, then, I could show you a different way. "He pulled a pen from his white coat and took a piece of paper from the file, looked at both sides of it, and seemed to decide it was not important. Then he drew an oval on the back of it and put an x on toward the top. He looked at her. "That's the clitoris. In order to tighten the vaginal opening, we make v-shaped cuts here, here, and here," he said, "avoiding places where sensitivity is more pronounced than at others. It is not unlike doing an episiotomy during a delivery."

He went on to explain that some of the muscle is excised, and then the vagina is stitched back together with very small stitches. When it heals there is virtually no loss of sensation and no apparent scarring, although there are some marks on the inside of the vagina from the incisions. The patient is instructed to do vaginal floor exercises before the procedure and then again after the wounds have healed.

"Is it very painful?" Ron asked.

"Well, it is done under considerable sedation," Dr. Hill said. "An anesthesiologist is present throughout and I guarantee you the patient is unaware that anything is happening at all." He wrinkled his youthful-looking brown forehead and crossed his arms. "But you knew that, didn't you? I suppose you were asking about the recovery."

"Yes."

"It's worth noting that the procedure was performed in our clinic, not in a hospital surgery. That is because it is not a complicated or unusually dangerous procedure. Of course we don't send anyone home until they are fully conscious and the anesthetics are completely worn off. And a friend or relative has to take the patient home, of course--or an ambulance."

"And who picked Mrs. Rosa up?"

"It says here that a Mr. Figueroa picked her up, and signed here," he said, gesturing to the file.

"Was he a young man?"

"Oh, I am sorry to say I would not have been there as Mrs. Rosa left," he said. "You might ask one of the orderlies, but it was a while back. But you never know, someone might remember."

Sue asked about how Mrs. Rosa would have felt post surgery, and what kind of medication she would normally be prescribed.

"It is not as painful a recovery as, say, a hernia repair," he said, "because the muscles involved are quite small, and although the pelvic floor is part of the musculature involved in walking and a variety of other things, such as a bowel movement, most of the uses do not involve distending the area."

Ron said they really didn't need to get into that sort of detail. "What we need to know is whether Mrs. Rosa would have been taking pain medications."

"We gave her prescriptions for a couple of different medications to help make her more comfortable," the doctor said, pulling out a sheet from the file and perusing it. "You know, people are quite different about these things. Some people resist taking these medications and others just have a very hard time dealing with the discomfort, especially as the anesthesia wears off. The second day can be much more bearable for some people. We can't predict how particular individuals will handle this. I can tell you that the discomfort level from the type of surgery she had is lower than with many surgeries. I have done numerous of these procedures, and from what the patients tell me, it is comparable to the discomfort from a delivery that requires an episiotomy. And an episiotomy is done at the last minute, as it were, where the work we do in a vaginoplasty is very deliberate and careful, and the closure--the stitches--finer and more of them. Both procedures tend to heal fairly rapidly because of the type of tissue that is involved."

"Can you tell us which medications were prescribed for Mrs. Rosa?"

He handed them the file, which had a prescription for five days of Vicodin and another for two days of OxyContin. Mrs. Rosa had been instructed in their use by the anesthetist and the head nurse.

"Would there be other alternatives?" Sue asked.

"I'm not sure I understand," Dr. Hill said with his head cocked to one side.

"Aspirin? Generics? What about fentanyl?"

"Aspirin is contra-indicated because it is a blood-thinner and is likely to increase the tendency to bleed. Generics? Sure, but they would be approximately the same drug as either Vicodin or OxyContin. There was no fentanyl prescribed. It could have been, because it is in the same general family of opiates as OxyContin, but no pharmacist could make that substitution. Why do you ask?"

Ron explained that there were fentanyl patches found in the house and car.

Dr. Hill looked confused. "Unless this file is incomplete, I don't see fentanyl as a prescribed drug."

"I believe we were told by a physician at Harbor General that most likely Mrs. Rosa would have been given a couple of fentanyl patches, or even had one put on and then given one or two more," Sue said.

"That seems unlikely to me," he said. "The nurse would have instructed her on OxyContin, along with whoever picked her up, this Mr. Figueroa. It looks like P Figueroa."

"Well, there was a fentanyl patch in her car and at least the scent of fentanyl in a storage area in the house, and it seems likely, since Mrs. Rosa had no other surgeries recently that we know of, that this would have been the only opportunity for her to get it, at least legally."

"Well, I don't know what you are implying," he said. "I can only tell you what it says in the file."

"Someone on staff here told us that it is not unusual to use fentanyl in situations like this."

"That would be correct. It is not unusual. What would be unusual would be for the file to say OxyContin and the nurse to hand out fentanyl. They are both opioids and they serve similar purposes, but they are not the same drug."

"Do you keep fentanyl here in the office or in the clinic?" Ron asked.

"Almost certainly in the clinic, and there are usually samples in the office--kept locked up, obviously, and with the appropriate logs," he said. "In either case, there would be records of how it was dispensed and who got it."

Ron told Dr. Hill that they would need to have access to the records, to check the batch numbers against the fentanyl patch that was found in Mrs. Rosa's car. "You should talk to the clinic administrator in that case," he said.

They thanked him for his time and courtesy in seeing them right away and said that they might have more questions later. He nodded.

"So," Sue said when they got to the car. "Figueroa. That's a new name, I think, not one of the phone numbers we found."

"Common enough name," Ron said.

They inched their way back onto the 405 and Sue called Denis. She summarized what they had learned from Dr. Hill and then asked him if he knew anyone named Figueroa.

"Not well," he said, "but that is our gardener's last name .Why?"

"Is it possible that your gardener picked up Elissa at the clinic in Westwood after her surgery last spring?"

"I suppose it's possible. Maybe she would not have wanted to ask one of the kids to pick her up after that kind of procedure. I don't know. Why him? No idea. He has been taking care of the yard for years."

They asked what he knew about Mr. Figueroa the gardener and he answered that he actually knew very little about him. He had been there the previous week to mow the grass in the front yard and possibly Sue would have seen him there.

"You mind if I stop over when we get back to Lomita? I'd like to kinda review the bidding."

It was OK with Denis. "Maybe I can finally make that cioppino."

"Maybe," she said. "Sounds great."

She told Ron, "Figueroa is the name of their gardener. Maybe he drove her home after the surgery."

"In that case," Ron said, "we need to speak to him."

The ride back to Lomita was faster than the ride to Westwood had been, one of those semi-mythological "windows" in traffic, and they pulled into the Lomita station before six thirty.

When they went inside, there was an envelope in Ron's mailbox. He looked at the contents briefly and then handed them to Sue. Mamie McCormick had been cited twice for driving under the influence, the first time suspended, but the second time she was ordered to serve one hundred hours of community service. Marcus McCormick had been arrested in 2005, but apparently never charged in a family dispute that sent Mrs. McCormick to the hospital with a broken rib and various cuts and bruises. She later said she tripped over a chair and fell.

Denis recruited Matt to go with him to the market to pick up the supplies for cioppino: fresh fennel root, mussels, clams, tarragon, flat parsley, Italian bread. He quickly checked to make sure he had the other items in the pantry and fridge and decided it wouldn't hurt to get some more tomatoes. They took off, and were walking back into the house when Sue pulled into the driveway. She walked in with them through the garage. The dogs greeted them as though they had been gone for a week.

Matt excused himself and went to see how Josh was getting along with the website project while Sue and Denis went into the kitchen.

"So you need to know about Mr. Figueroa?" he said. "How does he figure into this?"

She explained that someone by that name, Figueroa, picked up Mrs. Rosa after her surgery at UCLA and drove her home. They wanted to ask him if he remembered some of the things that might have happened that day.

"Well, you're in luck, because I think he will be here tomorrow," he said, pointing to the calendar.

"Tuesdays, I think. They're sure it was him? He is a fit guy, hauls around his equipment like it was weightless, but he is not someone you'd pick to do that, I think. He is short and gray-haired, just doesn't look like my picture of the person who would haul someone out of a wheelchair or whatever."

She said there was no reason to believe that he would have had to lift Elissa after the surgery. They had spoken with Dr. Hill that afternoon and the way he described the procedure, she most likely would not have been incapacitated, even if she was sore, or possibly in pain.

"Interesting," he said. "Maybe I'm just squeamish, but it seems to me if he was cutting her between her legs it might be pretty uncomfortable."

She smiled and nodded. "I have to say the whole discussion gave me the willies. "She did not mention the new information about the McCormicks.

He was scrubbing the mussels with a kitchen brush.

"What are you doing?"

"Mussels tend to have seaweed-like appendages that are sometimes called beards. I am scrubbing them off and generally trying to get any little pieces of shell or whatever at the same time."

"One at a time?"

"No other way. You can't just rinse them, the beards would not come off that way."

She had found it interesting when she was a child to watch her mother cook, but her mother was a meat-and-potatoes cook, nothing as exotic as what Denis was doing. She poured each of them a glass of red wine while she watched.

He rolled garlic cloves in a little rubbery plastic tube and it peeled them without a knife; he then dumped them out one by one onto a cutting board. When there were twelve of them, he pulled out a long knife with a relatively triangular blade and chopped at them until the twelve cloves were all in very small pieces. She shook her head as his hands flew over the parsley and then cut the whole fennel root into chunks that were about the size of baby potatoes in a stew.

"You know," he said, as he was chopping up the fennel, "I feel kinda silly buying this at the market because it grows wild everywhere, but I didn't feel like scrambling down the cliff to grab some."

"Really?" she said.

"Yes, most Californians call it licorice plant. It's that ferny-looking tall plant that is by every roadside. It has yellow flowers in the spring and summer. This is the root, and probably a lot more tender than what I would dig up outside, and cleaner by a lot, too, but the same plant."

He threw the garlic into a blue oval roasting pan that was sitting astride a large burner. It had olive oil in the bottom with a sprinkling of red pepper flakes and it started to hiss and crackle. A couple of bay leaves went in, followed by a small tin of anchovies, which melted like butter into the oil. A sprinkle of kosher salt. A few sips of wine later, the fennel, four chopped-up tomatoes, two fresh jalapenos, and some roughly cut celery. He was like a sorcerer, throwing little bits of this and that into the pot and talking to it, stirring the potion, which had begun to smell, well, bewitching. Josh and Matt came out of their cave, Josh buttoning his shirt.

"What is that glorious smell?" Josh sang across the room.

"It is going to be cioppino," Denis said. "Why don't you guys set the table?" Saying that

rocketed him back to when his children were young enough to be happy to be at home for dinner.

He stripped the leaves off the tarragon stems, chopping them into small pieces, and the delicate smell of tarragon mixed with the smell of the garlic as he scraped it into the pot. He opened a can of crushed tomatoes and dumped that into the pan, and then about half a container of chicken broth. "I ought to use fish broth," he said, "but I like it better with chicken broth, makes it taste more buttery." He put the lid on the roasting pan, but crooked so that it let steam out. He looked at Sue. "Now you watch that and if it starts to bubble up, take the lid off and stir it.

He peeled more garlic, put it on the cutting board and crushed it with a wooden spoon, then chopped at the mash with the knife. He scraped that into a cereal bowl and dumped in half a stick of butter, then sliced up the bread, but left it sticking together and buttered in between the slices with the garlic and butter mixed together. He wrapped the bread in foil, opened the oven and threw it in, set the temperature for 300.

"How's that doing?" he asked her. The boys were staring over the pass-through, breathing in the fumes.

He took out a skillet, put some oil in it and put it on a burner, turning the flame up to about medium, then dumped all the mussels and clams into the skillet and gave them a stir with a wooden spoon. He grabbed a pair of tongs and said, "Now we wait." All eyes were trained on the shellfish, and he stirred them. One by one they popped open, and as they opened, he picked them up with the tongs and dropped them into the tomato brew in the roasting pan, giving the pan a stir. All but one of the mussels opened up and he dropped the holdout into the trash. "We don't want the ones that stay closed," he said. All the clams opened, but they took longer, and fairly soon all the shellfish were in the liquid. He stirred it around a bit and sprinkled all the chopped parsley over it, stirred it again, looked up like he was saying a prayer, and said, "OK, let's eat."

He dumped the bread into a woven Mexican basket with a dishtowel for a liner and then they were ready to eat. They sat at the table like a family and Denis passed the wine around. He served the cioppino into soup bowls and put a pasta bowl in the middle of the table. "That's for shells," he said. Even Josh served himself, but took none of the shellfish and had a glass of water.

Denis raised his glass to them, "Amen. Dig in."

It was a feast fit for a hardworking farm family--or a king. No one said anything for several bites and each one grabbed at the garlicky bread and dunked it into the apple skin-colored broth. The dogs sat at attention in the TV room.

Sue broke the silence. She swallowed a big spoonful of the cioppino and tossed a mussel shell into the bowl. "Can I take you home with me?" she said, grinning from ear to ear.

"Careful what you ask for," he said, looking at her from the corner of his eye.

Chapter Nineteen

The boys started cleaning the kitchen and kept nibbling at the leftover garlic bread, dipping it in the pan.

"We saving this?" Josh yelled into the TV room.

"Saving what?" Denis asked.

"The leftovers," Josh said.

"There aren't any leftovers," Denis said.

"There's sauce," Josh said, his mouth full of garlic bread and sauce.

"No," Denis said. "Throw it out. No one wants yesterday's shellfish stew. Or you can stand in there and keep eating it until you burst. I promise I will make it again if you like it and next time I'll put some shrimp in."

He and Sue sat at the table while the boys cleared and cleaned up. They sipped on the Rhone wine that Denis had picked out.

"Sorry to venture back into the real world after that heavenly dinner," Sue said. "But Ron and I spent a good part of the afternoon with Dr. Hill up at UCLA. We didn't learn a lot that we didn't already know, but his files say there was no fentanyl prescribed for Mrs. Rosa after the surgery. His file indicates that the prescriptions were for Vicodin, which we found in the medicine chest, and OxyContin, which the dogs sniffed in the wine room, but which we have not seen anywhere. If that is true, we have no idea right now where the fentanyl patch that was in the car came from."

"But that was fentanyl they stuck on me, too."

"Yes, so it is tempting to say that the patch in the car may have come from the same place as the patches that were found on you," she said. "Fortunately the one in the car was in its original package, so it has a batch number on it and we are tracing it to find out who sold it."

"So if Elissa filled the prescriptions, she would have had some OxyContin someplace, right?"

"Well, maybe yes, maybe no, because Dr. Hill said the prescription she was given was only enough for two days. So if she used it and threw the patches out after they were used, there might not be any trace of it anywhere. We need to talk to the pharmacy that dispensed the Vicodin and find out if they also sold her the OxyContin and if so, how much they gave her."

"But even if she used it and threw out the patches afterward, that could account for the dog smelling OxyContin in the storage room, right?"

"Well, only in the most literal sense. Yes, it is possible. But what is the likelihood that if he gave her enough OxyContin for two days and she used it right away, she would have stored it in the wine room?"

"Or in the attic, I guess. Same thing."

"Right."

Sue said she had to get home since she had to be back tomorrow morning with Ron to talk to Mr. Figueroa.

"I could set the alarm, or just wake you when the sun comes up," Denis said.

She ran her fingers through his hair. "Not tonight," she said. "Not because it's not a good idea and not because I don't want to. But not tonight. Not until we start to work our way through what happened here. I don't want some defendant's attorney asking me questions about the two of us during the investigation. There will already be questions about Matt, but that also explains why I have been here so often and why we are friends."

He nodded and shrugged, kept nodding.

"We're still not any closer to figuring out why there were drugs in the attic or why there were drugs in the storage room," he said. "Or why there was fentanyl here when the doc didn't prescribe it."

She said she was trying to withhold attempting to make a decision until there was more evidence, more clues. "I think we are getting closer to finding someone who can point us in the right direction," she said, as she stood up. "Walk me out?" She waved to Matt and Josh, who both trotted over for a filial hug.

When they got to the car, she held her hand out. Denis took it and kissed it, looking at her while he brushed his lips across the back of her hand.

"Charmed, I'm sure," she said, smiling, pressing her key control to blink the lights and unlock the door. And then she drove off. He walked back into the house.

He woke up the next morning when the dogs were scratching at the door to get out, the first time they had done that.

He opened the door rubbing his eyes and they ran to the front window, put their paws up on the ledge and peered outside at the gardener unloading his equipment from the back of an old green pickup truck. He looked at his watch: eight thirty. He walked back into the kitchen and put a pot of coffee on to brew and then headed for his bathroom to brush his teeth and take a quick shower. Sue and Ron were due there in half an hour or less. He heard the lawn mower start up and knew that Mr. Figueroa would be mowing the side yard on the other side of the house first. There was no grass on the pool side of the house, and although the front yard had grassy areas, the largest stretch of grass was on the side, where they had played tag football when the kids were young.

He loved the smell of pine tar in the T-Gel shampoo, took him back to summertime at his grandfather's ranch in Texas with pine tar soap in a bar, the bitter, turpentine smell a good start to a day. But he rushed through his shower and threw on his jeans while his hair was still wet. He dropped to the floor and did three sets of crunches, then pulled on a black T-shirt, part of the New Yorker in him.

When he hopped out to the front yard, slipping his shoes on as he went, Ron and Sue were already getting out of their car. He made a comb out of his fingers and pushed his hair straight back, opened the door and walked over to the car in the driveway.

"Wake up late?" she asked smiling.

"A gentleman wouldn't notice," he said, sniffy.

"I'm not a gentleman," she said, "in case you didn't notice."

"I hear a lawn mower," Ron said.

"Yes, he got here at eight thirty and he is mowing the side yard. But I think what you are hearing is an edger, so he is probably getting finished over there. You want some coffee?"

"Maybe after," Ron said. "We need to talk to Mr. Figueroa."

"Should I come with you?"

"Sure, but once we are introduced, maybe you could wait inside the house?"

They walked around the side of the house and Mr. Figueroa was edging the lawn with an electric edger. He was wearing safety goggles, and Denis stood well away from him and waved. The gardener shut the edger off and took off his goggles.

"Hi, Pedro," Denis said.

The gardener smiled and looked inquiringly at the two strangers.

"This is Detective Mason and Detective Furman," he said, gesturing to them one at a time. "They are looking into Mrs. Rosa's death and the attack on me. I sure will appreciate it if you can take a few minutes to talk to them."

Mr. Figueroa nodded, put his edger down, and walked over to them, taking off his striped denim gardening gloves. He was shorter than any of them, about 5'7", lean, strong-looking, and bronzed both from his natural coloring and spending years outdoors. He was smiling, but clearly anxious. As he walked up, Denis held his hand out and Pedro shook it.

"I'm going to go inside and finish my coffee," he said. "If you can just answer some questions for them, it will be real helpful, Pedro. Thanks." He turned and walked around the corner of the house.

Sue suggested that maybe they could go and sit out by the pool so they would be more comfortable and noticed that made Mr. Figueroa more anxious as he realized that the questions would not be just a couple of quick queries. They walked around the house, through the gate on the side, and sat down at the round teak table by the pool.

They asked him how long he had been working for the Rosa family and he said he thought about fifteen years. They asked him if he had other clients in the neighborhood.

"Oh, yes," he said. "I work for other families here on Rocky Point, too, yes. You know, they see my truck in the neighborhood for many years and they ask me to help them with something sometimes, and I do. And then sometimes they ask me can I take care of their yard."

They asked him about his family and he said he and his wife had three children, all grown.

"I was born in East LA," he volunteered, and he pulled out his California driver license to show them his birthplace.

"Oh," Sue said, "I was born at Good Sam, downtown, not very far. But we were not worried about where you grew up, Mr. Figueroa."

"Well, you know when the police stop me, they want to see my license and they always ask me whether I came here from Mexico, but I didn't. I was born here like you and I went to high school at Salesian High School on Soto Street. The fathers were good to us there. I was an altar boy, too."

"Mr. Figueroa," Sue said. "We believe you. It's not fair for people to question you because you are Chicano and that is not why we want to talk to you."

He held his hands in his lap and his shoulders were slumped. She reached over to him and put her hand on his shoulder lightly for a moment. He looked at her and managed a smile. *He's been pulled over a lot in that rattletrap truck of his and he probably works harder than ninety percent of the people here on Rocky Point.*

"How often do you come here to the Rosa house?" she asked him.

"Oh, every Tuesday," he said. "And sometimes more. When I need to prune the roses over there, I come on a different day, or if I need to thin out the branches on the trees, or if I need to set out plants. Mrs. Rosa always wanted me to plant tomatoes in the springtime. It's not the best place for tomatoes, I always told her, because the sun, it's not so hot here, but I planted them for her anyway."

"Did Mrs. Rosa ever ask you to do other things for her, like maybe pick something up for her?"

He looked vague, as though he did not understand.

"If she needed to buy something, for instance, did she ask you to help her bring something home? Her husband was not here for the last several years and I just thought maybe you would help her with things, that's all."

He said he helped her clean out the garage sometimes and that he put up some shelving in the garage, too.

"Do you have a key to the house?" they asked.

"Oh, yes, I do," he said, and he pulled out a keyring that must have had thirty house keys on it, each one with a number written on it in fingernail polish.

"When Mrs. Rosa had some surgery last year, did you bring her home from the hospital? We know she was not allowed to drive herself."

"No, I did not," he said. "But I asked my son, Pablo, to help her with driving sometimes, and he did take her to the hospital at UCLA and then brought her back home after."

They asked about Pablo, and he said the boy was twenty-two, going to school at El Camino College, a two-year school just down the hill from PVE. "He is a good boy," he said, "but he does not know what he wants to do. His two sisters both finished college, but they are older, and he was our youngest. So he helps me with my work. He lives with us in Wilmington. He is a good boy."

Sue asked if he had a picture of Pablo and of course he did. The picture looked recent and the man in it was tall and muscular with the good looks that they had seen in Ricardo Espinosa and some others. She looked at Ron and showed him the picture.

"Handsome boy," she said. "I bet he has lots of girlfriends."

Mr. Figueroa looked down again and his shoulders slumped. "We thought maybe he would be a priest," he said.

"Ah," Sue said and paused. "No girlfriends." He shook his head slightly. "My son the same, no girlfriends," she said. "He is a good boy, too. Not everybody is the same. That's fine."

"We don't want to alarm you at all, but we would like to be able to talk to Pablo, because we have some questions about the day Mrs. Rosa came home from the hospital. Would it be possible for us to meet him?" Ron asked.

He looked up and nodded. They arranged to visit the house that afternoon, when Mr. Figueroa indicated Pablo would be at home.

"And which other families around here do you work for?" she asked.

He responded with a list in which one name stood out: McCormick.

"I know this is an awkward question," she said, "but did you ever see Mrs. Rosa with another man--that is, a man other than her husband?"

He clearly felt trapped, looked down at his hands and would not look up.

"Mr. Figueroa? Mrs. Rosa is dead now and we are trying to find out whether her death was an accident or if perhaps someone intended her to die. We know you are uncomfortable answering the question about her, but it would be very helpful to us if you could just tell us what you know," Ron said, as matter-of-factly as he could.

He slowly looked up at Ron, and nodded his head.

"Sometimes there were younger men here when I would come on Tuesdays. I have seen her having breakfast with a man sometimes."

They asked if he recognized the man. He shook his head. "There were maybe four or five different ones and they all looked like beach boys," he said, looking down at his hands again.

"Beach boys?"

"You know, young, tanned, movie star-looking, lots of muscles."

"Did you ever see Mr. McCormick here?"

He looked up with a puzzled expression. "No," he said, shaking his head. "Well, maybe one time when I came to plant that queen palm over there," he said, gesturing to a lush palm tree."There were a few people here, and maybe Mr. McCormick was one of them."

"Maybe?"

"Yes, it was him."

"And the others?"

"Nobody I knew, those young beach boy kind of guys."

"Would you be able to recognize any of the beach boys if you saw them again?"

He shrugged and shook his head. "Maybe if it would help find out what happened to Mrs. Rosa. She was always good to me, and Mr. Rosa, too."

Sue smiled, and thanked him for his help.

Sue and Ron walked Mr. Figueroa back around to the side yard and he took up his edging again. They walked around to the front and rang the bell. Denis answered the door and stood back to invite them in.

"That was interesting," Sue said. "It was his son who picked up Elissa at the UCLA Medical Center last spring. That makes more sense than her taking the gardener up there. And from what we saw in a photo of young Pablo he was what we might call her 'type,' as well. I'm not entirely clear, but perhaps from what he said, though, Pablo may be gay."

"Was Pedro OK after the talk?" Denis looked concerned. "His son has helped him out here. No idea about his personal life, but he seems to know all about gardening. But I would not want Pedro to be upset. He has been working for us for a long time and has always been the best of the best."

"As far as I can tell he was OK," Ron said. They sat down in the living room. "Initially he seemed to be anxious that we might question him about his citizenship or his work permit, but I think he stopped worrying about that. He was not particularly happy to be talking about Mrs. Rosa, because he seems a decent man who would not gossip, but he gave us helpful answers to our questions."

They told Denis that Mr. Figueroa had in fact seen Mrs. Rosa with young men at various times when he was there on Tuesdays to do his work. He had indicated that the young men looked like movie stars with lots of muscles which fitted with what was already known about her preferences, or at least her choices. And they told him that on one occasion Mr. Figueroa had seen Marcus McCormick with Elissa at a time where there were various other guests there as well.

"Did you know he had a key to the house?" Sue asked.

"No, I didn't," Denis said, cocking his head to one side. "But I guess it makes sense because we keep the gardening supplies in the garage and the only way to get into the garage without a garage door opener is through the door on the side, which has the same key as the other doors."

"Who else might have keys?"

He said that was a good question. Certainly Paul, Rich, and

Maggie would have keys, and he had always had one himself. Elissa did have help with housework, but he did not think that the people who came to clean rugs or wash windows would have keys.

"You understand why we're asking?"

He nodded and said he would try to make a list when he talked to the other members of the family. But since he had installed the new security system, no one else had the ability to disarm the system once it was turned on, so it was unlikely that even someone with a key could get in without being announced and photographed.

The doorbell rang. He opened the door and it was Maggie with a casserole dish covered in tinfoil.

"I hadn't talked to you and wanted to make sure things were OK, Dad. How is your arm? You're not wearing that sling?" There was a warm father–daughter hug and she gave him the sort of appraising look that women give men who can't be trusted with their own welfare. "I made a tuna casserole for you. Kinda like coals to Newcastle since you're a gourmet chef, but you never know. Can I put it in the fridge?"

They walked off toward the kitchen. Sue and Ron excused themselves to go to the Lomita station, and then go to talk to Pablo Figueroa. Waves all around. Frick and Frack wandered into the room to inspect the new arrival and she gave them her hand to smell.

"Nice," she said. "Yours?"

"Not mine, no," he said. The dogs waited outside the kitchen and then wandered back down the hall toward the guest room.

Chapter Twenty

Maggie was very solicitous, and he realized he had been too wrapped up in other things and had been neglecting the family at a time when they needed attention. It was getting on toward noon and he said, "A tuna casserole, eh? Why don't we have it for lunch?" He pulled the foil top off. "Slivered almonds. This looks good and I didn't have breakfast."

She smiled the smile of a child who has been recognized and complimented, took the oblong Pyrex dish from him, and put it on the counter. "We can just nuke it when we're ready. It's all cooked, of course, just needs to be warmed up. Maybe put some butter pats on top when we nuke it."

She took his hand and pulled him toward the TV room. She sat on the edge of the sofa and he sat in an overstuffed wing chair.

"Dad, you know we're worried about you. And we're all wondering what you're planning to do. I know you've been talking about selling the house and Paul tells me you have listed it already with someone. Are you sure that's what you want to do? There is so much family history in this house. You grew up here. We grew up here, and now our kids are growing up thinking of this house as the family home."

She looked out the window at the pool. "I know, it's not really home anymore since you've been living back east, and now Mom is dead. And I really understand that it is just a place, not a living thing, but it just makes me want to cry to think about it being sold to someone we don't even know. And the places on your closet where you measured us when we were growing up would get painted over and that would be the end of that."

He listened, didn't say anything until she had been quiet for a while. "It is a beautiful place, Maggie. And it would never not be home to me. Mom and I didn't get along, and although the house was always mine by inheritance--not ever community property--she needed it to be hers. She was always unsure of herself, but the house was her sense of who she was. She cared about it, different from the way I cared about it, but she cared. She wanted me to take all of Grandma's china and crystal to New York, and I did, and I took a lot of the art, too. My apartment looks like an old-fashioned art gallery with pictures from the floor to the ceiling virtually. Could I put Humpty Dumpty back together again? I don't know. I'm not young, you know."

Tears ran down her cheeks, but she did not sob, just leaked. She wiped her eyes.

"You know, Dad, I came over here to find out how you are doing. So how is your arm? Are your wrists healing up? Can you drive? Are you scared at night?"

"I'm still sore from the shoulder. My wrists are still angry-looking because of the amount of skin that was rubbed off, but I can do anything I could do before with my hands, including type on the computer. I wouldn't want to do pull-ups and I have not been to a gym in two weeks, but I'm OK. And no, I am not afraid at night. First of all, there is a pretty thorough new security system here now with cameras and lights and sirens, and it calls the police automatically if anything happens. But more than that, Sue Mason's son and his boyfriend are staying here in the guest room, and so are their two German shepherds, the dogs you saw in the living room. Smartest dogs I have ever met. Would I be scared if they weren't here? That's a real question and I don't know the answer. It is a big house and it is a lonely spot out here on the end of the point. And someone tried to kill me here. That's pretty creepy."

"You know you could stay with us, Dad," she said, smiling and eager.

"Would that be the point at which we switch roles and you become the parent and I become the child?" he asked, and caressed her hair. "No, I don't think so, and if I didn't live here, I would go back to New York anyway, although I would come to visit a lot more often. This old house, though, it has a lot to say to me. I have conversations with it, and I can even visualize your mother when we were young when I am here, and sometimes she seems to be here with me anyway. I know it's hard to believe, but we loved each other."

He stood up, walked back into the kitchen, and picked up the casserole dish. "How long do you think?" he asked.

"Oh," she said. "Just put it on high for about five minutes."

He put the dish into the microwave, pressed some buttons, and it made a soft purring sound as it turned on.

"We can eat at the counter. I'll tell you the rest of what you need to know and that is that if I sell the house, it will bring in something more than six or seven million dollars, according to Jim Kearney, the real estate guy I have been talking to. Considering that my whole net worth is about $1 million and most of it is not in things that can be turned into cash, that's a lot of money. And it is a lot of money for you and your brothers, too, someday."

The bell on the microwave chimed and he grabbed a kitchen glove, taking the casserole out and putting it down on the granite counter. "Your mother had this granite put in," he said. "It looks good and it's very functional. This all used to be old-fashioned kitchen tile and a very fifties kinda flesh-colored pink when you were a kid, and going back to when I was a kid. The granite makes it look modern."

Matt Mason ambled down the hall in jeans and a T-shirt, barefoot.

"Hey, Matt, someone here for you to meet. Matt, this is my wonderful daughter, Maggie, or Mags. Mags, this is Matt Mason. His mom is Sue Mason, the detective who is investigating what happened to mom and then later to me." Maggie looked skeptical, but stuck her hand out. Matt shook it. He whistled, and the dogs came loping in.

"Maggie, say hi to Frick and Frack, man's best friends."

"Yes, we met. They're beautiful." She smiled and petted them.

"They would not let anyone in the house who did not belong here," Matt said. "And they sleep with your father, between him and the door."

Maggie looked at Denis for confirmation. He nodded.

Matt squatted down and said to the dogs, "Get Josh." They took off down the hall and re-emerged about thirty seconds later with Josh in tow.

"Oh, my," Josh said in a barely audible voice, "we have company," obviously realizing that he was not wearing a shirt. "Shoulda done more sit-ups" flashed across his mind, but did not come out of his mouth.

"Maggie," Denis said, gesturing from one to the other, "Josh."

"Josh and Matt and the dogs are making sure I'm not a sitting duck out here on the point. And I'm kinda hoping we can have a pool party for everybody in the family one of these days. Josh and Matt lean toward being vegetarians, so there would be lots of hummus and veggies with the hot dogs and burgers."

"Oh, if I had known, I would have made that a string bean casserole instead of tuna," Maggie said.

"It's OK, we're gonna leave you to it anyway," Matt said, herding Josh and the dogs out of the room.

"The point is, kiddo, that I'm in good hands here, at least for now. The bad guys are gonna have to go through the dogs and the security system, and even then they're gonna have to get around those two hunks in there, and at least one of them is a black belt in karate, I think."

Maggie smiled and teared-up again. "We just worry about you, Dad, that's all. And I worry about what you're going to do. Because I bet these two guys and their dogs are not planning to spend the next few years protecting you from boogeymen."

"Well, as of right now, I'm planning to sell the house and put some of the money into educational funds for the kids," he said. "And unless I decide to pack it in at the business--which I could--I will be moving back to New York, where the boogeymen would have a considerably harder job trying to get at me in my apartment. And by the way, from what I am hearing, no one would move into this house if I sold it. It's the land that would bring the money and the house is probably a tear-down."

He dished out portions of the casserole onto two plates, then went to the fridge and pulled a fat tomato out of the vegetable bin and sliced it onto the two plates as well.

"A tear-down?"

He nodded. "This casserole is good, sweetie. Very thoughtful of you to bring it. I like your cooking, reminds me of Grandma. Maybe in a few months you guys can come visit me in New York and I can take you two girls to a Broadway show." He ate some more of the casserole. "Oregano, right? Fresh? Your garden?"

She smiled and nodded.

Meanwhile, there were surprises for Ron and Sue at the office. First, there was a report on the batch number of the fentanyl patch that was found in the trunk of Mrs. Rosa's Jaguar. They had assumed that it was given to Mrs. Rosa by the staff at UCLA when she had her surgery, but in fact it was part of a batch that was delivered to a pharmacy in Inglewood a month later and reported stolen after a break-in. But interestingly enough, there was a prescription written by Dr. Hill's office for fentanyl patches on file there for Mrs. Rosa, and a box of the patches was picked up in June. There was a fuzzy, but helpful picture of the purchaser taken by a pharmacy surveillance camera. Young, Chicano, fit, the type that Elissa Rosa seemed to have preferred. Unfortunately, there were no good face shots, although the lab was working on trying to isolate one from the digital images on the pharmacy's backup files. They figured it could have been Pablo Figueroa.

Then they headed to the PVE police to compare notes. While they were there, they ran a report on Pablo Figueroa. Nothing very interesting came back: no arrests as an adult, although there was a juvenile case that was sealed. They asked the PVE police if they could get a judge to unseal it so they could see what it was and Sergeant O'Leary agreed to give it a try since it was part of a potential murder investigation.

The pharmacy in The Plaza was where the Vicodin prescriptions were filled. The bottles in the medicine cabinet that had apparently not been used still had the cotton in the tops. They had examined the bottles and the contents, and they were intact. So they walked from the PVE police over to the pharmacy and asked to see the pharmacist. They presented a search warrant and requested all the files pertaining to Elissa Rosa. The pharmacist, a heavy-set Asian woman with beautiful, dark mahogany-colored hair, tapped into the computer and printed the files out. There were the prescriptions for Vicodin that they already knew about, as well as a prescription for two days of OxyContin patches that had been filled. There were some estrogen supplements that are frequently taken by post-menopausal women, not unusual, and two antibiotics a year earlier. She had also taken flu shots and a pneumovax shot, and there was a notation for Ciclopirox.

"Is there a way of finding out what these antibiotics were for?" Sue asked.

"You could get in touch with the prescribing physician, but the prescriptions are for Cipro, which, along with the estrogen, probably indicate urinary tract infections. They're common."

"And the Ciclopirox?" Ron asked.

"It's a topical antifungal ointment. There is also a prescription two years ago for Ciclopirox nail paint. She probably had a fungal infection under her fingernails or her toenails. Also common. Most doctors don't want to prescribe internal medications like Lamisil for that, because it can be dangerous to the liver and kidneys."

The printout also indicated the prescribing doctors if they needed to get in touch with them.

"That, of course, does not tell us why the fentanyl came from Inglewood. Couldn't be because she didn't want it to be known she was using opioid drugs because she bought the OxyContin at The Plaza."

They got back in the car to drive to Wilmington to meet the younger Mr. Figueroa. Wilmington is an old town, but it was heavily industrialized way back when a large oil field was discovered there in the 1930s and there are still at least eight major refineries there. It has charm and history in some areas, including a Civil War barracks and a mid-nineteenth-century historic home built by Phineas Banning that looks for all the world like it was lifted up from the antebellum South and set down in California. William Wrigley, the chewing gum man, built innovative homes in Wilmington. But these days it is, for all intents and purposes, an area of low-income homes fitted in and around old-fashioned industrial refineries and factories. For that reason it is heavily minority, and has been for decades. It figured in the Zoot Suit Riots during World War II. It has also become part of the City of LA, even though it maintains its name.

The Figueroa home was a craftsman-style house set up and away from the refineries on a parcel of about one and one-half acres, much of which was devoted to a small truck farm type operation. Mr. Figueroa's hand was evident in the front yard, which featured a well-manicured lawn and a wide variety of leafy, flowering plants, from sky-blue plumbago to camellias as tall as the house, and a row of perfectly aligned queen palms on both sides of the driveway, which was old-fashioned, made of two strips of concrete with a strip of grass in the middle. His truck was parked at the curb.

They parked easily; there were plenty of curbside places and no meters or no-parking signs. The Figueroa house was not typical of the street. Most of the other houses were on small lots and they were more like bungalows, where the Figueroa house was somewhat bigger, with better finishes--a double front door, for instance, with polished brass door handles.

Pedro answered the door, asked them in, and took them to the living room, which was furnished primarily with two couches in an L configuration opposite a flat-screen television. A young man whom they recognized from the photo as Pablo was sitting in an overstuffed easy chair that was on the third side of a large, square, wooden coffee table. He stood up.

He was taller than his father, about 5'11", and lean. He had the swarthy good looks of a Chicano man: straight dark hair brushed right back, broad shoulders, and high cheekbones that were probably inherited from Native American ancestors. Overall his features were regular European: hazel eyes, a straight nose with a narrow bridge, and a dark shadow that evidenced a heavy growth of beard. He regarded Sue and Ron as equals and held his hand out.

"Pablo?"

"You can call me Paul, that's what my friends call me."

"Paul, then," said Ron. "Thanks for letting us come by to ask you some questions. We are investigating the circumstances of Mrs. Rosa's death last month, and of an attack on Mr. Rosa ten days later in the back yard of the house on Rocky Point. You're not a suspect, so don't worry about that."

Paul gestured for them to sit down and said, "It's OK, Pop, I can handle this." Pedro nodded and left. They heard the front door shut and saw him walk out toward his truck and start to unload his equipment.

"Your father told us that you were kind enough to drive Mrs. Rosa to Westwood last spring for some surgery that she was having and to take her back to Rocky Point afterward. Is that correct?"

"Yes."

"Can you tell us what happened that day?"

"Just what you said. I drove over to the Rosa house and parked my car on the street. Mrs. Rosa was ready to go. It was early, maybe six o'clock. She had a Styrofoam cup of coffee for me, and we switched to her car and I drove her up there. I waited while she was having the surgery and then when they brought her out in a wheelchair I took her home. Then I drove my car back here. That's pretty much it."

"Did you stop on the way home?"

He looked upward. "Yes, we did. We stopped at the drugstore in The Plaza and picked up a prescription. That is, she stayed in the car and I picked it up. Then I took her home."

"Did you have occasion to put anything in the trunk that day?"

He looked directly at them. "I don't think so, no."

"And the prescription from the pharmacy, what was in it?"

"Um, I don't really know. I gave them the prescriptions and they gave me back a bag. It sounded like it had bottles of pills in it, but I think there was a box of something too, a small box. It was stapled with a receipt on it, and I gave it to her when I got in the car."

They asked whether Mrs. Rosa seemed groggy on the way home.

"Not particularly, I guess. Maybe a little. I don't know."

"Did she sleep?"

"Not that I remember, but that was a long time ago. Her car is a little car. It might be hard to sleep anyway. I think she put her chair back, but I was driving and she put the radio on to some classical music station and I don't remember much else."

They asked him how big the prescription bag was. He didn't remember, maybe like a bag with a couple of Subway sandwiches in it, but not like a grocery bag.

"No idea how big the box inside was?"

"Sorry."

"So when you got back to Rocky Point, what did you do?"

"I went home."

"Did you help her into the house?"

"Oh, yeah. She was kinda wobbly and I helped her get into the house and into her bedroom, and then I left."

"Left her alone?"

He nodded.

"Did you think she needed someone to stay with her in case she had a problem of some kind?"

"She told me she was OK, so I left."

"And how much did she pay you to do all this driving and so forth?"

"I think $200."

"Cash?"

"Yup."

"Something else," Ron said. "You do some work for the McCormicks, too, as I understand. Is that right?"

He looked up at Ron without lifting his head. "Not exactly."

"I'm sorry, but I don't understand what you mean."

"Well, my dad takes care of their yard, and I work with my dad, but I don't work for Mr. and Mrs. McCormick."

"But you know them?"

"Yeah, I guess. "He looked like he was being backed into a corner, but he was not worried or anxious, just careful.

"OK," Sue said. "That was very helpful. Thanks."

"One other thing," Ron said. "Did you ever do any other work for Mrs. Rosa, other than helping your dad?"

"Like what?"

"Oh, I don't know," said Ron, "like picking up prescriptions for her, maybe in Inglewood?"

"I don't know what you're talking about."

"We just thought maybe you did her a favor and picked up some medicine at a pharmacy in Inglewood. We think that because there is a surveillance camera at the pharmacy and someone who looks very much like you picked up a box of fentanyl patches prescribed for Mrs. Rosa last June, well after the surgery."

"Maybe I did."

"Maybe?"

"Yeah, maybe. I don't remember."

"Interestingly, there was also a box of fentanyl patches reported stolen by the same pharmacy at about the same time," Sue said.

"I don't know anything about that," he said. "But she did ask me to pick up a prescription for her in Inglewood."

"Did she give you a prescription to take with you and have it filled, or did you just go and pick up the medications and someone else had already given them a prescription?"

"She didn't give me anything, just the address and her name. It was paid for in advance and everything."

"Why didn't you want to tell us about it?"

"Because she paid me too much to do it, so I knew it wasn't just a regular prescription, and besides, what rich lady gets her prescriptions in Inglewood?"

"But you didn't say anything at the time?"

He was sweating profusely. "She told me not to say anything."

"Did you think she was going to use that whole box of patches?"

"I didn't know, I just needed the money and she told me there wasn't anything wrong with it, but she gave me $200 for picking the stuff up. My dad's gonna kill me when he finds out about this."

"You may have more to worry about than your dad," Sue said. "But for now we're just asking you to go back to the Lomita station with us to answer some more questions." She explained that he was not being arrested, not being charged with anything, but that they needed to continue the interview at the station, where they had better facilities for taking notes, recording conversations, and so forth.

They walked out to the car and Paul got into the back seat. Pedro came around the side of the house and broke into a trot. "Wait!" he shouted.

They paused, and when he got closer, Sue told him that they

needed to finish talking to Pablo at the station but that he was not being arrested. She told Pedro he was welcome to follow them to Lomita if he wanted, but that they would need to talk to Pablo alone. He looked at his son, saw that he was worried and anxious, and told them he would meet them at the Lomita Sheriff's station.

"No, Dad," Pablo said. "You're busy and I'm gonna be OK. If I need something I'll call you." He brandished a smartphone.

When they got to the station they went into an interrogation room with a table and four chairs and sat down. They offered him some water or a soft drink and he said water would be good. He admitted to them that he was suspicious about driving to Inglewood to pick up the fentanyl, but Mrs. Rosa told him that the price was better there than other places; she had looked around on the Internet. He was more suspicious when she told him she would pay him so much money, but he did it anyway.

"I gave her the box. She gave me the money."

"And the other box?"

"What other box?"

They told him again that the pharmacy had reported a box of fentanyl had been stolen.

"Look, I picked up what she told me to pick up and I took it to her and that was it. When I got back, I went to help my Dad."

"You usually help your Dad?" He nodded. "Where was it that you met your Dad to help him?"

"Just on the same street as Mrs. Rosa, the McCormicks."

"Did you see Mr. McCormick that day?" He nodded.

"By any chance, did you tell him that you had been in Inglewood to pick up something for Mrs. Rosa?"

He looked puzzled. "I don't remember, sorry. We were working on the yard, setting out some plants in the border, I think. You can ask my Dad maybe."

"Did you know of any relationship between Mr. McCormick and Mrs. Rosa?"

He didn't answer, just looked at them and wrinkled his forehead as a physical question mark.

"Were they friends?"

"How would I know that?" he said.

"And you don't remember whether you told Mr. McCormick that you had done an errand for Mrs. Rosa? You must have been excited that she paid you so much money."

He scratched at his cheek and shook his head a bit.

"Paul, can you answer the question please?"

"I might have, I just don't remember."

"You might have?"

"Maybe I did."

Pedro was waiting in the station lobby when they escorted Pablo out. They left together, talking, Pablo taller and meeker, Pedro older and more stern, a picture of concerned father and scared son.

Chapter Twenty-one

There was a report waiting for them on the Inglewood pharmacy that had sold the fentanyl patches to Mrs. Rosa. They were dispensing a lot of opium-based drugs, mostly fentanyl and OxyContin, far more than other pharmacies their size. It was not unusual for patients using drugs on a regular basis to shop around for the best price; the Internet made that relatively easy if you took your time and were careful. But it is common for certain pharmacies to be dispensers of drugs that can end up being street drugs because it takes a certain mindset to dismiss the potential harm that is being done. Fentanyl patches bring hefty prices on the street, about a dollar a microgram. Ron and Sue looked in the medical formulary at the station and read the entries, but that didn't tell them much about the real world.

They found a detective, John St. Clair, who had worked in the narcotics department for years, and asked him for a quick education on fentanyl and OxyContin. He said they were basically lower-level drugs from a cost point of view, but very dangerous, and increasingly common with very young users: teens and even pre-teens.

"The type of patch that you're asking about," he told them, "has a time-release dose of the drug at various strengths, but this one, at fifty micrograms, is one of the most common dosages. Where the drug is in a pouch or pillow within the adhesive border in some types of patches, and easy to drain out, in the Duragesic patch like the one you're asking about, it is spread throughout a bandage-like plastic matrix and more difficult to remove from the patch. It is supposed to be absorbed into the body at a predictable rate and it's a very effective painkiller. For comparison, it is about one hundred times more potent than morphine, which makes it a very powerful drug.

"There are a variety of things they take them for, but basically, since they are opium derivatives, they are painkillers, and they put the outside world at a distance from the user, who can dream or hallucinate, especially if the dosage is not controlled. Some people pierce the patch and drain the drug onto a flat surface and then wait for it to dry out, or use a hairdryer to dry it out. That's more difficult with the Duragesic patches, but it can be done. Once it is dried, it can be smoked. Some kids chew on the patches and suck the drug out, which means they often get enough drug to kill them because the drug is supposed to be time-released. It's sometimes used as it is designed, by just sticking the patch on the buttocks, stomach, the lower back, or even the thighs. It has the potential to put you to sleep, or induce a dreamy, semiconscious state. It can be used to come down from a high, but it is very dangerous, and there are a lot of deaths even with first-time users. A couple of states' AGs have launched investigations into the diversion of fentanyl to illicit uses, and we may be on the verge of doing the same here in California when we have some budget dollars."

Sue asked, "The box that was sold to Mrs. Rosa and picked up by Pablo Figueroa had twenty patches in it, each for fifty micrograms, I believe. We think the street value of that would be about $1,000, which is not a huge amount, especially since Pablo told us that she paid him well to pick it up. Are there other uses for the drug?"

"It's common," St. Clair told her, "to cut heroin with dried fentanyl to boost it, or to use fentanyl to cover up inferior quality heroin, sometimes where even talcum powder has been used to stretch it. But those users don't pay more for it than the kids who chew on the patches and drop dead. I think you're right when you say about a dollar a microgram. Of course, all of it is made in medical grade if it is real, but there are counterfeits, too, sometimes. I think with fentanyl, there are not so many counterfeits for whatever reason, maybe because there's not so much profit in it."

"Maybe it was for a test, to see if it was the real thing," Ron said. "Then they could go back for more. We need to see if there were quantities of fentanyl sold by the pharmacy right after this one."

"Could be, especially if they were buying from a pharmacy that looked the other way when quantities were sold. If you could get a few boxes of fentanyl patches and get MediCal or your insurance to pay for it, and then sold it on the street, you could make some money. Or if you just stole it."

Sue told him that the pharmacy had reported a theft of fentanyl a couple of days after this prescription was filled and that one of the stolen patches was found in Mrs. Rosa's car months later, after she was found dead in her hot tub.

"And," St. Clair added, "they had probably sold hundreds of boxes in the meantime. But you need to look at what they mean by a box, because fentanyl can be shipped in larger cartons. And dollars to donuts that if some fentanyl was stolen, other drugs went missing at the same time."

As it turned out, the pharmacy had reported a break-in through a rear door that did not have a camera. A long list of painkilling drugs was taken including the fentanyl, as well as methadone, oxycodone, and a case of Ritalin, a stimulant that is really a form of speed, commonly used to treat children with ADHD, but increasingly abused by college students who want to study all night before exams. All those would commonly be distributed by pushers working with younger people. The Inglewood police were investigating, and it was not the first time that pharmacy had been robbed.

"I think we ought to look at Paul Figueroa's phone records for the day he picked up the fentanyl," Sue said. "I would be interested to see who he was talking to that day. And I think Denis Rosa may be able to help us tie some of this together, too."

They called the Figueroa home and asked to speak with Paul, who happened to be home studying. Could they come over and ask him some more questions? No, he was not under arrest, and no, he was not obliged to answer questions, but it would help them if he would agree.

"OK," he said, "but I have to be at class at El Camino at four."

No problem, they told him, and emphasized that they would only take a short time away from his studies. When they got there, Pedro

Figueroa's truck was in front of the house and Pedro met them at the front door. He ushered them into the living room, looking sour every step of the way. Sue and Ron said nothing beyond a greeting. Once they were seated, Pedro left and returned almost immediately with his son.

"Mr. Figueroa, we would like to speak with Paul alone," Ron said.

"I stay here. It is my home and my son."

Ron nodded and directed his attention to Paul. "Thank you for agreeing to see us again, and we both know this is stressful for you, so we will try to keep it brief." Pedro stood by the living room door with his arms crossed and the son sat down and nodded to the detectives.

"Paul," Ron said, "we want to ask you some questions first about the day you picked up the prescription in Inglewood for Mrs. Rosa. I believe you told us that the prescription was prepaid and all you did was pick it up and then deliver it to Mrs. Rosa. Is that correct?"

"Yes," he said.

They asked him if he had discussed the trip to Inglewood with anyone else other than Mrs. Rosa. Pedro's arms remained folded, but he looked puzzled. Paul said he didn't remember discussing it with anyone.

"I didn't even tell my dad. He's hearing about it for the first time now."

"Are you saying you discussed it with no one at all other than Mrs. Rosa? I should tell you that we have subpoenaed your telephone records, so we will know the people you talked to."

"Why would I talk about that with anyone? I picked up a prescription for Mrs. Rosa, that's all."

"And she paid you $200 to do that, is that correct?"

Pedro's arms dropped and he looked at his son, who looked down at the floor. "Yes, that's right."

Ron told Paul that the pharmacy where he picked up the prescription was robbed that same night and among the drugs that were taken was the drug he had picked up for Mrs. Rosa.

"I didn't rob anyone, if that's what you're saying."

"No, we're not saying you robbed anyone. But we wonder if you spoke with anyone about picking up the prescription. If you lie to us, you may be making yourself an accessory to a crime, Paul. Just tell us the truth."

The young man was very frightened and his eyes flitted around the room as though he were trying to find a way out.

"Paul," Sue said, "we're not trying to scare you. We are trying to find out if anyone knew that you had picked up that prescription."

He looked at the floor again. "I told Mr. McCormick."

Pedro made a noise, not a word, just a noise that sounded like a question mark.

"Why Mr. McCormick?" Sue asked.

"He told me he was keeping an eye on Mrs. Rosa to make sure she was OK and told me he wanted to know what was going on with her."

"When was it that Mr. McCormick told you he was keeping an eye on her?"

"It was right around the time that she had that surgery and I drove her," Paul said. "We work for Mr. McCormick right after we leave the Rosa house, and he knew that."

"So Mr. McCormick knew she was having the surgery because you told him that, as well?"

"No, he already knew that. I thought he was keeping an eye on her because she was alone, that's all."

"Paul, I have the feeling you're leaving something out," Sue said. "You might as well tell us the whole thing, because we're going to find out anyway. And we have already subpoenaed your phone records."

"You can't wiretap into my phone calls from last summer," Paul said, with an edge of uncertainty in his voice.

"Probably not," Ron said, "unless someone you spoke to was already being monitored." He paused and looked at Paul, who flinched. "But we can see the numbers you called, how often you called them, how long you spent with them, and whether you sent any data packets."

"Look," Paul said, "Mr. McCormick was paying me to tell him what was going on with Mrs. Rosa."

"Paying you?" Pedro said in a crescendo that rose to a full-throated yell, his face turning red under his deep tan. "Paying you to spy on that lady who was so good to us?"

Ron Furman stood up and looked at Pedro. "Mr. Figueroa, please give us a few minutes with Paul alone. We can't have him feeling like you're intimidating him while we talk."

Pedro stomped out of the room and out the front door. They could hear his boots on the wooden floor of the front porch and then walking down the steps.

"He found out about me and he said he was going to tell everyone if I didn't help him keep an eye on Mrs. Rosa."

"Found out what?"

There was a long pause and a sort of strangulated sob. "You can't tell anyone, please."

"If it doesn't have anything to do with what we're investigating we will keep your secret," Sue said.

"I'm gay," he said in a rush, "and Mr. McCormick saw me watching some guys swimming in his pool and he guessed."

"I take it your father doesn't know this? Or you don't think he does?"

"No, of course he doesn't know it. He would kill me. We're Catholic."

Sue said calmly, "Parents know more than you think, Paul. Just because you haven't talked about it doesn't mean he doesn't know."

"What I want to know," Ron said, "is why Mr. McCormick would blackmail you to get you to spy on Mrs. Rosa. Were they having an affair?"

"I don't know," Paul said in a low voice. "How would I know that? Mrs. McCormick hated Mrs. Rosa and my dad said Mrs. McCormick thought they were doing it, but I wouldn't have asked Mr. McCormick that."

"Now here's the big question, Paul," Ron said. "What else happened the day you picked up the prescription?"

The boy slowly pulled his smartphone out of his jacket pocket. "I didn't delete it. I tried to forget it was there and I thought I would just drop it in the toilet, but I didn't."

Like a lot of young people, Paul conducted much of his life on his smartphone and there were hundreds of files. He handed it to Ron.

"Show me," Ron said, and handed the phone back to him.

Paul flipped through the files, found one, and opened it. There were photographs of the inside of the pharmacy. They looked like random shots.

"And this is?" Ron said.

"Pictures of the place where I picked up the prescription." He flipped through them and handed it back to Ron. He had forwarded to several exteriors, including the loading dock in the back.

"And why did you take these pictures?" Ron asked.

"Mr. McCormick told me to do it."

They told Paul that he was potentially an accomplice in a robbery, but that they were not going to arrest him, provided he would continue to talk to them about what had happened.

"What am I going to tell my father?"

Sue shook her head. "Can't help you with that one, except to say I think most parents are more reasonable than a lot of kids think. Whatever you say to him, do not talk to him about what Mr. McCormick asked you to do at the pharmacy. Do not mention it and do not allude to it. Do you understand?"

He nodded.

"And do not have any further communication with Mr. McCormick unless we are present. Do you agree with that? We will be monitoring your calls in and out."

He nodded again, then looked at them questioningly, "What if he calls me?"

"Don't answer it. Tell us, and we'll go from there," Ron said. "And you should realize that it is possible that you could be in some danger if you let this leak out. Remember that Mrs. Rosa died and someone attacked Mr. Rosa and left him for dead. This is not a game, Paul."

He started to sob.

"You're going to have to put a brave face on, Paul, so take a few deep breaths. If you want to come down to the station, that's OK."

They heard Pedro's boots on the porch and the front door open. He walked into the living room from the central hallway with a face that looked like a thundercloud.

"Come in and sit down, Mr. Figueroa," Ron said. "We need to talk."

Pedro sat across the room from his son and continued to stare at him.

"Mr. Figueroa, the situation is that there may be some connection first between what we have heard today and what happened to Mrs. Rosa, and Mr. Rosa after that. What happened is not Paul's fault, as far as we know. It involves other people. Mr. Rosa told us that there were three men who attacked him on the deck by his pool, and while they were wearing ski masks, he did not recognize any of their voices either. We believe that Paul has probably helped them with information, most likely without realizing what he was doing. Mr. McCormick could be involved."

Pedro looked away from Paul and at Ron. "What do you want me to do?"

"We want you to go about your work just like normal and not to discuss this with anyone who is not in the room right now. Send Mr. McCormick an email that you will not be able to do your work for him this week because you have some family issues to take care of--and then stay away from Rocky Point for the next few days."

"Is someone going to hurt my son?"

Ron told him that they hoped things would go on as normal and there did not seem to be any reason for anyone to hurt Paul.

"You and your son need to trust each other and you need to talk to each other so you can support one another," Sue said.

"He doesn't like girls," Pedro said. "Is that why this is happening?" Paul looked up with wide eyes.

"That does not have anything to do directly with what happened as far as we know, but it gave Mr. McCormick a hammer to hold over Paul's head."

Pedro stood up and said to his son, "You crazy sonofabitch. Did you think we were blind? Did you think we didn't know? Did you think we didn't love you?" He held out his arms and Paul virtually flew to him, sobbing and shaking. Pedro patted his head like a child. "We thought maybe you would be a priest, but then your mom and I realized that wasn't it. You are our son. How would we not love you? We would throw you out? You don't believe that."

"I knew it was bad what I was doing, Dad," Paul said. "But I thought Mr. McCormick just cared about Mrs. Rosa and it would be OK."

Sue handed both of them her card and Ron's. "I know we already gave you our cards, but I want you to keep these handy and contact us if anything happens that we should know about. We will try to answer quickly if you call, but we are trying to unravel what is going on at Rocky Point and that is our first priority."

The Figueroas, father and son, walked them out to their car on the curb, then turned around and went back into the house together as Ron and Sue pulled away.

Chapter Twenty-two

Denis decided to take the dogs for a walk if Matt or Josh would allow it. It was broad daylight, no ninjas in sight or expected. Even so, Matt thought it would be best if he went along. After all, he said, the dogs can pull hard if they want to and Denis's shoulder was still healing. So they agreed that Denis would take Frick's leash in his left hand and Matt would hold onto Frack's leash. They set off to the right and decided to take the passage up to Paseo del Mar, the broad street that ran along the cliffline, and then go down the easy path to the beach along the edge of the ravine created by rainwater runoff in the soft earth. The cliff varied from 150 to 200 feet in height, so the ocean views were spectacular, but you could still hear the surf and smell the tide pools from the top.

The dogs were frisky, but would not pull on the leash as long as the walker held the leash firmly. The two men walked along the street, which tended uphill slightly, mostly watching the dogs sniffing the curb, plants, mailboxes, and even decorative rocks in the gardens.

"If you're a dog, that's how you get to know the neighbors," Matt said with an amused smile. "You think she was pretty, the dog that peed on that rock? Some bitch, eh?"

Denis had been living in New York long enough that the extraordinary variety of flowering plants in California had escaped his memory. Even late in the calendar year, landscapers used plants that hugged the ground and provided a nearly year-round display of color. And of course, there were the cascades of chrysanthemums trained to grow high on trellises and then allowed to tumble down to the ground in sheets of yellow and orange and purple and pink. The ivy geraniums added to the display, and the cymbidium orchids were spiking in their ceramic containers, ready to start their gaudy display around Christmas. The paperwhite narcissi were starting to bloom and the heady smell wafted out to the sidewalk-less curb.

"Denis, haven't seen you in ages."

Denis felt the voice like a knife between his shoulder blades, but tried not to react. He turned around to see Marcus McCormick behind him.

"Why, Marcus," he said, and then remembered to say, "Your yard looks perfect, as always."

McCormick held out his hand, and Denis shrugged, "Consider it shaken, Marcus. I had an accident with my shoulder, can't really shake your hand right now. How's Mamie?"

McCormick shrugged in answer to the question about his wife. "We were sorry about Elissa," he said.

Denis glanced down at the street. "Nice of you to say that, Marcus."

"She was a lonely woman."

"Lonely women are easy prey for unscrupulous men, or so I am told," Denis said, looking straight at Marcus.

"Don't let me keep you," McCormick said in a jocular voice. "Just wanted to say hi, glad you're back with us, at least for a while. I heard you are listing the house, probably get a pretty penny for it, best view in PVE. Beautiful dogs. Big."

Denis introduced Matt Mason, and the two men nodded as Marcus McCormick headed back up the flagstone steps toward his front door. Denis and Matt continued on their way.

"I have to talk to your mother," Denis said, and then in a whisper, "That was the voice I heard the night they tried to kill me. No question in my mind, no question at all."

They walked on, and made their way between two big homes up toward Paseo del Mar turning right before they got to the street, so they could walk in the weeds and grasses, and low chaparral.

When they were safely out of hearing distance, Denis said to Matt, "Do me a favor and dial Sue on your phone so I can talk to her." Matt complied and handed the phone back to Denis.

"Hi Sue," he said. "Yes, it's me. Matt was kind enough to let me use his phone because I forgot mine. I just ran into Marcus McCormick while Matt and I were walking the dogs. It was him, Sue, it was him. The man who talked to me that night, it was him...no, how would I prove it? I just know it. You don't forget a voice like that talking into your ear...yes, we are going to walk the dogs and then go back to the house...I'll be goddamned if I am going to let that man scare me now that I know who he is. We set out to walk the dogs and that's what we're gonna do. Besides, I doubt he knew I recognized him."

As they walked, Denis split his mind between the extraordinary sights and oceanic freshness of Lunada Bay, and wondering what would have possessed a prominent man like Marcus McCormick to attack him with a ski mask on. He kept coming back to one word: drugs. He wanted it to appear that they were involved, but anyone who knew Elissa's proclivities would have put the lie to that right away. That's why it was so good for him that Mamie caused a scene in public.

But there was no indication that Elissa was using any kind of drugs other than marijuana. Traces of it had been found in her shoe closet and there had been that container of leaves in the freezer too. Recreational quantities of marijuana were usually considered harmless from a legal point of view. Elissa had been a cigarette smoker when they married, but she said she had stopped after he left and as far as he knew, had never touched a cigarette again. So it was highly unlikely that she was a pothead, and there was no paraphernalia in the house--not to mention no marijuana beyond what the narcotics dog could smell. Maybe it was bait for her boy toys.

Matt was the perfect companion. They walked gingerly down the ravine path to the rocky beach, the dogs off their leashes and dashing ahead.

"Penny for your thoughts," Matt said.

"Aaahhh," Denis said, drawing the syllable out. "Might not be what you're thinking. I was wondering why. Why he did it. Why Elissa did whatever she did. Why even after she was dead it was worthwhile to try to kill me. Morbid I guess, but also just interesting to someone who went through it."

"Gotcha," Matt said. "You know I didn't have a dad, but I had some great teachers in high school and college, men who gave me something to look up to the way some dads do for their sons."

"My father was a real father in an older sense," Denis said. "He was distant, but mostly fair, didn't talk much, and I always remember him as slightly disapproving, no matter what I did. He was rigid about some things, but he provided for us, and he had a good sense of humor. But my real dad in a way was my grandfather. He was the one who taught me how to fish, how to sit still, how to shoot a rifle, how to tease a cat with a piece of string, how to poke a blackberry bush to make sure there wasn't a snake hiding under it."

They climbed around on the rocks and Matt whistled a couple of times when the dogs wandered too far away. They came panting back and Denis looked at them. *Oh, if they could talk, what a good time they would say they were having.* He thought back to when he was a teenager playing with Old Duke, the Labrador who didn't like to swim. He talked to Duke, and Duke listened, wagging his back end.

Now knowing that Marcus McCormick had attacked him it was interesting to see how he felt about it. Angry, because he barely knew the man other than as a neighbor with a beautiful yard and a somewhat snobbish personality. Obviously, there had been more between Marcus and Elissa than the occasional howdy-do, but he was having a hard time visualizing them as lovers. But who knows? Hormones lead people down strange pathways. And lovers are the most common killers, aren't they?

Matt was skipping flat rocks over the surf. It was low tide, the tide pools were teeming with critters, and gnats were buzzing over the kelp that had been stranded by the tide. *The pungent smell is friendly.* He looked up at the cliff rim, at the parade of houses that lined the top all the way out to where Rocky Point curved around out of sight. When he was a kid, most of that expanse of cliffline was empty. The point had been subdivided in the early 1950s and the lots sold off to individuals to build houses on spec. Even when Maggie was born, there were empty lots on the cliff, though not many, as he recalled. It was wise of the city elders to have preserved the cliffline on Paseo del Mar. Well, the land was probably not stable there anyway, with several small ravines piercing the soil and acting as picturesque drains from the hills above. When he was a kid, no one cut the chaparral in that area and it got to be tall and fragrant with anise, mustard, sage, and a variety of lupine and wildflowers, as well as the ever-present castor bean trees: beautiful but poisonous. On any summer weekend night, you could walk along the cliffline and see couples doing what couples do in the grass, oblivious of kids with big eyes.

"We should get back up to the house, don't you think?" Matt called out. Denis nodded and started back toward the ravine path. Matt pulled the leashes out of his jacket pocket and waved them so the dogs could see. They came running and panting, happy animals with wet fur drying in the sun and ocean breeze. Denis looked at them fondly. *They'll smell like wet dog for a while.*

As they walked back, Matt's smartphone buzzed; it was his mother. "Yes, we are walking back to the house now, Mom," he said. "Yes, he's right here with me, everything is OK. Yes, we will meet you at the Rocky Point gates," he said, referring to two large structures of PV stone that had been erected by the developers at the point where Yarmouth Road turned into Rocky Point Road. But there was no actual gate. They walked over to find Sue Mason and Ron Furman in an unmarked car waiting for them. Matt motioned that he would walk the dogs from there and Denis got into the back seat of the car.

"You're certain that Marcus McCormick is the voice you heard that night?" Sue asked. "As I recall, he didn't say much, that man who grabbed you."

"He didn't say much, and yes, I'm certain."

They drove out to the Rosa house on the end of the point and pulled in the driveway. Sue got out of the car with Denis and walked with him to the front door. He unlocked it, disarmed the alarm, and they went inside. Ron Furman made a circuit of the yard around the house, making certain that the cameras were all working and the motion sensors were all functioning properly. Then he knocked on the front door and they let him in. Shortly after that, Matt returned with the dogs. Josh woke up and padded out to see who was there.

"Why all the sudden precautions?" Denis asked. "I think I told you that Marcus probably did not know that I recognized his voice."

"The point is," Ron said, "that if you are sure he is the one who tried to kill you, we need to tighten security because he lives about the length of a football field away. And if he was friendly with your wife he may well have keys."

Denis nodded.

"That means if there is something in the house that he needs, he has to get inside to access it. I think we have to assume that the night he attacked you he needed something from the house, and we know something was removed that night. We just don't know exactly what it was. Certainly he did not string you up like a spring lamb to get his hands on a thousand dollars' worth of fentanyl."

Denis rightly said that they had been over the house like a fine-toothed comb, and with the exception of some old things up in the attic, there did not seem to be anything amiss. "So maybe he got what he wanted that night."

"And maybe not," Ron said, "since we don't know what he was looking for. We can sift through the contents of the house again, but we might not know if we found it, whatever it is. It could be a phone number, or a receipt, or a key, or a computer file. It does not have to be a physical pot of gold."

They asked what his plans were for moving forward with showing the house. "For obvious reasons, we would want to make sure that there is not a steady stream of people poking around the house right now."

Denis explained that he believed that there would be no "For Sale" sign on the house, that the only people who would see the house would have appointments, and that their credit would be checked since the price tag on the house would be beyond the reach of most homebuyers. He said he would call Jim Kearny and get details.

"Even so," Sue said, "it would be best if you stayed close to Matt and Josh and the dogs for now." She directed her gaze to Matt, who nodded. "Or if you prefer, move to a different place for a while. If there is something here, we can be sure that McCormick or someone who works for him will be snooping around to get it."

"I can't--and won't--hide out like Butch Cassidy waiting for a showdown that might never come," Denis said. "I have to do something about getting my life together. I need to sell the house--or not sell it and figure out a way to keep it. Right now I think I need to sell it. And I have a business in New York that will not maintain its own equilibrium without me indefinitely." He began to chew on the knuckle of his index finger on his left hand.

"Denis, we fully understand all that," Sue said. "There are, in fact, some other pieces of evidence that are beginning to put together a picture for us and we expect to know more in the next couple of days, so we're not suggesting you settle in for a long winter's nap. And if you want to go back to New York, that's OK, although it might be better for the investigation if you are here. You were the victim, after all, and you are the only witness, which can be important, as we learned this afternoon. Just to be clear, some of the other evidence that we are piecing together makes sense with your recognition of McCormick."

"Can we go out to eat?"

They explained that if Denis and the boys and the dogs went out, the best thing would be to post guards in the house while they were gone.

"Guards? They can't hurt me if I'm not here."

"But someone could break in and take whatever is worth taking, even if we can't figure out what that is. No one can break in while you are here without alerting you to the fact that something is happening."

"OK," Denis said, "Well, since we don't have any armed guards other than Frick and Frack, I am making dinner, and I hope you will stay, because I am feeling very nervous right now. If I felt this nervous in New York, I'd go to an action movie or the opera--something loud that keeps my mind from turning somersaults, or my stomach."

He wandered over to the pantry and opened the doors. "There are several cans of salmon. I could make salmon cakes. And there's some Gimme Lean here, so I could make soy protein cakes at the same time for Josh and Matt. I'll need help, though. Someone to snap the string beans and someone to mash potatoes and cauliflower."

There were plenty of volunteers. There's nothing like a communal cooking project to make it easy to talk. Denis chopped onions and flaked the salmon, dumped them both in a bowl. Then he chopped celery and parsley, and mixed in thyme, oregano, and some Old Bay seasoning. Two finely minced jalapeno peppers went in next, and a couple of cups of dried breadcrumbs and an egg. Portions of each also went in with the soy protein.

"What do you suppose could be so all-fired valuable that we can't even see? I find it hard to believe it is a phone number. A key I could understand, maybe to a safe deposit box or something, but not just a name and phone number. At any rate, we know that whatever they wanted wasn't in the wine room because they went through that. They also went through the closet in the bedroom and poked around in the attic," Denis said. "The garage, I don't think they searched the garage, and the storage bins are only used for things no one would ever need, like old photographs and hurricane lamps for parties. The old Christmas decorations should be out there instead of in the wine room, and all those Christmas dishes too."

Matt spoke up. "There's nothing of any interest in the room we're staying in and the bathroom is a bathroom, not even anything in the cabinet or under the sink except toilet paper and soap." He was snapping the string beans while he talked, and Josh was peeling potatoes. Sue was cleaning and cutting up a head of cauliflower, and Ron was watching.

"OK, when you finish those potatoes, cut them up into chunks and put them into a ceramic mixing bowl you'll find under the counter there, throw in the cauliflower and some water, and then nuke it on high for about ten minutes," Denis said. "The string beans go in a saucepan with a steamer basket in it, look under the stove in the cabinet. Water. Put it on one of the back burners at medium heat, my hands are all covered with fishcakes."

When the potatoes and cauliflower went into the microwave Denis called an intermission and poured himself a scotch on the rocks. Most of the others had wine, but Sue had a soda with lime.

"Tell me, in your professional opinion, what could we have missed in looking through the house? Gold bars? I doubt it," Denis asked.

Ron answered. "I can't get away from the idea that we are looking for drugs, or a key to drugs, or some piece of evidence that would lead us to someone who has been dealing drugs. In that case, it would likely be Marcus McCormick, or someone he has been working with. Consider that he was here the night you were assaulted, so if your identification of him is right--and we assume it is--he has to be connected to it. We will be doing some further research on McCormick through the national fingerprint database and the FBI, and we could come up with something. But why this house? Did your wife have access to money? Did she leave bank accounts full of money or did she buy things and pay cash for them?"

Denis said that her financial records were pretty meticulous and nothing out of the ordinary. They had been filing jointly even after they separated, and there was nothing to indicate that this year was much different from the year before, other than a larger outlay for medical costs due to the two surgeries. She drove a luxury car, but it was twelve years old and had been paid for in the distant past. She didn't wear jewelry much, and her closet had a lot of shoes in it, but not up to the Imelda Marcos level, and she did not have a closetful of designer clothes. She basically had no shelter costs because he paid the taxes, utilities, and the credit line from his office in New York.

Denis walked back into the kitchen and extracted a big skillet from under the stove, put it on a front burner, and put a wad of Crisco in it. "I'm gonna start making the fishcakes. Josh, can you mash the potatoes and cauliflower together please--there's a masher in the drawer--and put some sour cream, a dash of milk, some white pepper, and some salt in when you mash them--and about a quarter of a stick of butter. Mash them until they're smooth. Matt, please drain the string beans, put them in a covered dish from the cabinet over the counter, and put some butter on them. Sue, put about a cup of mayonnaise in a bowl and mix in some pickle relish with a dash of Tabasco sauce. And then we will be ready to eat."

He fashioned the cakes with his hands, making balls of the fish and breadcrumb mixture and flattening them. He put them one by one into the skillet with melted Crisco and they started to sizzle as soon as they hit the hot oil. Ron set the table. The dogs sat at attention clear across the room where Matt had put them. The fishcakes cooked quickly and the soy protein cakes sizzled away in a smaller skillet. When they sat down to eat it seemed like they were a family.

Chapter Twenty-three

Matt and Josh volunteered to clean up, and Denis, Ron, and Sue went out to the garage to look in the storage cabinets that lined one side of the garage. One by one, he unlocked them and they looked in the boxes that contained old clothes, toys, stuffed animals, an electric train set, a box of sports trophies from various high school varsity teams over the years, and a box full of high school yearbooks. There was a large box of photos that were completely unsorted, some looking like they dated back to before World War II from the look of the cars. There was a lot of darkroom equipment that had been purchased when Elissa got a new camera for Christmas one year, but was not useful in an age when cameras stored images on digital media instead of film. There were two sets of Christmas dishes and two boxes of ceramics that Maggie had made in high school. But there was nothing that looked like someone would want to steal it, or hide it.

They looked up in the garage rafters, which were open, and there were some old suitcases, which they hauled down and opened up to find them empty. The washer, dryer, and hot water heater were there, and one wall had a bunch of old paint cans lined up on the floor. Ron pried open two of the paint cans and they did indeed have old paint in them. It was a three-car garage that was home to only one car, and there was a variety of old furniture stacked up, as well as some rolled-up rugs.

They gave up on the garage for the time being.

"Diamonds," Denis said.

"What?" Sue said with a puzzled look.

"Diamonds. The only thing small enough to go unnoticed," Denis said, smiling mirthlessly. "It was a joke."

They poked around in the wine room again, but nothing jumped out at them. There was some clutter, but mostly there were cases of wine stacked in their original wooden crates and a bunch of paintings piled against each other. There were a couple of chairs and some odds and ends, a couple of big ceramic vases. They looked over and under and inside everything other than the wine cases.

"Should we open the wine cases?" Denis asked.

"No point," Ron said. "If there were drugs in them, the dog would have told us. And I'm not going for the diamond theory. First of all, there's nothing that points to jewelry here, and second, if whoever was here was looking for jewelry, they would have taken the good pieces out of the bedroom, where they were almost in plain sight in those mahogany boxes on the dresser. No, I'm sticking with the drug theory. We don't have a lot to go on, but we do know there was a box of patches that disappeared and a supply of patches that were stolen from the pharmacy. That's not a lot, but it points toward drugs. I think there has to be a connection with this house."

Sue's phone pinged and she walked into another room to answer. When she came back, she asked Ron to step outside with her for a minute. "Nothing about you, Denis, just information that needs to stay inside the department."

When they got outside, she told him that their research into Mr. McCormick showed some six-figure tax problems with the State of California and a pending tax levy against all of the McCormick bank accounts. It seemed that McCormick's charity clients had made a change in Sacramento, and he had closed his office near LAX and fired all the staff about two months prior. His house on Rocky Point Road was refinanced at about the same time to nearly eighty percent of its appraised value, which meant that there was basically no leverage--no borrowing power--left in it.

"That doesn't mean that he has no other assets," Sue said, "but what kind of big mucky-muck sucks all the equity out of the house he lives in, closes his office, and fires his staff?"

The financial stress did not seem to jibe with the fancy museum fundraising party he was preparing when he and his wife agreed to be interviewed the previous week.

"Maybe he has another source of income," Sue said. "We need to find out. But if he doesn't have another source of income, he also has nothing to hold him here if he has gotten the last dollar out of the house and has closed down the business. That's especially true with a big tax levy coming."

They agreed, however, that they did not have enough evidence to charge McCormick with anything. If Denis was right, it was McCormick who led the attack against him, but there was no way to prove that, given that the attacker only said a few words. And although it was obvious that the intruders had been looking for something, it seemed unlikely that they had found it, whatever it was. So that meant it was increasingly likely that they would try again.

"I'm gonna stay here tonight," Sue said.

"You don't have to do that. I can stay and help keep an eye on things," Ron said.

"You can't make it look like a date, though," she said. "And I can. Less suspicious that way. Take me home and I will get my car and come back. Then we can play it by ear from there. My son is here in addition to Denis Rosa, so I have a personal interest in what's going on."

They went back inside and Sue took Denis aside, told him that she was going to leave and come back, and that she thought the bad guys would try again to find whatever they were looking for, especially since it turned out that the tax heat was on McCormick.

She and Ron left. They all went out front and said their goodbyes on the sidewalk so that anyone in the neighborhood could see Ron and Sue leave.

Denis re-set the alarm system and threw the double bolts on the outside garage door, the front door, and the door from the wine room that led to the side yard. Matt called the alarm company to make sure the connection was on.

Denis explained to Matt and Josh that, based on what Sue and Ron had found out, there might be another attempt to find whatever contraband had been missed the night they had left Denis hanging on the pool deck. They thought there was something hidden in the house that they wanted or needed, and that it could be drug related. The canine drug sniffer had not come up with anything and had been all over the house except in the attic crawlspace, and although there had seemed to be something removed from the attic due to the way the dust on the floor had been disarranged, there was nothing visible in the space other than a few old boxes, most of which held unused Christmas ornaments.

"So they are speculating that what they could be looking for might be a key or a phone number or a notation that tells them where something is stored or hidden," Denis told them. "We searched the garage pretty thoroughly, and we had another look through the wine room, but there doesn't seem to be anything in it, and there sure as heck is nothing in the room where you guys are staying, or you would have found it, and as you know, there is almost nothing in the other bedrooms which basically haven't been used in years."

"Could there be something buried in the yard?" Josh asked.

"Well, you would think if there was something buried in the yard, Mr. Figueroa would have come across it at some point. We can ask him, but I kinda know what his reaction is going to be. He is just going to be puzzled. Certainly no one dug holes in the front yard because the neighbors would have seen it. Same for the side yard by the garage. And almost the entire pool yard is paved with stone decking except where the bougainvilleas and a couple of queen palms are planted, and those have been there for decades."

About an hour later, they heard a car pull into the driveway and Matt ran to the front window. "It's Mom."

Sue had changed to jeans and a form-fitting sweater. Denis waved the boys off and went out to meet her alone. She kissed him full on the mouth. "Give them a show," she said to him. He kissed her back and ran his right hand over her breasts while he held the back of her head with his left hand. "Wow," she said, "you're good at this. Now let's go inside. But before we do, go get my duffel bag from the back seat and let me have a chance to have a quick look around." She wandered off looking at the garden and picked a few chrysanthemum blossoms, putting one in her hair. He brought the duffel and carried it while he put his arm around her waist and walked her to the door.

"Hanszen is watching anyway," he said, gesturing with his eyes to the house next door.

"That works. I suspect he is a good conduit to the neighbors," she said with a wide-eyed, knowing, hungry smile, running her fingers through his hair. She pecked him on the mouth as he opened the front door, then released her grip on him after the door closed.

"Hey, I was getting used to that," he said, not entirely in a good-humored way.

"So was I," she said, squatting down to pet the dogs. She looked back at him with the same look she had given him on the stoop.

"Tease."

Big grin and she shook her head vigorously. She walked over to the front window and closed the miniblinds purposefully, looking back at the room while she did it. Then she went to the side windows and closed those blinds, as well, looking for all the world like Jezebel seducing her lover in a 1950s Hollywood biblical epic, eyes flashing, lips moistened and red.

"Where did you learn to do that?" Matt asked.

"Oh, God," she said. "In high school. Didn't you?" When she closed the final set of blinds, she flashed her service revolver, stuck in her right boot leg. Then she reached into her handbag and pulled out three clips of ammunition and put them on the coffee table. "Let's have a little strategy session," she said.

"I'm here because we believe that there is likely to be an attempt made to either break into this house, or in some other way to get hold of something that we believe has been secreted here. That much I already told you. We think we know at least one of the people who is involved in this, and it's no secret among the four of us that it is Marcus McCormick. Denis recognized his voice as the man who grabbed him the night he was assaulted on the pool deck."

She explained briefly that McCormick had some financial problems, had closed his business and leveraged his house up to the limit, and had a significant tax bill with the state. That meant he was in hot water with the IRS, too. Having been a guru for nonprofit charities for years, he knew a lot of the "right" people and was continuing to maintain his position, which was probably the reason behind throwing the big museum party the previous weekend.

"But as far as we can tell, he is scraping bottom on cash," Sue said, "so we're thinking that whatever he was after in this house is likely to be more attractive now than it was a couple of weeks ago.

"Unfortunately, we don't know what it is, and we've done several fairly thorough searches to see if there is anything that pops up. And when he was here the night he assaulted Denis, he didn't seem to even look through most of the house--or the garage for that matter. So he must have some idea at least where whatever he's looking for is. We think he took some painkillers that night, and that they were hidden in the wine room. But there was probably not a big stash there, although it could have been a few thousand dollars' worth, maybe enough to help put on the party."

"And why don't you just arrest him?" asked Josh.

"Just don't have enough evidence to convince a DA or a grand jury. Our strongest evidence is Denis's certainty that he recognized McCormick's voice as the man who assaulted him, but that would probably not be enough. He has no record of anything that would make him a suspect, and of course his wife was involved in a yelling match with Mrs. Rosa. A good lawyer could make that look like a reason for Denis to lie about recognizing his voice. It's easy to discredit most eyewitnesses, and in this case, Denis would be an ear-witness."

She explained that if they waited, she and Ron believed McCormick would risk coming back to get whatever it was he left behind before.

"So we play Scrabble until he breaks the door down?" Denis was sounding out of sorts.

"More or less," she said. "I am taking a few days off and I'm going to stay here 24/7 for now. If anyone calls for me at the station, they will take a message and say that I am taking some time off. Then they will let me know who called to ask, because of course they can see the origin of any call that comes in. Everyone in the neighborhood will have reason to believe that Denis and I are going at it hot and heavy, and since my son is living here, too, McCormick may think we're looking for whatever he's looking for--that is, if we play our cards right."

They did in fact play a game of Scrabble and Josh won by converting "site" to "exquisite" on a triple word square.

"Pure luck," Matt said, dashing off. "You got all the high-score tiles." Josh chased him to the bedroom.

Chapter Twenty-four

The night was balmy and Denis and Sue walked out by the pool, making sure the lights were on. They could see the Hanszen house over the fence, so she threw her arms around his neck and kissed him.

"Just in case someone was watching," she said with a grin. The dogs wandered around the perimeter sniffing at the plants.

"Want to go for a swim?"

"Don't want to get my gun wet," she said, "and not gonna go anywhere without it either." She kissed him again, and then strolled back into the house. The dogs followed.

He offered her a nightcap and she declined. "Have one yourself, though. I'm kinda on duty, even though I'm off duty. If something happened, I wouldn't want to have a blood test make me look like I didn't know what I was doing. You understand, I'm sure."

He poured himself a Ramazzotti neat in a sherry glass and sipped at it. "Every old Italian will tell you that these are good for the digestion," he said, gesturing a toast to her. "I don't want to be indelicate, but what are our sleeping arrangements going to be, Officer Mason?"

"I'm going to sleep with you, if that's all right, but in spite of the fact that I would like it to be romantic, it's not going to be, and I am going to have my service revolver under my pillow. Plus the dogs will be there with us to let me know if anyone comes creeping around outside. You have a shirt I can wear to sleep in?"

He nodded, and handed her a long-tailed dress shirt on a hanger. She took it, stepped into the bathroom, and slipped it on, emerging barefoot. She took her revolver out of her bag and slipped it under the pillow, tucking the three extra clips in the drawer of the bedside table. She pulled the sheet down and slipped into bed.

"I'll be here," she said. "Leave the door open while you're in the bathroom. I promise not to peek."

He took a shower. *I've never felt more awkward in my life, getting into bed with a beautiful woman who's got a gun under her pillow.* She did not make it any better when he got into bed, studiously looking the other way, and she scooted over to him and kissed him full on the lips. He looked at her with a big question mark on his face.

"Me, too," she said. "Not the way I would have scripted our first night together. Give me a rain check on what you're thinking."

"I'm going to read for a while if you don't mind the light being on," he said, and hauled out his book about a man walking around the coast of England. She scooted back to her side of the bed and turned over.

"G'night," she said. He patted her butt gently and said nothing. She wriggled slightly and soon was breathing very evenly.

He read a full chapter about the coastline near St. Michael's Mount, and then felt like if he turned off the light, he might have a chance of falling asleep. He did turn off the light and lay on his left side facing the outside of the bed. He did not go to sleep easily like he usually did, but stared out the window at the encroaching fog and the few stars that were able to shine through it. The last time he had been with a woman in this bed, she had been Elissa, and twice when he arrived after her death, he had seen incorporeal images of her here in this room. He felt as though he was being watched and was hyperconscious of the strong woman whose back was to his now. He thought of taking aspirin, which usually did the trick if he had trouble sleeping.

He waited for the fog to swirl up, waited for some kind of connection with her. They had had a good marriage for years and he found that what he remembered most about her was laughter and kisses. She was never interested in food, not really--just ate to live, as they say, didn't live to eat, although she loved restaurants. They had honeymooned in Mexico on a very shallow budget and stayed wherever they could find a hotel or motel. In one place, Punta Penasco in Chihuahua, they had stayed in a room over a disco that blared rock music most of the night.

They ended up going downstairs for alcohol, but all of the patrons were locals and very few people spoke much English. They ordered cervezas and chugged a couple of them, went back upstairs and fumbled over each other in the slightly neon-pervaded shadows, laughed a lot and finally must have fallen asleep, because it was morning and quiet.

That night, the fog did not swirl over the clifftop in tendrils; it crept in on little cats' feet and just got thicker and thicker with no drama to it. Sue snorted lightly and turned over without waking up. He glanced at the dogs, curled up together on the old bathmat he had put out for them. He got out of bed and walked over to the window. The fog hovered over the pool and the hot tub, but did not obscure them, and the underwater lights in the pool were on, which made it look like a setup for a movie, or maybe a commercial. Both dogs looked up at him, but did not uncurl themselves. He slipped back into bed and realized she was awake.

"Everything OK?" she asked, alert.

"Yes, just looking at the fog. Sometimes it takes a while to go to sleep. I was thinking about old times, that's all."

She turned back over to face the edge of the bed and didn't move. He did the same and began to feel drowsy. He fell into a dreamy state, but felt as though he were still awake, although the room morphed into something different, and he could see the Dodger poster that was on his wall as a kid. Then he was climbing on the cliff with his friend, Norman, whose family had the first swimming pool in the neighborhood. He begged his father for a pool, but there was no possibility because he had been told that the cliff would destabilize from the weight, and especially if there was a leak. At that point, the back yard was a garden with grass, and his father had planted two peach trees that were pretty in the spring and had big peaches on them in the summer. One of those trees was cut down when they put in the pool and the other one was threatening to be taller than the roof.

He and Norman had a clubhouse in the cave behind the slight ledge a few feet down the cliff from the house. It was damp and you had to crawl in it, but it was secret, and the view of the ocean went on for 180 degrees. They could watch the teams trying to dismantle the *Dominator* at a time when the police weren't allowing tourists onto Rocky Point in order to control the crowds. Eventually it lost its charm and the crowds dispersed; he and Norman got taller, and as they closed in on their teens, they became less interested in having a hideout and more interested in girls.

One of the dogs was pushing his cold nose into Denis's face .He woke up, puzzled, going from a sunny day on the cliffs to a dark foggy night with a dog ready to lick him. He sat up abruptly and looked at Sue, or where Sue had been, because she was not there. He looked at the digital clock: it was two eighteen. The dog was intent on telling him something.

"You need to go outside?" he asked the animal. The dog wagged his tail. The other dog was not in evidence and there was no way to tell which was which in the dark. *The other one must be with Sue.* He got up and looked out into the mist. Nothing, no lights from the motion sensors, no alarms. He opened the bedroom door and walked into the living room. There was no one there.

He squinted into the living room and saw Sue with the other dog peering out the window toward the street from a position on the floor so that she could see between the bottom of the venetian blind and the windowsill. She hissed and waved him over to her. The dog went with him; it was Frack. "Good boy," he whispered, and rubbed the dog under the chin.

"No alarms have gone off, so I need to check whether everything is turned on." She took out her smartphone, pressed a redial number, and the alarm company answered quickly.

She dropped to the floor and spoke briefly to them. The control panel near the front door blinked off and then rebooted, and she hung up. "All the alarms are reporting in," she said, "so I guess they are all armed."

They looked back out of the crack between the blind and the windowsill. The mist was thickening, but they could still see the streetlights and the porch lights of the neighboring houses. The Hanszens were either watching TV late or had fallen asleep with the TV on, because the flickering light in their family room gave them away. The dogs continued to lope around the living room and TV room as though they were greyhounds looking for a rabbit.

The alarm box lit up and a pair of spotlights flicked on in the pool enclosure. They moved cautiously toward the now-lighted glass doors, and peered out from a dark corner of the kitchen pass-through. They saw nothing, but the lights remained on.

"An animal?" Denis said. "A cat?"

"The alarms are set to ignore small animals like cats or rabbits, or birds for that matter," she said. "The bushes are moving on the other side of the pool."

"Wind?" he asked.

"Wind doesn't set off the alarms. More likely there is someone out there who jumped behind the bushes when the lights went on. Stay behind the counter," she said. He saw that she had her service revolver drawn.

"You gonna call for help?"

"Not yet," she whispered without diverting her gaze. "I want to make sure I know what's going on. You go back and watch the front yard without getting too close to the blinds, and remember that the lights around the pool will backlight you, so be sure you stay in the dark side of the living room."

He crawled back into the living room and maneuvered to the side of the room that was not illuminated by the pool lights shining through the house. All he could see was mist. Both dogs were with him. "Get Matt," he said, and they took off down the hall silently. Within a minute, he was aware of Matt and Josh in the room with him, and one of the dogs was nuzzling him. He reached back and patted the dog on the head. "Good boy," he whispered.

"Wait a minute!" Denis said in an emphatic whisper and crawled back toward the TV room that opened onto the pool. "Sssssst," he whispered to Sue, who turned to him with her back to the couch. "You know there's a ledge in the cliff face just a few feet down from the yard. You can't see it from the water and you can't see it from the top, but it's there. And there is a narrow little path down to the ledge behind those bushes."

She looked puzzled. "What good would it do to get onto the ledge?" she asked, and crawled back to the dark safety of the kitchen counter. "Can you climb back up the cliff face to a different place in the yard?"

"Not without a rope you can't, and even with a rope it's iffy because the top of the cave and the cliff slant out from the ledge, which is why you can't see it unless you know where it is. So even with a rope, you can be virtually dangling over the rocks, although there is room on the ledge to break a fall. I never thought much about it, but there is a shallow cave, or an eroded area that would pass for a cave, behind the ledge. We had it reinforced when we put the pool in so it would not collapse, because we would have lost eight feet or so of the yard if it caved in, although it would not have endangered the house or the pool. My friends and I used it as a clubhouse or a fort when we were kids, and so did my kids. It doesn't get wet in the rain and it would be an OK place to store something if you knew it was there. It just never occurred to me because I haven't thought about it in years."

Matt hissed from the front window where he had taken over the watch. They crawled into the living room and saw that he was waving them toward the window. There was a man with a dog standing on the curb across the street, gazing at the house.

"Can you tell who it is?" Sue asked.

"It could be Marcus McCormick, but I'm not sure."

"If it is McCormick, we need to wait until he comes over here before we make a move. We don't want to scare him off. I'd guess he is trying to decide whether, with the alarm lights on, there is anyone home here, or whether we are all asleep."

Sue told Matt to stay low and watch the pool area, and Josh to go into the garage and make sure the door to the side yard was locked and secured, and then to go to the guest bedroom and watch out the side window.

All was quiet. The man across the street paced up and down with his dog and Denis tried to see enough of his face to be able to say he could identify him as Marcus McCormick, but the man stayed at the darker end of the penumbra of the closest streetlight, effectively blocked from much of the light by the ferny foliage of a *schinusmolle* or pepper tree, common in landscaping in southern California. The dog was getting restless, and he walked it on a lead up the road into relatively complete darkness, and then kept returning to his position.

The alarm lights in the pool enclosure turned themselves off, meaning that the motion sensors were not picking up any further motion. Sue hissed to Denis, who crawled toward the room where she was mostly obscured behind the couch. "This will make us easier to see from the outside," she said. "Stay close to the floor."

Denis felt his eyes drooping as nothing else happened and the stationary observer in the front remained at his post. Apparently the man's smartphone buzzed, because he pulled something out of his pocket and put it to his ear. Then he took off up the street into the darkness and Denis could see him in the light of the next streetlight a couple of hundred yards away. He crept back toward Sue and stage-whispered the news from the corner of the kitchen pass-through.

"Stay where you are, keep an eye on the front. I think they are going to try to move something out," she said.

A car appeared around the curve in the road and pulled over to park in front of a house two doors away. No one got out of the car and the driver turned the lights off. The car was not near enough to a streetlight to see the make or model, but Denis was not enough of a car person to have been able to tell the difference between look-alike models anyway. Sue hissed at Denis again and he crawled back toward the TV room.

"Can someone in that cave exit on the other side of the house?" she asked.

"The cave is entirely behind the pool area. It does not extend as far as the back of the house, much less to the other side. If you rappelled down the cliff you could take things out that way if you could anchor the rope, but other than that, you probably have to come back up the same path, unless you are willing to try to climb out of the cave at a pretty scary angle." He told her about the car parked up the street with the driver in it.

The alarm lights snapped back on in the pool area.

"They're ba-ack," Sue whispered. They strained to see any movement, but between the fog and the glare of the lights, it was hard to see anything happening. "I'm going out the front door to see if I can see anything on the side.

"Whoever is in that car will be able to see you."

"First of all, it's foggy. Second, I'm betting that whoever is in that car is not going to be interested in being part of what's going down here," she said, and she pulled out her smartphone. She called Ron and told him that she thought the bad guys were back and trying to move something off the premises. She explained that there was a car up the street that looked like it was part of the group. "Yup, lotsa noise and lights. Wake up everybody in the neighborhood. Both ways around the circle." Then she dialed again and whispered to the phone that they should cut the alarms in the front of the house. Then she slunk along the back wall toward the bedroom and came out with jeans and a dark shirt on, revolver still drawn. "You stay here," she said to Denis. "The alarms are off in the front, so there will be no protection if you don't keep your eyes open. Lock the door after me."

She opened the front door a crack and checked that the light was not on. It was dark, and she moved quickly out and along the wall to the cover of a clump of large cacti, and ducked behind them. No reaction from the driver of the car. She moved quickly toward the tall grape stake fence that enclosed the pool area and ducked behind an Italian cypress at the corner of the house where the fence started. Still nothing from the car. Most likely his view was bad because of the fog. She peeked through a crack between the grape stakes. The floodlights made it difficult to see with the fog, but whoever was back there would be having the same problem, possibly worse, because the floodlights were pointing in their direction.

As she was straining to see through the crack, the unmistakable sound of Frick and Frack barking was followed by a slight rumble of glass door, and the dogs bounded out into the yard, heading straight for the bushes near the cliffside. There was something happening, and she decided to give herself away to make sure nobody got hurt. She opened the gate to the pool area, and almost immediately, as though she had flicked a switch, the engine of the car parked up the street started, although the lights did not come on. She crouched close to the ground and entered the yard with both hands on her service revolver, which was pointed directly in front of her. She weaved slightly as she walked into the yard and yelled, "LA County Sheriff. Put down your weapons!"

She realized that there was a figure between her and the house, as well as the probable person or persons behind the bushes, but if there was someone there, he or they were not responding to the dogs.

"Sue, it's Denis," the voice said. "I opened the door to see if I could see better and the dogs ran out. I think there are people over there."She couldn't see him distinctly but he appeared to be pointing toward the bushes.

"Get back in the house!" she yelled. "Whoever is back there, this is your last chance to come out. I have backup on the way." A siren piped up in the distance, as though summoned by her voice. No movement in the bushes .She crept toward them and realized that Denis was to her right going in the same direction. She hissed at him, "Get down!" He dropped to almost flat on the ground, but continued to inch forward toward the bushes behind the diving board where it would be difficult for him to be seen.

The siren was distinctly louder, probably waking up everyone in Lunada Bay, but still not close.

There was no real cover for Sue, who stayed at least partially behind the corner of the kitchen that stuck out into the pool enclosure. Denis continued to inch forward closer to the bushes. Sue saw him gliding across the flagstones like a low-lying iguana and did not create a ruckus on the chance that whoever was behind the bushes could not see him, but she muttered strong words under her breath. Then she saw him begin to rise up a bit as he got close to the bushes--not standing up, not even crouching, but like a house cat after a bird, wound up like a spring.

"You jerk," she said to herself. "Your shoulder is going to come right out of the socket if you do that."

Then she realized that Matt was crawling out the door on all fours behind Denis. The dogs were growling at the bushes and lowered into fighting position, and she could see the fur standing up like crests on their necks. Their growls erupted into short, sharp barks, alternating one, then the other. And the two human creepers got closer and closer.

The sirens were in the next block and coming from both directions. The street was a big uneven circle, so you could turn either way at the entrance and end up in the same place.

"OK, whoever you are, the jig is up. This place is going to be swarming with guns in about one minute. Come out and throw down your weapons so I can see them," Sue yelled. At the same moment, Denis sprang up like a puma from the ground and into the middle of the laurel bush. While he was in the air, two figures stood up with their hands raised. Denis tackled one of them, who turned in fright and pushed him away toward the cliff. His eyes grew wide as he lost his balance and his footing on the crumbly cliff edge. He grabbed his shoulder and slid over the edge of the cliff with a brief scream.

"Bastards!" Sue yelled and charged the two. "You've killed him!" The two stood stock-still and Matt sprang up, ran to the cliff, and looked over at the water.

"It's too dark, I can't see him," he said. "All I can see is rocks and waves."

The gate burst open and there were a handful of helmeted police with revolvers drawn in the yard.

"They pushed him off the cliff!" Sue yelled, and ran to the edge. "Denis, can you hear me?" she shouted into the night.

"Yes," he said. "My shoulder hurts."

"Your shoulder hurts? Where the fuck are you? You sound close."

"I'm in the cave," he said.

The dogs bounded over the bushes and down the narrow path to the ledge.

"Boys!" Denis yelled, "Good boys! And I think we've found the treasure."

Chapter Twenty-five

They had been walking around on top of the cache of drugs all along. Denis had been strung up and covered with painkillers so that he would not be aware of what was going on as the cache was being put into its seascaped hiding place. The area that Denis had always called "the cave"--the only area outside the house the drug dog never got near--was a warehouse that held hundreds of plastic-wrapped bricks of white powder.

Denis struggled up the path to the pool area holding his arm folded across his chest. He was covered with the white chalky dirt from the cliff face. Sue handed him up across the bushes as the PVE cops were handcuffing and frisking the two black-dressed, hooded men who were face down on the stone paving by the pool. The fence gate swung open and Ron Furman sauntered in with Marcus McCormick in tow, cuffed and silent.

"Look who I found parked a few houses up waiting for someone," he said to Sue.

The two prone men looked up at McCormick and the PVE cops pulled their balaclavas off like waiters serving a fancy meal. They were both dark-skinned Latinos, and they both looked directly at McCormick.

"You know these men?" Furman asked McCormick.

"I'm not talking to you until my lawyer is here."

Furman asked the two men on the ground, "Do you know this man?"

They looked at each other and then back at McCormick. One nodded.

"Take these men in and book them, and take them in separate cars so they can't talk to each other," Furman said.

"You look like someone who fell in a vat of flour," he said to Denis.

"He's hurt," Sue said, dialing her phone. "I'm calling for an ambulance."

Josh and Matt stood in the doorway with the dogs.

"What happened?" Furman asked.

"He slid off the cliff," she said.

"On purpose," Denis said, pausing for effect. "It's a trick that my friends and I worked out in high school to freak people out. If you slide face-in down the cliff over there, you land on the ledge that's only about eight feet down, and then you roll into the cave, so if someone runs over to the edge and looks down, you aren't there and they think you hit the rocks 200 feet down. I thought my mom was going to have a stroke when I showed her."

"He's hurt," Sue said.

"I fell on my shoulder when I rolled into the cave," Denis said. "I'm OK. I can ride in a car sitting up."

Sue apologized to the person on the phone and said they wouldn't need an ambulance after all.

The PVE cops marched McCormick and the two black-clad men out the gate one at a time. Furman followed them to the gate and watched as they were put into three separate cars.

"Did you recognize either of them?" Sue asked.

"Never saw them before," Denis said. "But I don't live here. Probably it would be better to ask the neighbors or, for that matter, the dogs. I bet Albert Hanszen will know if they have been here before."

Ron said his bet was that they worked for the catering company that Cruz, Dominguez, and Espinosa worked for.

Denis asked if he could get cleaned up before they went to the PVE police station and Sue said she would stay with him and take him over there so Ron could go ahead. They walked out to the front where Albert Hanszen was taking in the scene from his TV room window. Denis waved. Albert waved back. A tow truck was hooking up McCormick's car to take it in as evidence.

Albert opened the front door and trotted over toward Denis and Sue.

"Were those guys the ones who tried to kill you?" he asked.

"No way to know right now," Denis said. "I was the only witness and I never saw their faces."

"Because they work for your gardener, I think. I didn't get a very good look at them because it's dark, but I think they do."

"Would you be available to come down to the police station and look at a lineup?" Sue asked." Maybe right away?"

Albert nodded vigorously. They arranged for him to go to the PVE police station in forty-five minutes and then they headed back into the house. The dogs were sitting as though they were at a tea party, looking at Josh and Matt. Denis headed into the bedroom to wash the film of white diatomaceous earth off. He stripped and stepped into the shower, where the water was, blessedly, hot right away. He found that he could lift his arm, so he washed his hair quickly and rinsed off, and stepped out to towel off.

"Can I give you a hand with that?" Sue asked, standing outside the shower looking at him.

"Uh," he said, and instinctively his hands covered his crotch.

She picked up a towel and dried his hair, then walked behind him and dried his back, his buttocks, and his legs. She turned him around and started to dry his chest, but he said, "I'll do that," and grabbed the towel with one hand, keeping the other strategically placed just below his center of gravity. He watched the smile light up her face and she turned and walked out of the bathroom.

"You got to feel me up," she sang out from the other room. "It was my turn."

He smiled slightly and dried himself off, his shoulder aching more than he thought it would. He grabbed a terrycloth robe from the back of the bathroom door, wrapped himself up in it, and stepped into the bedroom. The door to the TV room was open and there were voices out there. He went into the closet, flicked on the light, and dressed in jeans and a shirt that buttoned down the front so he could get his arm into it.

He picked up a pair of socks and walked out to the TV room.

"Sorry," he said, "I need some help with these."

Matt scurried over and Denis sat down in a straight chair. Matt knelt down and put the socks on his feet.

"Thanks." He went back into the bedroom and slipped on a pair of shoes, put his wallet and some cash in his pockets, and grabbed a lined suede jacket.

"Ready," he said.

Sue beamed at him. "You never looked better, handsome," she said.

She turned to Matt and Josh. "I think it's all over here, but I want you to stay alert, because until the PVE police cart off all that cocaine or whatever Denis found down there, anything can happen. Keep your guard up and let the dogs out in the back yard."

As she finished saying that, a car and a van pulled up in front and they looked out the living room window. Both were marked PVE Police, and the van had CSI on the door. Seven people got out, all in uniform, and walked up to the front door. Sue opened it before they rang the bell.

While they were standing in the doorway, a Sheriff's van pulled up and six men with automatic weapons stepped out and took up positions in front of the house.

"I think you're in good hands now," she said to Matt. She knew two of the Sheriff's Department officers, but she checked credentials of all of them before leading them to the back yard and showing them the path to the cave. Two of the officers set up video cameras on a tripod, focusing on the beginning of the path, and the other officers set up high-intensity lighting to facilitate removing the drugs without mishap, since the cliff was well over a 200-foot drop.

"Don't worry about the shrubs," Denis said. "We're going to be re-landscaping anyway." He watched as two of the uniformed officers with orange jumpsuits and rubber gloves disappeared down the path with cameras to shoot photos of the cache tucked into the side of the cliff. Matt and Josh held the two dogs on their leashes and watched the whole proceeding.

"We're going down to The Plaza to make a statement and lend a hand with interrogations," Sue told one of the PVE cops. She and Denis left, Denis looking over his shoulder from curiosity. They got into her car and she put the Cyclops on the roof and pulled away from the curb with the light spinning. When they passed the Rocky Point gates and pulled onto Yarmouth Road, she turned on the siren and they picked up some speed. Denis watched, buckled under his shoulder strap and very conscious of his painful shoulder.

"Did you arrest Marcus McCormick?" he asked.

"Ron did, yes."

"What are you going to charge him with?"

"Well, there's a range of things, I suppose, depending on what happens with the interrogations. At a minimum, selling illegal drugs, or holding them for sale. But maybe attempted murder. Maybe murder. Maybe conspiracy. Maybe RICO. That's going to be up to the DA or a Grand Jury. We'll hold him for whatever we can hold him for most easily."

"So you think he killed Elissa?"

"I didn't say that, and the truth is that's the only part that doesn't seem to make sense. If he wanted to continue to use her house to store his drugs, the worst thing he could do would be to kill her and have the house change hands. But then, of course, when it did change hands, someone tried to kill you. Something about it seems like overlapping events, not completely connected, if you follow."

"It was him that was holding me that night. It was Marcus who stuck that needle in my neck."

She nodded. "But that does not mean he killed your wife. It may mean he doesn't have any idea who killed your wife, in fact."

She was concentrating on driving and they were picking up speed on the curving roads that followed the cliffline. When they pulled onto PVE Drive just before Bluff Cove, she said, "I can't talk to you now," and hunched over the wheel watching the sides of the road, the cars ahead, and the side street at the end of the cove.

Denis did not like being in a speeding car a heartbeat away from a 300-foot cliff, but it was clear that Sue knew what she was doing. He turned and looked out his window at the hillside above them, the stunted pine trees that had been blown toward the hill by the prevailing winds, and the buzz cut of eucalyptus trees lining the hilltop. There was a full moon over the trees and he stared consciously at that as they careened up from the cove onto the back road to The Plaza and away from the cliff. The route was shorter, but ran through entirely residential streets, so she slowed down, aware that a tricycle or a skateboard could appear from anywhere, even at night.

"So we go back to the list of boys she was seeing?"

She did not look at him because she was watching both sides of the road. "Maybe, or, like I said at first, it could have been an accident. Or there could be someone else involved, although I don't know who it would be."

They cruised down Via del Monte, turned on the road before the library, and slowed down for the last two blocks to the PVE police station. They pulled up in front and parked in a space reserved for police. She turned off the ignition and turned her whole body toward Denis.

"Somebody said that when you eliminate all the impossible things, then what remains, however improbable, must be the truth," she said. "That's over simplified, but in a way, it works here. Unless there's something I'm missing, there would have been every reason in the world for Marcus McCormick to opt for the status quo--a tipsy, horny woman living alone above his warehouse for whatever kind of drugs that turns out to be. The craziest thing he could do would be to kill her, unless, like I say, there is something we're not seeing."

"Like what?" Denis asked, wrinkling his nose and scrunching his eyebrows together.

"I don't know. Maybe she could have found out what was going on and become dangerous. But in that case, the thing to do would have been to call the police, not to fling what you know at someone you know to be dangerous. And from McCormick's point of view, if he thought she was a danger, even if he was really boiling angry, he would have moved out his inventory before he killed her, don't you think?"

"I don't know, maybe they had a fight?"

Sue said that the way she saw things, everything pointed to the idea that McCormick had no idea who was responsible for Elissa's death. "Or it could even be that he thought you did it," she said.

234

He stared at her."Me? Why? I wasn't even here, and we got along OK the way we were."

"I don't know, the house is valuable, and maybe you needed the money?"

He put his forehead into his palms. "Is that what you think?"

She unhooked her seatbelt, reached over and put her hand on his head. "No, I don't think you were involved. What I said was I think McCormick may think you were involved. Look at me."

He looked at her.

"No, I don't think you had anything to do with it."

He exhaled slowly and took her hand and kissed it. Then he unhooked his seatbelt and opened the door. They walked into the PVE police station.

Chapter Twenty-six

They were directed to the observation room next to an interrogation room, where Marcus McCormick was sitting alone, aware that he was being monitored from behind the two-way mirror.

"Can he hear us?" Denis asked in a whisper.

"No, the room he is in is soundproofed completely and everything that happens in there is videotaped from three cameras. We are here to observe."

The door to the interrogation room opened and Ron Furman walked in. He did not glance at the mirror but sat down and put a manila folder on the table.

"Did they offer you some water, or soda, or coffee?" he asked McCormick.

"Yes."

"Did you hear and understand your Miranda rights?"

"Yes."

"Have you asked for an attorney?"

"Not yet."

Ron told him that he needed to ask him some questions about what had happened earlier in the evening.

"Now I want to talk to my lawyer," he said.

"OK, I will arrange for you to call him and we will not ask you any further questions until after your attorney is here," Ron said. "Meanwhile, we will be questioning the two men who were arrested at the Rosa house this evening and who seem anxious to cooperate with us."

"What's that to me? Couple of Mexican wetbacks, they'll say

anything to get themselves off."

"Interesting, Mr. McCormick. What makes you think these two fellows are Mexican?"

"All drugs have something to do with Mexicans, I guess."

"And what leads you to think there are drugs involved?"

"I want to talk to my lawyer."

"Certainly."

Ron exited the room and went into the observation room. "Well, that would not necessarily convince a jury, but it sure convinced me," he said to Sue.

She nodded.

"He tried to kill me," Denis said. "I don't have to be convinced more than that. He strung me up like a side of beef and stuck drug patches all over me and left me to die."

"And that's a crime that will put him in jail for a while," Ron said. "And if we can connect him to the drugs, that will put him away until he is old enough and feeble enough that if he gets out, he will have to use a walker and have someone to remind him to put his hearing aid batteries in."

Denis looked at Ron. "You don't think he killed my wife either, do you?"

"I don't really have an opinion on that, other than to say that I think he would be smarter than to wring the neck of the goose that laid the golden egg, especially after he went to the trouble of supplying her with pain patches and marijuana."

"So are you thinking he went after me because he thought I killed Elissa?"

"No idea," Ron said, "but you were certainly in his way with the drugs and he was in an increasingly desperate situation financially. Of course, someone has to sort all that out, too, because the façade he put up made it seem like he was pretty well off."

Ron and Denis went into the second observation room to watch Sue talk to one of the men who was taken at the house earlier. She walked in and stood, looking into a manila folder. "Ramiro Ramos?"

He nodded.

"How old are you?"

"Twenty-three."

She verified his residence address and glanced down his list of priors.

"You've been run in before for drugs."

He nodded.

"Do you understand your right to remain silent, your right to an attorney, and that anything you tell us may be used against you in a trial?" she asked.

He nodded.

"I need for you to answer that out loud, please."

"Yes."

"Who hired you to move the drugs from that cave below the Rosa house?"

He looked at his hands and said nothing.

"We have taken two other people into custody at the same time that you were arrested. One of you will decide to tell us what happened and that guy will have a chance at a better deal than the others. Up to you."

Denis stared intently at the man, but said nothing. "Does he seem familiar to you?" Ron asked him.

"Vaguely," Denis said. "Maybe he was one of the guys that the gardener brought around to help, but I'm not sure. Actually, I bet Albert would know because he makes a point of noticing things. Certainly more attentive than I am."

Ron nodded.

Ramiro was looking more anxious as Sue continued to talk to him; he was glancing around the room, up at the ceiling, then down at his hands. Trying to decide what to do.

Ron took Denis to the viewing room next to the second interrogation, where Marcus McCormick was sitting alone. He fidgeted, looked at his watch several times, and glanced around the room, looking intently at the mirror which hid Ron and Denis. He looked alternately angry and curious. "We're letting him wonder what's going on," Ron said.

Meanwhile, Sue left Ramiro, and a pair of young officers took him out of the interrogation room and into a holding cell. They brought the other young man who had been taken at the house in for questioning. He was considerably less calm than Ramiro, looking caged and worried. Sue entered the room with a manila folder. She stared at him for a minute, as he became more fidgety and clearly shaken.

"Fernando Gomez?"

He looked up, startled, and nodded.

"Do you know why you were arrested?"

He nodded again.

She repeated his Miranda rights, and he acknowledged them.

"I'm going to give you one chance to tell me what happened. Otherwise, I will bring Ramiro back in here and he will tell me. You're younger than he is, and I'm guessing you did this because you had no choice, so we can work with you to get a deal. But if you don't cooperate, it'll be all over and you'll do hard time. Do you understand?"

He nodded again.

"Answer out loud please."

"Yes, I understand," he said audibly but without energy, blanching through his leathery, tanned skin.

"I think we have one here," Ron said to Denis in the viewing booth.

"If you tell me what you know, we can try to get you a deal," Sue said.

"What kind of deal?"

"No guarantees, but if you help us, we will help you."

"He'll kill me."

"Who?"

"Him. McCormick. He said he would, and he has a lot of friends. I'm not saying anything."

They tried, but could not get anything more out of him on that subject. He had family, a sister and a mother, and he was afraid for them. There was no way to convince him that McCormick in jail was not a threat. So they changed the subject.

"You worked with Mr. Figueroa, the gardener, at the house where you were arrested, the Rosa house?" she asked.

He nodded.

"He's a good man, Mr. Figueroa?" she asked with a friendly smile.

"He works hard and he's a good family man. He didn't have nothing to do with this. He never would."

She picked up the cue. "We're investigating him because he has a direct connection with McCormick. He did a lot of work for him. He was the best man to know what was going on at the Rosa house because he worked for Mrs. Rosa for a long time. So I have to say he is a person of interest, maybe not a suspect, but someone we have to keep an eye on."

"He didn't have nothing to do with it," Gomez said.

"Did you know Mrs. Rosa was found dead a few weeks back and it turned out she had been drugged?"

He stared at her, clearly wondering what she was looking for.

"She drowned in her hot tub in the back yard, and someone had given her a date rape drug."

He looked at her upward, catching her eye as his face was down. "You didn't need no drug to get in that lady's pants," he said. "If you wanted to."

"Did you get in that lady's pants?"

"No way," he said. "I ain't no pervert."

She asked what he meant, and he said she had a reputation for wanting kinky sex from younger guys. "I got a girlfriend, and not gonna let some old rich woman get me to do her."

"And yet," Sue said, "you didn't mind helping move a ton of cocaine or so."

"It's different. You help somebody move something, you still the same after you do it. I thought it was most likely drugs. Like I wasn't asleep when I was growing up. I know what drugs are, and a lot of people do them, and a lot of people sell them, but not me."

"But not everybody works with Marcus McCormick," she said, circling back around.

"Ain't gonna talk about that," he said.

"Then we're going to remand you to custody and charge you with aiding and abetting, drug trafficking, and possible accessory to murder and attempted murder."

He wrinkled his brow and said, "What? All I did was help move those bricks, lady."

"We don't know that, do we?" she said.

He looked at his hands.

"You're illegal, aren't you?" she asked. "If you are, you'd still have to serve your sentence here before we deport you. But if you cooperate with us, we can get all that changed. You might not be charged with anything at all, and we might give you a chance to go home on your own, not be deported. Under the new laws, you might even be able to apply for citizenship if your record is clean, and I see there are no arrests on your record up to now."

He looked like a kid all of a sudden. A defeated, naughty tagger kid caught with a can of spray paint or something like that. Not a killer.

"So you were not there when Mrs. Rosa was killed?"

"No, I steered clear of that lady and wouldn't have nothing to do with her."

"And you were not with Mr. McCormick when someone tried to kill Mr. Rosa out by the pool?"

He looked at her quizzically. "What?"

"We believe Mr. McCormick and two Latino guys tried to kill Mr. Rosa, who came out here from New York after his wife was killed."

"They shoot at him?"

"No, they strung him up and dosed him with drugs and left him to die."

"I told you, that guy is a bad guy and he's gonna kill me if I say anything, so I guess I go to jail, but I stay alive."

Sue stood up and told him she would be back, left the room and joined Ron and Denis in the observation booth.

"What do you think?" she asked Ron. "Did you recognize his voice?" she asked Denis, who shook his head.

"I think the way to get him is to tell him you're going to spring him and arrest McCormick .He'll know what that will tell McCormick."

She smiled and said, "Great minds, you know, Ron. I was thinking the same thing. "She headed back to Gomez's interrogation room.

"Good news," she said, smiling. "We're planning to release you.

We're going to charge McCormick, who was at the scene with you, and he knows we have been questioning you and your buddy, so we think he will want to get a deal."

"But you're gonna tell him I didn't say nothing, right?"

"No. Not right. I'm not going to lie to him. You did tell me he threatened your life, but I'm not going to go into details about our talk."

"Then he's gonna kill me, and maybe my sister, too."

"Why your sister?"

"Because she been doing it with him sometimes, and she knows about him, too."

Sue glanced at the mirror, and Ron picked up the phone to send a sheriff to take Miss Gomez into custody. "We knew that, and we already have her in custody, but now that we have what we need, we may let her go, too. She's illegal, as well, so we will probably just turn both of you over to Immigration."

He started to sob, big wracking, chest-shaking sobs.

"I told you we can help you," she said. "You're doing this to yourself."

He continued to cry, but said, "OK, I'm gonna tell you what you want to know, but you gotta get me and my sister out of here so he can't find us."

She brought Ron into the interrogation room and together they took his statement. He told them that Marcus McCormick was importing cocaine from a Guadalajara gang that brought the stuff in trailing behind fish boats, and then handed the line off to a day boat, landing it in Redondo Beach. Then a motor boat dragged it to Lunada Bay, and they carried it up the cliff and stored it at the Rosa place in that natural shelf below the pool area. It stayed dry, and as long as Mrs. Rosa was cooperating by drinking and spending time with Latino boys they brought her, the coast was clear.

He had heard that McCormick intended to kill Mr. Rosa, but did not know he had actually done it. Nobody had said anything about Mrs. Rosa, though, and that didn't make sense because the whole plan depended on her staying busy and letting them store things there.

Denis watched from the observation booth. That put him back at square one about Elissa. He knew it was Marcus who tried to kill him; he had recognized the voice that day when Marcus was walking his dog. No surprise there. No real surprise that Marcus was such a bad guy, considering that he had strung him up on his own house and left him to die.

But he did not kill Elissa. There was no scenario that made sense that included Marcus killing Elissa. So did that mean it was one of the boys she was seeing? No need for date rape, as Gomez had said, if she was spreading her legs for all of them anyway, and she had not been harmed, other than the fact that she drowned, so no one had gone bonkers and killed her like that.

Maybe it was a mistake and she had done it to herself like Sue had said at the beginning. But that was out of character, too, at least from what he remembered, and from what the kids said about her. The drug that killed her was surprisingly like the drug that would have killed him if he had been left hanging.

Connect the dots. But he couldn't see the other dots.

Sue came into the booth with Ron.

"He's being processed now," she said. "He's going to be charged with aiding and abetting, and we are going to recommend that it be dropped. As long as the charge is there, he has to cooperate with us or lose all hope that he or his sister will be able to get green cards."

"But it all adds up to Marcus having nothing to do with killing Elissa, right?"

She nodded, but said, "We don't have all the pieces yet, though. Obviously there is more to it than we can see, because none of the people we have talked to would have had any reason to drug her or kill her. No wacko that could have just reversed course on her while she was in the hot tub naked. She had had sex, we know that from the autopsy. Unless she bought the GHB herself and then put it into her drink, there had to be someone else involved. But the guy she was with would have had no motive--they had already had sex--and from what it seems, she was willing to have sex pretty much on demand with a certain type of potential partner. I think we need to go back over everything we know, but that's going to have to be tomorrow because we're not powering on all cylinders right now, and we need to look at it when we're fresh."

Chapter Twenty-seven

The PVE officer drove Denis back to Rocky Point. *It could have been a suicide. Or it could have been an accident. That vodka could have been spiked at any point by someone who knew she drank vodka. Or she could have dropped a pill into it to relax with, maybe.*

But she had had sex that same night. She was naked when she died, maybe just jumped into the hot tub from bed.

Not that it meant anything, but he walked backward in his mind to the times when he had imagined her in the house, in the Jacuzzi. She looked so real and so beautiful. She had undergone that surgery to make herself more appealing to the younger men, and she apparently had enough lovers to keep her going. They had only scratched the surface and had turned up more than a handful. How many Mexican gardeners worked in the neighborhood? A lot.

But there was no reason for any of them to drug her because, like it or not, she was available to any or all of them.

He flipped on the classical music station on his iPod and heard a Mozart clarinet concerto, calming and beautiful. He lowered the window and let the cool sea breeze flow up his sleeve and through his hair. He asked the patrolman to pull over at Bluff Cove and he stared at the surf pounding on the ochre-colored rocks that lined most of the beach a couple of hundred feet below. The sound of the surf was bewitching, rhythmic but changing, powerful and soft, with velvety overtones that stretched out behind each crash.

They drove home on Paseo del Mar, the roadway that skirted the cliffside.

Sue was thinking about the same puzzle as she headed back to Redondo Beach. She planned to call Denis when she got home and see what he was up to, and to see whether he had any ideas that had not already been discussed.

Where Denis was running through what he imagined of Elissa's experience, Sue was having another careful look at the people they had talked to: the bartenders, the gardeners, Marcus McCormick, the next-door neighbor, the dog-walking neighbor. She pulled over in Hollywood Riviera and parked on the curb in an illegal spot, but with her Cyclops light on the dashboard. She walked over to the low bluff that overlooks the white sand Torrance Beach there and looked out at the lights on the fishing barge a mile out on the water. The tide was coming in and a lot of the sandy beach was underwater. You couldn't see it.

She cocked her head and remembered something. She got back in the car and made a U turn with the light flashing and headed back into PVE. She called Ron and asked him to get a car out to the Rosa home on Rocky Point.

"I'm on my way out there now, too," she said. "Can't explain right now. Gotta drive. Look up to see if McCormick has made any airplane reservations and let me know."

"He's on a seventy-two-hour hold here," Ron said. "He can't go anywhere."

"Check anyway," Sue said, and turning on her siren, sped up through Malaga Cove and onto the winding PV Drive heading for Bluff Cove. She turned off the siren, but kept the whirling light flashing on her roof and drove fast toward Rocky Point.

After the police officer dropped him off, Denis hit the garage door opener. The door obediently ran up the guides and onto the top of the garage. He walked into the garage and over to the door into the house. He hit the garage door close button, watched the door close, and then opened the door into the house. Something hit him on the back of his head and he fell to the floor.

Sue pulled up outside the Rosa house in time to see the garage door in the final stages of closing. She lurched into the driveway, ran to the front door and rang the bell. No answer. She removed her service revolver from her waistband and crept around to the side of the house, aware that the house alarms would trip the searchlights around the pool if she opened the gate to the back yard. The fence was made of grape stakes and she could see fairly well through the spaces between the staves. She could also see the front door from a fairly sheltered crouch and the curtains in the living room were not drawn.

There was someone in the house. It could not be Matt or Josh, because they had gone back to Redondo Beach to pick up some things and taken the dogs with them since the "bad guy" had been caught. She kept to her crouch. The front door opened cautiously, and a figure crept out slowly, keeping close to the wall of the garage, heading toward the street. It was a woman. Bingo.

"Freeze!" Sue yelled. "LA County Sheriff!"

The figure stopped and Sue stepped out from behind the shrubs with her gun in a two-handed, body-centered stance. It was Mamie McCormick. Everything dropped into place. Sue held her gun on Mamie and called in for help. She moved cautiously to the woman and cuffed her, saying nothing other than, "I am arresting you for the murder of Elissa Rosa." They stood facing each other.

"So you're the new squeeze for the old man," Mamie said. "We'll see how long that will take to come out." She was a picture of fury: shaking and flushed.

"Denis!" Sue yelled at the top of her lungs.

No answer.

A siren whined in the distance and Sue edged toward the front door, which was slightly ajar, service revolver pointed at Mamie constantly. She kicked the door open and yelled again, "Denis!"

A man's voice made a strangulated sound like someone yelling in a nightmare.

The siren was close. The lights came flashing around the bend on Rocky Point Road and there were two cars that screeched to a halt in the driveway. Five uniformed men popped out, crouched, and moved forward. Sue yelled, "Over here!" Ron Furman came around the corner at a run and spotted Sue and Mamie. He pointed his gun at Mamie, and Sue yelled, "Possible injury inside," and popped through the open door calling for Denis Rosa.

The weak voice guided her to the hallway outside the wine room, next to the garage, where Denis was trying to get to his knees and make an attempt to crawl. The back of his head was bloody and there was a ring of blood on the floor.

"What happened?" he groaned.

She knelt down, took his hand, and helped him sit up on his haunches. He was still bleeding, but not badly, and his left ear had a drop of blood crawling toward the earlobe. She reached over and wiped it off with her hand.

"Stay here. Someone hit you. I think you were knocked out, but you're probably OK because you have a hard head," she said.

He managed something close to a smile, but crooked, and with his head bent forward.

"I gotta get out of here. It's dangerous in this house," he said, and indicated a chuckle.

"I think that's all over now," Sue said. "I think we got the bad guys and you're gonna be OK. Let me get someone in here to have a look at you," she said, and backed down the hall. She met a pair of uniforms in the living room.

"He's hurt, need to call for an ambulance," she said, and one of them turned back and dashed out the door. She and the other officer went back to find Denis sitting up with his hand on his head. He pulled his hand around in front of his face and looked at the blood.

"I think it was Mamie McCormick who hit you, and if we look around we'll probably find out what she hit you with, so don't touch anything, and stay where you are. The guys will be here with a gurney in a few minutes. Do you want some water?"

He stared at her.

"How did you get here?"

"I was thinking about who could have been responsible for your wife's death, and there was basically only one person, Mrs. McCormick, who obviously disliked Mrs. Rosa intensely, and clearly believed her husband was attracted to her. My guess is that Mamie had no idea her husband was storing drugs at this house and thought he was having an affair."

"Sorry, you're way ahead of me," he said, but he sounded more alert, like he had waked up.

Two paramedics ran in with bags of gear and took charge. They inspected his head and put some butterfly bandages on his scalp, wrapped his head in a slick-looking white bandage cloth and lifted him onto the gurney, then wheeled him down the hall and out of sight.

Sue and one of the officers slipped on latex gloves and moved slowly toward the garage door, careful not to step anyplace there was blood or a blood splatter. She pulled on the door, which was not latched, and it slid open. There was a baseball bat on the garage floor with blood on it, and blood splatters on the dryer and the wall next to the door.

"All yours," Sue said, and headed back outside.

"Need a CSI in there, looks like we found what hit him."

Two officers ran toward the hallway.

Sue walked back to the front, where Mamie McCormick was being held exactly where she had been apprehended. Ron Furman was there.

"We have arrested Mrs. McCormick for the attack on Mr. Rosa and she acknowledged her rights when we read them," he said.

"They have the baseball bat that she hit Denis Rosa with in the garage and they're dusting everywhere."

Mamie glared at her, but said nothing.

"I'd say run her down to The Plaza and let's have a frank and earnest conversation with her," Sue said.

"Why did you do it?" Sue asked.

No response.

"I hope you didn't think Mrs. Rosa was having an affair with your husband, because she wasn't."

That got Mamie's attention, but she said nothing.

"She was getting involved with every young Mexican stud in the neighborhood, but not with anyone older than about thirty."

"Marcus couldn't resist coming over here to be with her," Mamie said. "After all the years we were together, he flaunted her in front of me. He had a lot of girlfriends, but none of them was as slutty as that one."

"You mean Elissa Rosa?" Ron asked.

She stopped talking and looked down.

"Just so you know, Mr. McCormick was using this house as a depot for the drugs he was dealing and Mrs. Rosa was a patsy who let him do it without ever realizing what was going on. So when you slipped her that mickey, you actually ruined your own livelihood, and that's why Mr. McCormick had to start liquidating everything," Sue said. "You're the one who pulled the rug out from under your own husband. That'll be interesting when he finally figures it out, don't you think?" Sue sucked on her tongue behind her front teeth and made a brief tsk-tsk sound, then turned on her heel and walked back toward the front door as Mamie was escorted to a police car for the ride to the PVE Police Department.

Chapter Twenty-eight

"Mr. and Mrs. Smith, I guess," Sue said to Denis as he was enduring having his head bandaged.

He looked puzzled.

"A movie," Sue said. "Brad Pitt and Angelina Jolie. They played a couple who were both hitmen who had been hired to hit each other. Stretching a point, but kinda like that, Marcus and Mamie."

He looked at her, his gaze hitting her directly and inquiringly.

"Yes," she said. "Yes."

He smiled and grimaced as the smile deformed his scalp and he felt the pulling of the stitches.

"Oops," the resident said. "You're gonna find that scalp stitches can be more uncomfortable for a few days than regular stitches. Unfortunately, that's because there's not a great deal of skin on your scalp, and when you have to sew it together, it makes it tighter than a drumhead sometimes."

He wrinkled his forehead and looked upward at the resident, who was smiling. "OK," he said.

"You've been kind of a punching bag through all this," Sue said, and put her hand on his cheek. He took her hand in his, held it down, and looked at it. Nails clipped short, no rings, no polish, but an amazingly feminine hand considering that she was strong and could wrestle a grown man to the ground with very little apparent effort.

"No ring," he said.

"No."

"Well," he said, "you gonna let me make dinner?"

"You mean tonight?" she asked, cocking her head.

He smiled and grimaced again as it pulled on his scalp. "Gotta stop smiling," he said. She laughed out loud and he smiled and groaned at the same time. "Stop it!"

The resident said it would be best not to be too active because there was still the chance of a concussion, although his eyeballs and reaction times did not indicate swelling in his head at this point.

Sue drove, since he had arrived in an ambulance, and shouldn't be driving anyway. She put her window down and rested her elbow on the door.

"So, Mamie killed Elissa?" he said, making a statement out of a question.

"Probably unintentionally," Sue said." She intended to make her vulnerable to whoever showed up, and she may have intended to watch or even take pictures, we think. Sort of a way to keep Elissa away from her husband with the negatives. She never realized until today that Marcus McCormick was throwing his fancy parties in her back yard with cocaine money and had no interest whatsoever in Elissa. And Mamie certainly had no clue that your house was her husband's drug depot."

"So she killed Elissa and her husband's candy store at the same time," he said.

She pulled over at Bluff Cove and they got out and looked down at the breakers a couple of hundred feet below. He put his arm around her shoulders and she cuddled into his armpit. "Chilly out here," she said.

"My mother said in the years she lived here it never got to eighty, and she was always cold. She grew up in Texas," he said. "Of course it does get to be eighty, but it has to be the coolest part of LA County, and it's almost always cool in the evening, which is why the hot tub was inevitably attractive after dinner."

"What's going to happen to Mamie and Marcus McCormick?" he asked her.

"We have enough to convict both of them five times, including Mamie's fingerprints on the bat and your blood on her blouse. I would say they are going to be guests of the State of California for the rest of their lives. No question in my mind on that at all."

"And the two guys who were with Marcus when he tried to string me up?"

"Gardeners, people who worked for him freelance in the drug business. All three of them red-handed, of course, and there was enough cocaine stored in their cliffside warehouse to give the Sheriff and the PVE Police Chief a remarkable press conference tomorrow."

He bowed his head and said, "Then it really is over?"

She nodded. His head was starting to throb.

It was clear to both of them that they were falling in love, but neither one brought it up. They got back in the car and drove on to Rocky Point Road, listening to some classical music on the radio. There were several cars parked in front and in the driveway, and Denis recognized them--all his children were there.

There was a scene like a thousand clowns pouring out of a small car as the family streamed out the front door along with Sue's boys back from Redondo Beach, Frick and Frack, and more than a few neighbors. It was a festive group, but largely quiet. When Sue and Denis got out of her car, he stood stock still and spread his arms like the statue of Christ over Rio de Janeiro. The whole crowd flew to him and he was engulfed in the love of the generations to come, the friends of the past and present, and two very well-behaved dogs.

He began to cry, not just a few tears, but big, wracking sobs. The crowd pulled back.

"No, goddammit," he said, "I am not sad, I'm happy. And I want everyone to hear it from me. Those two men, Matt and Josh, those two men are family. They may not be blood relations, but they are family forever. And the dogs, too." He looked at Sue.

"And this lady is more special to me that I can say. Not only," he said, as they started to applaud, "not only because she saved my life several times, but because she is someone I have been looking for but never even hoping I would ever find. I intend to court her mercilessly until she will have me. And just so we're clear, I am never going to sell this house. This is the Rosa home for generations to come. I'm putting the New York apartment on the market and moving my office back to California. I'm going to drive the Jaguar, an old man's folly."

"Here, here!" it was Ron Furman. "That's no lady, that's my partner," he sang out.

A burst of laughter, and Denis, bandaged like a fugitive from a mummy movie, put his arms in the air and snapped his fingers like it was midnight in Athens with Ouzo flowing fast. He danced forward on his toes.

"Opa!" someone shouted. Paul Rosa waddled forward carrying a bushel basket of mussels, and Matt Mason heaved a case of Retsina to his shoulder, then swung it down to place it at Denis's feet.

"Here, Dad," Paul said. "You said you were gonna make dinner and we're all hungry."

"And Josh and I both think you and Mom deserve each other. God knows you both have hard heads," Matt said.

More laughter.

Denis kissed Sue politely, and she grabbed him by the shoulders and planted her breasts into his shirt.

"I," she said, "am emphatically off duty."

The whole crowd sashayed toward the house and around it toward the pool, where Paul had built a fire in the fire pit.

Denis looked at the gathering marine layer sitting over the water about a half-mile offshore. He knew he could see Elissa there if he looked hard enough. He waved at the ocean.

"Ciao," he called. "Ciao."

About the Author

Joseph Allen grew up in Palos Verdes Estates and went to UCLA, where he studied Classics and English literature. He worked as an editor and marketer for scholarly and educational book publishers and then moved on to a career in public relations and investor relations, initially with large corporations, and for the last thirty years in a company he founded.

He has served on the boards of several small companies, and is co-author of a college text on systems life cycles and books on business communications and continuing education. He has written a book on sandcastles, and has written on a variety of topics for numerous periodicals. He is currently working on a family memoir and a second novel. He has been active in several charities.

Allen is a contributor to SeekingAlpha.com, and originated the blog, SmallCapWorld, to which he remains a principal contributor. He has been a contributing author for the Inside the Minds series of C-Level Business Intelligence™ books published by Aspatore Books, a Thomson Reuters business. He has two grown children and two grandchildren, and lives near New York City.

www.ingramcontent.com/pod-product-compliance
Lightning Source LLC
Chambersburg PA
CBHW051425170626
46809CB00006B/2328